Rico Jefe

American Kingpin

Tink Richardson

Society Ink Publications

Contents

Title Page 1

Copyright 2

Chapter 1: 7

Chapter 2: 16

Chapter 3: 22

Chapter 4 37

Chapter 5 54

Chapter 6 84

Chapter 7 111

Chapter 8 121

Chapter 9 125

Chapter 10 135

Chapter 11 144

Chapter 12 153

Chapter 13 168

Chapter 14 184

Chapter 15 201

Chapter 16 211

Chapter 17 234

Chapter 18 246

Chapter 19   254

Chapter 20   260

Chapter 21   266

Chapter 22   269

Chapter 23   274

Prologue

Downtown Federal Building, Present Day

If only Rico could have seen this coming. Right now, he was wishing he could go back and start over.....

"De'Rico Mitchell? My name is Agent Henderson, and this is my partner Agent Vega. I'm sure you know why you're here?" The agent asked.

Rico eyeballed the mixed looking guy in his face thinking *this nigga is such an Uncle Tom.* He maintained his silence and avoided eye contact.

"Ok...well, the reason you're here is because you're being indicted on numerous charges involving drug distribution, murder, and money laundering. Now, the federal government is aware that you did not act alone on these charges and is actually considering offering a plea deal. If you cooperate. Do I make myself clear?"

Rico knew that meant snitching on his people and that just wasn't going to happen. No matter how much time he had to do, he had a code he lived by. Even if that meant spending the rest of his life in prison.

"Listen...you can sit here and play mute all you fucking want. Either way, I don't give a shit because you're still going to prison. Now if I were you, I would think smart and take the deal. Forget your homies and whatever street code you live by." Agent Henderson continued probing but Rico kept ignoring him.

"Mr. Mitchell, we have a rap sheet long enough to get you the electric chair if we wanted to. If you can just please try and work with us, we can convince the judge to reevaluate your sentencing," Agent Vega added in.

Even still, Rico would not budge.

"Mr. Mitchell, where were you on the night of February 3rd at 10 pm?" Agent Henderson asked.

Nothing but silence.

"Do you know a man name Jackson Pelt?" The other agent asked.

The name rang a bell to Rico of course, but he wouldn't let it show.

"You know what? Maybe we should leave Mr. Mitchell here to think about what we said for a little while. By then, he should be able to talk and give us the information that we need."

The agents got up from the interrogation table and left out the room. Rico sat there thinking back on everything that led up to him being here.

How it all started...

Chapter 1:

Favelas, Santa Teresa, Rio de Janerio 2000

"Come on, Rico! Keep up!" Tony Mitchell yelled to his younger brother De'Rico.

The two boys were running through the neighborhood with their friends like all little boys did. De'Rico was struggling to keep up with some of the older boys, but he was determined to.

Tony was so hesitant to let Rico come along with him sometimes because he always had to basically babysit him. However, their mother Serafina would still make Tony take Rico along. Being raised in the rough part of Santa Teresa gave the boys the street knowledge they needed. Especially by them not having a father in their life.

"Hey, look what I found! Por aqui! (*over here*)" their friend Joshua yelled.

Their other friends Georgie and Tiago were crotched down next to him surrounding something small and motionless on the ground.

"What is it?" Tony asked, looking disgusted.

Joshua picked up a stick and began poking at it.

"I think it's just a cat. Somebody probably ran over it," Tiago said.

Rico stood next to Tony looking emotionless at the dead animal. They had seen plenty of dead wildlife when they went exploring but had never gotten this close.

"Hey Rico, I dare you to sniff it." Joshua said. All the boys looked at him waiting to see if he would chicken out.

"Wh...why?" Rico asked.

He hated being the youngest out the group because they were always daring him to do stuff.

"Because you're the youngest. Just a little sniff."

Joshua and the rest of the boys got up and made room for Rico to carry out his dare.

Rico leaned down putting his face really close to the cat. His stomach began to turn when he saw the maggots eating away at its flesh. Suddenly, Rico felt two hands push him forward and made him fall onto the dead cat. Luckily, he didn't fall into it face first, but now he was pretty sure his clothes would smell like dead cat guts.

He quickly moved from the top of the cat all while hearing Joshua and Tiago running away and laughing. He looked up and Tony was, of course, holding out his hand to help him up.

"You should've known not to fall for it. He gets you every time," Tony said. Rico brushed his shirt off but noticed a little bit of blood had stained it.

"You won't tell mom right?" Rico asked.

Serafina always told the boys before leaving the house to make sure they came back the way they left.

"Don't worry little bro. I'm sure she won't notice. Come on, let's go. That cat is starting to stink." They both ran off to catch up with Joshua and Tiago.

A few hours later, the four friends found themselves walking along the beach just as the sun was starting to set.

"Do you guys think if you swim to the end of the Earth that you'll fall off?" Joshua asked.

"Yeah, we're hoping you will. So, get to swimming," Tiago

joked.

"Foda-se.(*fuck you)*" Joshua responded and flashed his middle finger.

"I don't think there is an end to the earth. I think the ocean just goes on forever," Rico said.

He was actually fascinated to know himself. By the boys being out on summer vacation, their minds began to wonder about even the smallest things. Especially, what was outside of Rio.

"No one asked you what you think cat gut breath," Tiago said making him and Joshua laugh.

"Hey, lay off Tiago Just because your brain is made of mush doesn't mean my little brothers is," Tony said.

Rico loved it when his older brother stood up for him. Even though they had sibling rivalry at times, he still admired the only brother he had.

"Hey...veja. (*Look)*" Joshua said while looking straight ahead.

The rest of the boys looked in the direction that his eyes were pointed and stood frozen at what they saw.

Five older boys from a rival neighborhood that wasn't too far from Favelas were walking up the beach in the opposite direction. The four friends always would get into a squabble with them every time they crossed paths. No one knew exactly why the two neighborhoods had beef, but a lot of people believed it had to do with residents from the other neighborhood having more money. Therefore, they looked down on residents from Favelas.

"Come on. Let's just go," Tiago suggested.

"Tiago, you're such a cadela.(*Bitch)* We can take them!" Joshua boasted.

"How Joshua? There's five of them and only four of us." Tony said. Tony didn't want to back down from a fight either. After all, they were boys. What else was they supposed to do?

"Hey! What are you componesas *(peasants)* doing on our beach?" one of the boys asked.

"Your beach? This is our beach you bichano! *(pussy)*" Joshua yelled back.

Next thing he knew, the boy grabbed Joshua by his shirt collar, and they were nose to nose.

"What did you say?" the boy asked, clenching his jaw.

"Hey! Back off!" Tony stepped in pushing the boy away from Joshua.

"Or what?" The boy and his posse stepped closer to the four friends ready for a brawl.

Without thinking, Joshua jumped at the boy who grabbed his collar knocking them both down in the sand. Tony and Tiago jumped in and so did the other boys from the other side. Rico didn't know what to do, but he didn't want to chicken out. Especially, when one of the other boys started putting his brother in a headlock.

"Let go of my brother!" Rico jumped in knocking the boy down.

All nine of the boys ensued in a huge fight in the middle of the beach. People that were passing by thought they were just playing and let them have at it. Even though the four friends from Favelas stood their ground, they still lost the fight. By nightfall, Tony and Rico rushed home bloody and bruised up from the battle. As they got closer to home they could hear their mother calling.

"Tony! De'Rico...rapazes! *(Boys)*" she called out.
Tony and Rico instantly appeared.

"What happened?! Why are you two all messed up, huh?!" she asked, dropping the laundry basket in her hand.

"We...we uh..." Tony began to speak but was too scared at what his mom's reaction might be to hear they got in a fight at the beach.

"You know what, I don't even want to hear it. Both of you get inside. Eu juro que voces dois vao me fazer crescer cabelos grisalhos aos trinta, *(I swear you two will make me grow gray hair at thirty*" Serafina fussed in Portuguese.

The boys knew they were in trouble when their mom began fussing in their native language.

***

Later that night, Rico heard some noises from the other side of him and Tony's small bedroom. He was already half awake from the night-time humidity in the air. When he opened his eyes, he saw Tony putting on clothes and stuffing some items into his backpack.

Is he running away? He thought.

"Tony where are you going?" Rico whispered.

"Out. I'm going to Tiago's house. His mom is throwing a party and he invited us...well, me because you're too young to go."

"But, I want to go. I promise, I won't drag and will keep up," Rico said excited to go to a party.

Tony sighed not really wanting to take Rico along in fear they would get caught, but because of his bravery today when they fought against the boys from the rival neighborhood, he figured his little brother deserved a night of fun.

"Fine. Get dressed. And don't make too much noise or you'll wake up mom." Tony said.

Like lightening, Rico quickly got dressed for a night out on the town with his brother. They didn't have many clothes. Only what Serafina would find in the neighborhood donation bin or stuff other people's kids grew out of. Once he was dressed, they both climbed out their bedroom window and made their way to Tiago's house.

When they arrived, the party was in full affect. Grown-ups were hanging on the outside drinking and laughing, while the sounds of samba music played. Tiago's mom worked for a travel agency and had planned on moving her and the rest of Tiago's family out of Santa Teresa. When they entered the house, they spotted Tiago dancing with his little sister Nosha.

"Tiago!" Tony called out to him.

"Tony! Rico! You came." Tiago said walking over to them.

"Of course, man. We wouldn't miss this since you're moving pretty soon," Tony said.

"Yeah...hey you guys want some special punch?" Tiago asked.

"Special punch?" The boys asked, puzzled by what Tiago meant.

He led them into the kitchen where there was a second big bowl filled with red fruit punch. Tiago looked to make sure none of the grown-ups were looking and poured a cup. He gave it to Tony, who looked at his friend with worry. He shrugged his shoulders and sipped the red punch. When he did, he scrunched up his face with disgust at the bitter taste.

"Ugh what is that?" Tony asked.

"It's punch mixed with booze my dad brought home. I drunk a few sips and feel incredible," Tiago said with a wide grin.

Tiago's dad worked at a factory that made distilled alcohol

products and shipped them off to the states.

"Yuck this tastes terrible." Tony gave it to Rico for him to try some.

Rico took a sip and as soon as it hit his tongue, he wanted to spit it out. The two friends stood there sipping back and forth between each other. After a while, Tony and Rico got used to the taste and even wanted more.

"Tiago! Where are you filho? *(son)*" Tiago's mom called out.

"Uh oh."

Tiago quickly put the cup on the counter and the three friends hurried out the kitchen. As they tried to sneak out, they run into Tiago's mom, who had no idea what they were doing.

"There you are. Can you get some more chips out?" she asked.

"Yes, Mae," Tiago answered.

"And don't you be in the grown-up punch bowl. You understand?" she sternly said.

"Yes."

Tiago tried his best to not smile out of guilt knowing him and his friends drunk some of the punch. His mom eyeballed them feeling suspicious but decided to ignore her feeling and go back to partying.

As the night progressed, the three friends drunkenly partied and watched some of the grown-ups make fools of themselves. After a while, Tony and Rico had the urge to go to the bathroom really bad.

"Hurry, Rico. I have to pee," Tony said, standing next to his brother in the bathroom.

"Ok, ok." Rico shook out the last few drops of pee and zippered his pants.

"Ugh, finally." Tony quickly dropped his pants and began peeing next.

Pop! Pop! Pop!
"Ahhhhhh!"
Both of the boys jumped at the sound of what sounded like gunshots and screaming.

"What was that?" Rico asked.

"I don't know. Quick! Hide." Him and Rico climbed inside the bathtub and closed the shower curtain.

Pop! Pop! Pop! Pop!
The sound of more gunshots had the boys scared for their life. Who would shoot up their friend's party? They both sat there not knowing if this would be their last breath. Trying to hold it in Rico began to cry.

"Rico, listen to me. I need you to be brave ok? We're going to be ok," Tony comforted him.

"But, what if we aren't? Maybe we should have stayed home," Rico said, starting to shake.

"I promise you we are...now, stay here and don't move. I'm going to peek out the door and see if I see anyone—"

"Tony no!" Rico said, becoming scared all over again.
He didn't want to lose his brother.

"I promise I'll be ok. I'm not going out the door. I'm just peeking." Tony slowly pulled back the shower curtain and got out the bathtub. He walked over to the bathroom door and cracked it to peek out into the hallway. At first, he couldn't hear or see anything until a tall, dark figure walked by. Tony jumped back from the door hoping they didn't see him.

"Hey, did you check the bathroom?" he heard someone say.
Tony quickly went back and got in the bathtub next to his

brother who was shaking scared.

"They're coming. Cover your mouth and be quiet." Tony said.

When the bathroom door opened, the two boys made sure not to even breathe too hard. Tony looked through the small opening in the shower curtain and saw a man dressed in all black going through the medicine cabinet. He took everything off of the shelf and put it into a sack.

Tiago's house was being robbed.

When the robber looked at the bathtub, he slowly approached it noticing that the shower curtain was closed. He had a feeling somebody was behind it hiding. His goal was to make sure everyone in the house was dead and leave no witnesses.

"Hey, let's go! I think the cops are coming." The other robber said to him from the doorway.

Just as the robber was ready to pull back the curtain and reveal Tony and Rico hiding, he listened to his partner and left out the bathroom leaving the two boys there.

Tony and Rico sighed in relief but decided to stay put a little longer just in case.

After hiding for what seemed like forever, Tony and Rico got out of the bathtub. Tony went out first to make sure it was safe. When he saw that it was, he let Rico come out after him. The house was silent and an eerie feeling crept through the boys. They slowly walked back to the front of the house and was in shock at what they saw.

Tiago, Tiago's mother, Nosha, and Tiago's father were all shot to death and laying in pools of blood. The boys had never seen dead bodies up close before. Their dearest friend Tiago was gone.

Chapter 2:

Tony and Rico rushed back home before their mother woke up. The sun was starting to come up and they knew she would be up soon. They climbed up to their bedroom window and got into their beds. What transpired was heavily on their minds.

"Rico? You ok?" Tony asked his brother.

"Ye...yeah. Are you ok?"

"Yeah...look I know this is tough, but we cannot tell mommy what happened. She already worries too much."

Rico remained silent.

"Rico promise!" Tony demanded.

"Ok..." Rico lowly said.

Tony turned over and tried his best to go to sleep. Rico remained awake staring at the wall, until his eyes began to close.

~

"Tony! De'Rico! Café da manha! *(Breakfast)*" Serafina called to the boys.

It seemed like they had just closed their eyes to go to sleep and already it was time to get up. They sluggishly got out of bed and went to the bathroom to freshen up. Once in the kitchen, they didn't smell any food cooking and was puzzled as to what was for breakfast.

"Only two papaya's left for breakfast. Don't worry about me,

I'll be fine. You two just eat." Serafina said with much shame in her voice.

It pained her to have to struggle with her sons and she wanted to give them a better life. Something had to be done.

"Mom, can me and Rico go to the boardwalk today?" Tony asked.

"Tony, I needed you and De'Rico's help around here today," Serafina said but seeing the look of desperation on her son's face, she decided she could do the housework alone.

"Ok, you can go, but no fighting this time. And be sure to stick together," Serafina said.

"We will." Both the boys said in unison and headed out the door.

Tony figured a good way to get what happened last night out of his mind was to have as much fun as possible today. He had the whole day planned out for him and Rico.

Once they got to the beach near the boardwalk, they decided to go for a swim. The sun was high, but there was a cool breeze coming from out on the water.

"Come on in Tony! The water's great!" Rico loved to swim.

Tony had taught him how to swim last summer and he fell in love with it. Tony was happy to join Rico for a swim, but his attention was focused on the pretty girls running around the beach. Being thirteen, Tony's mind always wondered about girls and their body parts.

"Tony...Tony!" When Rico called out for his brother he didn't see or hear him.

Tony had wandered off after seeing a pretty face run by and had forgotten Rico was out in the water.

Shrugging his shoulders, Rico continued to swim further out into the ocean. He dunked his head under water a few times to see if he could see any fish swimming below. When he lifted his head back up, his eyes widened when he saw a huge tide coming in. Rico tried to hurry and swim back to the shore but got swept in by the water.

"Ton...Tony!"

He found himself completely under water but held his breath like Tony taught him to. The pressure of the tide being overwhelming caused him to accidentally inhale. Rico could feel his mouth and nose filling as he tried to get out the water. Suddenly, he felt someone grab a hold of him and pull him above. Once he felt the sand on his skin again, he couldn't be more relieved.

"Rico, que diabos?!! (What the hell) I told you not to ever swim that far out! You could have died," Tony scolded Rico.

He was upset that his baby brother went against what he said, but was glad he was ok. Rico coughed up more water and tried to catch his breath glad that his brother saved him.

"Thanks Tony for saving me," Rico said.

"Yeah, yeah. Don't get all mushy. Just next time listen to what I say. Come on, let's go," Tony said.

The two brothers made their way up to the boardwalk where there were all kinds of smells of delicious food. With their stomachs rumbling, but having no money, Tony and Rico tried to think of a plan. They knew it would be a while before their mother had dinner ready.

"Hey, you see that hot dog stand over there?" Tony pointed out.

A guy selling hotdogs had gone on break leaving the stand unattended. Tony saw it as the perfect chance to swipe him and Rico some lunch.

"Come on." Tony grabbed Rico's hand and they both ran over to the stand.

"Stand... watch in case he come back," Tony said.

He slid open the storage door and revealed what looked like a year's worth of hot dogs. He began stuffing as many as he could in his pocket.

Rico stood watch as he looked out over the boardwalk. He noticed there was many families out today. Him and Tony had only asked Serafina about their dad once. She assured them they didn't have a father, but in Rico's mind he knew it wasn't true. The boys both already knew how sex and babies worked when their friend Tiago's mom had her second child. Rico wondered from time to time about who his dad might be, where he could be, and why he wasn't with them.

"Hey!" Rico suddenly snapped out his thoughts and saw the hot dog stand guy running over towards him and Tony.

"Tony, he's coming!" he warned his brother.
Tony finished stuffing his pockets and took off running.

"Come on Rico! Run!" Rico couldn't believe his brother left him, but he didn't have time to think.

They both ran as fast as they could across the boardwalk to get away from the man. Tony almost knocked over a lady with an ice cream cone in her hand, and Rico almost slipped. When they both looked back and saw the man slowing down, they sped up the pace. With their chest pounding and out of breath, they finally lost him.

Once they saw it was safe to stop, they found a place under some trees along the beach.

"You did good little brother...but next time pay attention. Stay alert," Tony said.

Rico knew he made a slight mistake by getting distracted, but still, he couldn't help but still wonder about his dad.

"Here...eat; you deserve it." Tony got two hot dogs out of his pocket and handed them to Rico.

They both sat and feasted on the stolen hot dogs. As the sun started to set, they both decided to end their day and go home. When they got close to home, the smell of linguica sausage filled their noses. It disgusted them due to the fact they were still stuffed from lunch and just didn't have the taste for it.

"Soo...how was you boys' day today?" Serafina asked them, noticing they were not really eating. "Are you two not hungry? You haven't eaten since breakfast?" she said.

"No...we are." Tony said, giving Rico the look not to say nothing about them already having something to eat.

"Ok...I uh...have something I want to discuss with you both."

Tony and Rico both drew their attention to their mother who looked worried.

"I...talked with your father today and-"

"I thought you said we didn't have a father?" Tony interrupted.

"Listen...I know what I told you but...you both are old enough to know that sometimes things don't always work out between people. That's the situation with me and your father. Anyway, I told him that I think it would be best if you boys go live with him...in New York City."

When Rico heard what his mother said he couldn't be more anxious on the inside. After all this time he would finally get to meet his father and go to the states. He would always hear about how life over there was so different and wanted to go. Tony, on the other hand, was a ball of emotions at the moment. He was mostly mad at his father for never reaching out to them and now he has to possibly go live in a whole new environment.

"I'm not going." Tony said.

"**Tony**...não aja assim.*(don't act like that)* This is for you and your brother to have a better life." She said.

Tony was trying to listen to his mother and not be disobedient.

"I...heard about Tiago and his family. I don't want nothing to happen to you two. But how am I supposed to protect you two with all this violence going on? It would be best if you go and live in the states. I have Visa's for both of you." Serafina begins to cry making Tony get up and give her a hug. Rico also gave her a hug knowing he was going to miss his mom.

"I promise we'll be together again." She said and hugged her kids. She knew right now was one of the biggest sacrifices she had to make so that Tony and Rico could have a chance.

Chapter 3:

A few days later...

After a while, Tony and Rico had come to accept that they were going to the states. In a sense, something about over there excited them because they knew everything was so different. From the food, and music, and maybe even the girls.

"So you guys are really leaving?" Their friend Joaquim asked them.

"Yeah tomorrow. Our mom says she just doesn't feel safe with us being here anymore. Especially after what happened to Tiago." Tony said feeling sad for his friend.

"Wow. All the way to the United States? I hear it's like a different world over there. Even the food tastes different." Abel, Joaquim's twin, added in.

"And how do you know this?" Tony asked.

"We have a uncle who lives over there. Some place called California. Says it's a lot of movie stars over there." Joaquim said. Rico made a mental note to visit California one day to see what it was like.

"Well we're going to New York City." Tony said.

"Cool, that's where the rapper Notorious B.I.G is from." Abel said. Tony was amazed at how much the twins knew about the states and they had lived in Brazil their entire life.

"We're going to miss you guys. It won't be the same without you." Joaquim says. The twins gave Tony and Rico a hug knowing it would probably be the last hug they had for a while.

After walking along the beach and spending their last moments with their friends, Tony and Rico headed home to finish packing. That night Serafina tucked them into bed, something she hadn't done in a while. She was going to miss her boys dearly but knew this was the best thing to do.

The next morning, the boys and their mother caught a few buses to Tom Jobim International Airport. They had to stand in a long line to check in and get through security, but once they finally made to the gate things got emotional.

"Tony...De'Rico....I love you boys so much. Remember that. Promise me that you both will go over here and make something out of yourselves." Serafina said to her children.

"I...promise." Tony said choking up..

"I promise too." Rico added in.

"Ok, give me hug. Come on." She brought them in and squeezed them tight.

"Eu tea mo. (*I love you*)" Serafina said shedding a few tears. She finally let them go when they did a final boarding call for the flight to JFK. Tony and Rico walked to the desk, showed their passport and Visa's, gave their mother one final look, and disappeared through the plane door. Serafina said a silent prayer that her boys would make it there safe.

~

Sixteen hours later, the boys were getting off the plane. They looked around in amazement at what would be their new home. Following the airport signs, they went to claim their luggage and wait for their father to meet them where their mother told them to wait. After grabbing their bags, Tony and Rico went to wait for their father. They were both kind of hungry from the long flight and hoped whoever their dad was would buy them some McDonalds. They sat and waited, while watching the people walk by either coming or going. To them, this had to be one of the busiest airports they had ever seen. They waited....and waited...and waited. Hours went by before they noticed it was starting to get dark outside.

"You think maybe he forgot us?" Rico asked Tony.

Tony remained silent, while feeling angry. They were both hungry and exhausted. Until their so-called dad decided to show up, Tony knew he had to do something to feed him and his little brother. He noticed a small convenience shop a little ways from where they were sitting, and an idea sparked in Tony's head; he was known for having sticky fingers back home and was pretty sure he could get away with it in the states.

"Wait here." He told Rico. Tony got up and walked over to the small shop.

When he entered he saw the store clerk was busy helping a customer. Tony walked over to a rack with all kinds of candy bars on it. Taking one more quick look at the clerk, who still wasn't looking, Tony began stuffing a few Kit-Kat bars and Snickers in his pockets.

"Hey! You little thief!" Tony jumped when he saw the store clerk coming right over to him. Tony took off running bringing attention to him from bystanders.

"Stop! Thief!" He heard the man yelling but he just kept running.

When he got back to where him and Rico was sitting, a tall, dark skinned man with a beard was standing next to Rico. Tony stopped in his tracks as he stared at the stranger.

"Hey, stop! Thief! How dare you steal from me?" The clerk grabbed Tony by his wrist trying to pry the chocolate bar from his hand.

"Whoa, whoa...what seems to be the problem here?" The bearded stranger asked the store clerk, while removing his hand off of Tony.

"This boy stole from me!" The clerk said.

"Ok, ok...obviously he was probably hungry which is my fault due to me getting off of work late."

"And who the hell are you buddy?"

"Dewayne Mitchell." When both the boys heard that his last name was the same as theirs, they looked at each other. This was their father.

"If he doesn't pay, then he goes to jail." The clerk said not caring about what Dewayne had just said about them being hungry.

"Look here's two dollars. Take it or leave it." Dewayne said taking two bills out his pocket. The boys just kept looking on in amazement. They couldn't believe that their father was really in-front of them. The angry clerk stood there for a while and stared not sure if he wanted to take the money or not, but because it was almost closing time he snatched the two-dollar bills and stormed off.

"You two, let's go." Dewayne said to the boys in a stern voice. Tony and Rico grabbed their bags and followed after him.

They got to the parking lot and stopped at a 1981 green Volvo car. Rico had always thought his father might have been rich to live over in the United States and in a big city like New York. However, from the looks of things, those thoughts diminished.

The car ride home to Dewayne's apartment was quiet. Rico

looked out the window at all the lights and even thought he could see the Statue of Liberty. Tony, on the other hand, had many questions for his father like why did he leave? Why hasn't he come around before? Was he going to be super strict?

"You boys need to stay out of trouble while you're here. They have no problem with locking you up if you get into trouble. Especially two little colored kids." He chuckled at what he said. In the thirty-five years of him living, Dewayne never thought he would still see racism being a problem when so much had changed.

"By the way how's your mother?" He asked. Rico was about to answer but when he looked over at Tony he could see the "don't say a word" look on his face.

"Silent huh? That's ok. We'll work on that." He chuckled and continued driving.

Before going to his place, Dewayne stopped at the neighborhood carry-out and got the boys some Chinese food. He was used to the taste of it, but the boys ate it like it was their last meal. They had never tasted shrimp fried rice before and hoped they would be able to eat it almost every night. While at the dinner table, they were silent as they ate and still felt awkward about this whole situation.

"So...look I know this is all new for you boys and it is for me too. With that being said, you two should know I'm not one of those fun dads that will let you do whatever you want. There are some ground rules. Number one, no hanging out all times of the night and day. This is a dangerous neighborhood with a lot of drug dealers. You'll go to school and come home."

"School?" Tony asked. He was confused what Dewayne meant because in Brazil they had another month and a half before school started.

"Yes, school. Matter fact, I'm taking you two to get enrolled tomorrow. Tony, I know you're in the 7th and Rico you're in the 5th. There's a school right down the street from here but they stop at 6th grade, so Tony your school will be separate." The boys looked at each other in worry. All their life they had attended school together. That way if one got in a fight, the other would be there.

"But...me and Rico always stay together. Separating us won't be good." Tony protested.

"Listen, I understand you two are used to things and how they are in Brazil or whatever. But this is America and over here...you don't get your way. Especially at thirteen and ten." Dewayne glared at Tony for speaking against him. "Now as I was saying...tomorrow you start school because I have to work and I'm not leaving you two unsupervised. No telling what you might get into."

"But-"

Slam! Dewayne slams his fork down making it hit his plate.

"Boy, you better learn to stop talking back to me. Quick." Dewayne said pointing his finger in Tony's face.

Tony wanted to say something back but didn't want to make things worse for him and Rico than they already were. So, for now he would be quiet.

After Dewayne laid down a few more ground rules, Tony and Rico washed up for school tomorrow. Rico was semi-excited to go to school tomorrow and make new friends. Tony was the opposite because he would be away from his little brother and around a bunch of strangers.

The apartment only had one-bedroom, which Dewayne selfishly kept for himself and made the boys sleep on the pull-out couch in the living room. Listening to all the noises of police sirens, gunshots, and dogs barking was keeping Rico awake.

Tony decided now would be a good time to give him a few pointers.

"Look Rico, we're not going to be together tomorrow, so you have to listen to me. Just keep your head down, and don't talk to nobody. If someone messes with you, just tell me and I'll handle it." Tony said.

"But how I am supposed to meet people and make friends?" Tony slapped his forehead. He loved his little brother and understood he was only ten. But sometimes he was just so naïve to the world around him.

"Rico forget about all that. We're not back home anymore. This is different."

"...Do you think mom misses us?" Rico asked starting to feel homesick.

"I don't think. I know. We'll see her again, don't you worry. Now get some sleep." Tony said and covered himself with the thin sheet.

Rico sat up a little while longer staring out onto the fire escape. This new life was going to take some getting used to.

The next day, Dewayne got the boys up early to go enroll them in school. First stop was Rico since his school was only two blocks away. He made Tony sit out in the waiting area while him and Rico went to meet with the principal.

"So, you have...no previous records from his last school in Brazil?" The principal asked Dewayne.

"Uhh no, like I said my ex has all that information and I can't get it from her right now. But I assure you he's....really smart and can catch up quick." Dewayne said stretching the truth. He wasn't really sure if Rico was smart at all but he would say anything right about now so they would admit him and he can go to work.

"Ok but what I'm saying is it's going to be hard for us to know what grade he belongs in if we don't have his transcript." The principal said back. Dewayne was starting to feel inpatient with her, but tried to hold his composure and not flip out.

"Hmm...how old is he?" She asked.

"Ten." Dewayne said.

"...ok we can put him in the 4th for now and see how he does. If he does well we can skip him to his right grade before the end of the school year."

"Ok thank you." Dewayne said relieved.

"Just give me a minute to get his paperwork together and I'll let you take him to class."

"Uh actually I have to get to work and still take his brother to school. So, can he just wait here in the office?" Dewayne asked.

"Uugh, fine. Go. I'll make sure he makes it to class." The principal could tell Dewayne was going to be an issue as far as being a parent to Rico.

"Thank you. Rico...be good." Dewayne said before leaving. Rico sat there as quiet as a mouse as the principal kept eyeing him. She was nothing like his principal at his last school, who was more nice and friendly.

After what seemed like hours, the principal was walking Rico to his teacher Ms. Kenley's class.

"Ok everyone this is De'Rico Mitchell. He's all the way from Brazil." Ms. Kenley introduced him. Everyone oo-ed and ahhed at the interesting fact about Rico.

Rico felt a little bit better about everyone being I pressed by him being from another country. He now felt like he would like it there and all his feelings of worry were out the window.

The first part of his class was fun. Rico learned some new math problems, they read a book called *Moby Dick,* and had gym. It was now lunch time in the cafeteria, and Rico was sure all the kids would want him to sit at their table...or so he thought. After he got in line and got his lunch tray, he looked around to see if anyone would wave him over, but they didn't. When he saw a table with a group of kids from his class he walked over and tried to sit with them, but they just looked at him and continued to laugh and eat ignoring Rico.

After walking over to a few other tables to get a seat, Rico had no luck. Eventually, he wandered to the eating area outside where a lot of the older kids ate. He found an empty table by the dumpster and decided to sit there. Rico grimly picked at his food, sad that his vibe of being liked by his peers had went away.

"Yeah, yeah, yeah, oh I'm the best MC on the block know what I'm saying. I'll take ya girl from you nigga I ain't playing..." Rico looked over to where he heard music coming from and saw a group of boys with a boombox. He listened to the boys rhymes and had to admit they were pretty good. Rico walked over hoping they would let him join in on the fun. He stood there for a few minutes with just a grin on his face until the boys noticed the weird little fourth grader.

"Yoo, what do you want kid?" One of the boys said.

"I uhh...I like your rap." Rico said nervously.

"Yeah, whatever. Scram kid."

"Well, I was wondering if I can sit with you guys for lunch." Rico said. The boys looked at him and began busting out laughing. One of the boys laughed his way over to Rico dressed in a Adidas suit and a Kango hat. Suddenly, he pins Rico up against the wall by his shirt.

"What are you? Some kind of weirdo?" The boy asked.

"No I-"

"Wait, you're that new kid from Brazil aren't you?" A boy who looked around Rico's age asked.

"Um…yeah."

All the boys looked at each other with devilish grins and began beating up Rico. Rico figured if he just laid there they would leave him alone, but they didn't. They continued to beat on him, and even searched his pockets for money.

"Come on, let's go. This little foreigner ain't got shit." The boy with the sweat suit on said as they walked off.

Rico laid there for a while to try and regain his dignity. He could feel his nose and lip bleeding. He finally got enough strength to get up and go back inside when the bell rung signaling lunch was over. On his way back to class, a teacher noticed Rico's face was bruised a little and sent him to the school nurse. Some hours later, Dewayne came to pick him up. He scolded Rico like it was his fault and even yelled at him. This whole coming to live in New York situation was really starting to be tough, and it had only been twenty-four hours.

"I specifically said no fighting in school. I would expect for your brother here to get in one, but not you." Dewayne yelled at the dinner table.

"But it wasn't my fault. I-"

"I don't care who fault it was! No fighting and if you don't have a choice but to fight, then the least you can do is learn how to box or something."

"I told you we supposed to stay together." Tony mumbled hoping Dewayne didn't hear him, but he did. He grabs Tony by his shirt collar and drags him out the chair.

"Boy, didn't I say not to talk back to me! Huh?!" Tony just glared at Dewayne with so much resentment wondering why his mother just couldn't let him and his brother stay in Rio. After staring each other fiercely in the eyes Dewayne let Tony go.

"You know you boys think you're so tough, but you're not. You're not tough. Come over here Rico." Dewayne commanded. Rico sheepishly walks over waiting to see if Dewayne would spank him or not.

"Now I'm going to show you how to bob and weave. That's the basics. Now when I swing, you duck? Got it?" Rico nodded his head.

Dewayne lightly swings at Rico. He ducks but misses when Dewayne hits him with his other hand.

"See...never underestimate your opponent. Just because they miss with one hand, don't mean they're going to miss with the other." Dewayne can see the potential in Rico, but because he's still young it was going to take a lot of time and work to make him tough.

"You, Mr. Tough Guy, come over and let's see what you got." Dewayne said to Tony.

Tony walks over and stands in front of his father with his hands up. They start jabbing at each other for a minute while practicing bobbing and weaving. When Tony sees the perfect opportunity he jabs Dewayne in the side.

"Ahhh! Haha, well at least we know who can fight and....who needs some work. Come on. You two against each other."

Rico and Tony started boxing at each other with Dewayne coaching them on. Since being here over the past twenty-four hours the boys felt like they were actually bonding with their father.

The next day at school Rico is making his way to class

after eating the nasty breakfast they served in the cafeteria that morning. As soon as he turns the corner he bumps into one of the bullies from yesterday.

"Damn man, why can't you watch where you going?" The bully said. Rico found this as the perfect opportunity to redeem himself and stand up to the bully. Rico stood on his feet and put up both his fists.

"Haha, what are you doing? You want to fight me?" The bully asked. He wasn't that much taller than Rico and was only a grade above him.

Him and Rico stared each other down ready for a battle. They circled each other first and then Rico went in for the punch. The bully moved out the way making Rico miss his shot.

"Too slow fourth grader." The bully teased.

Rico tried again and this time landed his shot right in the bully's face. When he realized what he had done he felt proud until the bully tackled him to the ground.

"Hey! Hey! What is going on here?!" A teacher said coming to separate the two boys.

"Do either one of you want to tell me what it is you're doing in the hallway after the bell has rung?" The teacher asked him. They both remained silent.

"Fine, let's go to the principal office." He dragged the two boys down the hall to the office. Rico wasn't afraid; instead he felt proud that he was able to stand up for himself.

The two boys sat in the office awaiting the principal to come out. Rico looked over at the bully and realized he didn't seem so scary after all. The bully looked over and almost caught Rico staring at him. Rico quickly turned his head forward.

"What's your name kid?" The bully asked.

"Rico and I'm not a kid. I'm only in the fourth grade because they don't have my records from my other school." Rico said trying to sound tough.

"Cool...my name's Ricardo." Rico stayed silent not sure why he was even trying to talk to him.

"Why do you and your friends pick on me?" Rico asked.

"I don't know. I guess that's what makes us cool. Having people fear you."

"Oh."

"Yeah but...between me and you I think it's cool that you're from Brazil. What's it like over there?" Ricardo asked.

Rico and Ricardo spent the next half hour waiting for the principal and also getting to know each other. Ricardo told him all about how life was in New York, that he's half Puerto Rican and Dominican, and his father works at the docks. Rico tells him all of the cool things him and his brother did in Rio.

"Ok boys, now do you want to tell me why you two were fighting?" The principal asked. Both the boys looked at each other and figured since they had now become friends, it was no way they were going to snitch on each other.

"Fine. You're both suspended for two days." They both sighed. Ricardo knew his father wasn't going to be pleased seeing as though he just came off of suspension. Rico, on the other hand, wasn't so sure how Dewayne would react, but he was glad he made a new friend.

The next day, Tony went on to school while Rico was at home with Dewayne, who was upset about him having to miss work because of all this.

"I'm done." Rico said walking over to Dewayne who was sitting on the couch watching the Knicks game. Dewayne had instructed Rico to write a hundred times *I will not fight in school.* Dewayne snatched the paper out his hand, looked at it, and handed it back.

"Write it again." He said.

"But...can't I take a break? My hand hurts." Rico asked.

"Do it look like I give a damn about how your hand feels? I had to miss fucking work today because of you."

"But you told me to stand up for myself." Rico said.

"Boy are you dumb or just stupid? Go finish writing like I said." Dewayne said taking a puff of his cigarette. Rico walked back to the kitchen where he was sitting but then stopped to ask Dewayne one more question.

"Have you heard from our mom?" Rico missed his mother dearly and hoped she was doing alright.

"No I haven't. Now go finish writing." He said with his eyes stuck to the TV.

Rico walked back to the kitchen feeling miserable that he was stuck there with his dad. He took another sheet of paper from his backpack but decided to write a quick letter to his mother. He knew the mailman came around noon so he would just give it to him, along with the address, hoping his mother would get it.

TINK RICHARDSON

Teen years

Chapter 4

3 years later...

Dear filho,

So nice to hear from you. It fills my heart to know you and your brother are doing so well. You're thirteen now filho, and it's time you start deciding what you are going to do with your life. You'll meet many odds but that's ok. That is a part of life. I say a prayer for you, Tony, and even your father every night. As I promised, soon we will be together again. Enjoy your youth, and don't let nothing stop you from conquering the world.

I love you. Mamae.

Rico read the letter he received from his mother for the hundredth time. He missed her dearly and wondered how things had changed since him and Tony left home three years ago. They were both in high school now but still went to separate schools. Their father Dewayne ,who they'd developed a love and hate relationship with, still worked at the lumber yard. Now that the boys were older he worked the night shift most days.

Realizing what time it was, Rico stuffed the letter into his pocket. He felt like if he took it everywhere with him, the good spirit of his mother would be with him even though she was still alive. Tony had already left for school. He liked getting to school early to chill with the homies and check out a few hotties before class started.

Rico tiptoed past his father who was snoring on the couch. The boys finally convinced him to let them sleep in the room because of them being too big for the pull-out couch. Tony was about 5'8, had a cinnamon brown complexion and stayed with a fresh, wavy haircut. Now Rico, on the other hand, was 5'7, had smooth, silky light skin, light brown eyes like his mother, and had developed a little chin hair.

Once out the house, Rico met up with Ricardo at the corner store. Since the very last fight they got into, the two had become close friends.

"Maaaan, did you see Rowanda yesterday? Bitch was looking fine as hell! I'm talking muy sexy" Ricardo said in a Puerto Rican accent, while him and Rico walked to school.

"I mean she ight." Rico said. The whole thought of girls used to scare Rico, but now that his hormones were developing, there was one girl that seemed to catch his attention.

"Ahhh, you're just saying that because you're so hung up on Akeelah." Ricardo said and started making kissing noises.

"I am not. I just think, you know...she kinda fly." In all honesty, Rico wanted to downright get it on with her.

"Yo, she's a tenth grader. She doesn't even know you exist. And that's only because you haven't made it known yet."

"And what does that supposed to mean?" The two friends got on the public transportation bus and sat all the way in the back.

"It means if you want her to notice you, then speak up! Closed mouths don't get fed."

"I don't know...what if she rejects me or I say something stupid?"

"Older women love it when we say stupid shit. They think it's adorable. Look, all you gotta do is walk right up to her and say something like this.." Ricardo turns on his gigantic boombox that he borrowed from his brother.

Girl I like the way you do that right thurr (right thurr)
Swing your hips when you walkin, let down your hurr...

"Hey! Kid can't you read?" The bus driver yelled as he pointed to a sign stating that riders are not allowed to play boomboxes.

"Man whatever." Ricardo complied and turnt it off. He couldn't stand Benny the bus driver and all his rules every time they rode the bus.

"Ricardo, I think I can come up with some play on my own but...it's just gotta be the right moment."

"Fine and while you waiting for the right moment, some other guy is going to scoop her up and sweep her off her feet when you could have." Ricardo said. The bus stopped and the two friends exited out the back door.

All of the students piled into the front doors of the school. The line to go through the metal detector was out the door, but moved quickly. Ricardo turned his boombox back on and started blasting *Air Force One's* by Nelly.

"Awww yeah! This my shit right here." Ricardo said loudly attracting the attention of the security guard.

"Mr. Rodriguez, you wanna turn that down before I have to take it?" He said.

"Aww, come on Tatum. I can't live without my music." Ricardo joked.

"Yeah right, and I can't live without my wife's nagging. Now turn it off." Ricardo turned the volume down but still wanted to test his authority.

"I betchu' I can make your wife reaaal happy." Ricardo started dancing in a slow grinding motion.

"What you say?" Tatum came storming to Ricardo making him run through the metal detector. He looked at Rico with a mean glare. Since he was a friend of Ricardo's he was considered riff raft too[SC6].

"Move along!" Tatum shouted. Rico quickly got his book bag and speed walked through the detector and down the hall.

"Damn man. I don't know why Tatum gotta be sweating me so hard." Ricardo said as he turned his boombox back up.

"Maybe that's because you keep talking about fucking his wife all the time."

"Hey, don't hate the playa, hate the game." Ricardo joked. As they turned the corner they both bumped into Ms. Freely,, their Vice Principal.

"Ricardo what did I say about bringing that boombox to school?" She asked with her arms crossed.

"Uhh...don't have it so loud?" Ricardo asked in a confused tone making it obvious he forgot what she told him.

"I said if I see you with it I was going to take it. So hand it over. You can get it back after school." Ricardo sighed as he turned the boombox off and gave it to Ms. Freely. "Now you two boys get to class and be on your best behavior." Rico and Ricardo hurried along to their first period class.

"Good morning students. Please listen for morning announcements..." the loud speaker said.

While class was paused to listen to the announcements, some students were tuned in, while others took the time to horseplay. Ricardo found joy in eyeballing a girl named Crystal, who he thought looked good. Meanwhile, Akeelah was eyeing Rico. He could see her out the corner of his eye, and it made him nervous knowing she was staring at him. Rico could feel drips of sweat coming down his temple. Akeelah was a straight A student, top of her class, and most of all beautiful. Other girls either envied her or wanted to be like her.

"Rico." She whispered to him. He slowly turned to face her and saw her holding out a piece of folded paper. He contemplated on taking it not sure of what it would say, but by the bright smile on her face he just couldn't resist. He took the noted and unfolded it slowly. He could feel his heart racing as he finally opened it.

Meet me after school by the courtyard...

He looked back over at her and she flashed a smile. Rico loved how she had dimples in her cheeks, her skin was light like his, and she had long, brown hair. She was mixed with Cuban, Mexican, and Indian so Rico was definitely turned on. Him and Tony talked all the time about sex and girls. Although Tony has had his fair share of going beyond kissing a girl and was a junior in high school, Rico hadn't yet kissed a girl.

After the announcements were done, the teacher had begun her lesson, but Rico was zoned out. At first, he thought he should just stand her up and not go, but he knew he would never hear the end of it from Ricardo. He decided to man up and meet with Akeelah after school. When the bell rung signaling class was over, Ricardo caught up to Rico to ask him about the note.

"Sooo, what the note say?" Ricardo asked.

"What note?" Rico tried to play it off as if he didn't know what he meant.

"Don't act like I didn't see Akeelah pass you that note. What did it say? Tell me."

"Fine, it says she wants to meet after school."

"What?! Yo man that's great! I bet you she wants to kiss you." He says making smooching noises.

"Maybe not. Maybe she just wants to talk."

"Rico, come on. When a girl wants to meet up with you after school, it's not just to talk." This got Rico both excited and nervous. He had a crush on Akeelah ever since she transferred from a different school.

"Look, let me give you a few tips. Start off with simple conversation. Then you grab her, look her in the eyes, and say mi amor, then slob her down like a vanilla ice cream cone." Ricardo said.

"Yo, where do you get this shit from?" Rico asked.

"I see my mom and dad do it all the time." They both laugh as Ricardo continues giving him a pep talk.

The last bell of the day had finally rung and Rico's heart was pounding. The moment of truth had finally come. Rico waited in the courtyard as everyone else was leaving until finally it was quiet. Rico waited what seemed like forever and was starting to think maybe Akeelah stood him up.

"You came." A soft voice said from behind him. Rico turned around to see Akeelah standing there. She looked like a fresh cherry blossom in her floral dress and pink cardigan.

"Hey." Was all Rico could get out from looking at the beauty before him.

"Hey." She walked closer over to him, and they were now face to face. There was a silence between them for a while as they blushed at each other's presence.

"Soo um...did you have to tell me something?" Rico asked.

"I uhh...wanted to tell you...I like you Rico. I mean, my friends think it's silly for me to like a ninth grader but...you're cool, smart, funny...handsome." Rico could feel his face turn red with that last comment.

"Well, you know...I try." Rico tried putting on his player swag like Ricardo told him to.

"Do you...like me too?" She asked hoping he would say yes.

"Yeah...of course."

"Cool. So do you want to be like...boyfriend and girlfriend?" Rico felt like a damsel that wanted to faint when she asked him that.

"Uhh...yeah. Sure, I'm down."

"Ok." Akeelah smiled from ear to ear.

"Akeelah?"

"Yeah?" Rico wanted to ask her the ultimate question and hoped he'd get the answer he wanted.

"Can I...I mean if it would be ok, can I....I mean, can we-"

"Kiss?" Akeelah had been hoping the same thing as well.

"Do you...do you want to?" Rico asked.

"Well...I mean we are boyfriend and girlfriend.....sure."

They looked at each other and stepped closer until her forehead was to his chest. Rico poked his lips slightly out and closed his eyes. He waited for a while, and just when he was about to pull back, he felt Akeelah's soft lips over his. Rico had now gotten his first kiss.

After about two minutes, they both pulled back from each other and opened their eyes. Rico couldn't read the expression on her face right away, but when she blushed he knew he had done his job.

"So, I'll....see you tomorrow?" Akeelah asked.

"Yeah, I'll be here." Rico said smoothly.

Akeelah walked out the courtyard making sure to catch one last glimpse of her now new boyfriend. Rico couldn't be more thrilled. Not only did he get his first kiss, but now he had a girlfriend.

When he walked out to the front of the school, Ricardo was there waiting on him on the steps.

"Soo, how'd it go?" Ricardo asked.

"How'd what go?"

"You and Akeelah. Come on, man, tell me." Ricardo begged.

"I never kiss...and tell."

"What!? She kissed you?!"

"Yo, you are so nosey."

"Ahhhh! Did you do the thing I showed you with your tongue?"

"No. She probably would've slapped me."

"Man, if you would've did that she would've gave you more than just a kiss." They both laughed as they waited for the bus to go home. Later that night, Tony helps Rico with his algebra homework.

"Damn, this shit harder than the stuff they teach us at my school." Tony said trying to figure out the math problems.

"I know. Shit, Ms. Thomas be piling it on us." The house phone begins to ring.

"That's because y'all are ninth graders and gotta work y'all peanut sized brains." Tony said rubbing Rico's hair and picking up the phone.

"Hello?...yeah, ight." Tony quickly hung up the phone and sighed.

"Who was that?" Rico could see the look of worry on his brother's face.

"Dad. He said he's working late and want us to cook dinner-....or well me anyway because we know your ass can't even cook Ramen Noodles." Tony joked.

Rico gave him the finger. Tony went into the kitchen and began looking through the cabinets and refrigerator for food. Everything was empty. Their father only got $90 a month for food stamps and by the end of the month most of it was gone.

"What's wrong?" Rico asked.

"Nothing. Looks like dad forgot to go shopping again."

"So...what now?" Rico asked. Tony tried to think of how him and his brother were going to eat. He knew they couldn't rely on Dewayne to bring food home.

"I got an idea. Put your shoes on." Tony quickly put his tennis shoes on and so did Rico.

The two brothers walked out the apartment and down the street to New York Fried Chicken. Rico wasn't sure how they were going to get anything to eat without any money, but Tony knew.

"Come on." They both walked inside and were greeted by the cashier.

"Hi, can I help you?" A Latina chick said from behind the glass.

"Let me get one order of 10-piece chicken, a side of fries, two large Pepsi's, and a strawberry smoothie." Tony said with confidence.

"Ok, give it about 15 minutes and it will be ready." She said and went to the back.

"Tony, how are we-"

"Shhh. Don't worry, I got this." Tony whispered. After 15 minutes, the lady came back with their order. Now it was time for Tony to carry out the rest of his plan.

"That'll be $23.50." Tony walked up to the counter and pretended he was pulling some money out. Suddenly, he snatches the bag of food and ran.

"Hey! Hey!" The cashier lady yelled. Rico stood there frozen with fear until he saw the cashier lady coming from behind the counter and hightailed it out of there. After attempting to chase after them, the cashier lady said fuck it and went back inside. The boys kept running until they both were out of breath.

"Rico man, you got to stop with that frozen shit. When I say run, nigga run! If that lady would have caught you, we both would probably be in jail."

"Sorry." Rico didn't understand why Tony was so upset. They got free food, so why did it matter if he froze up a bit.

"Don't be sorry...just be better. Come on, let's go."

When they made it back to the house, they both feasted on the chicken dinner. Afterwards, Rico finished his homework, hopped in the shower, and went to bed.

Later that night, Rico was awakened from his sleep when he heard what sounded like his father arguing on the phone. He slowly got up and cracked open the door so he could hear better.

"Look man, I told you I'm going get you ya money!" Rico wore a confused look but continued to listen.

"Come on Tay, cut me break...you know I'm trying to make ends meet. Ever since those two brat sons of mine showed up, it's been hell." Rico shook his head and went back to bed.

It was a shame to him that his father always made him and Tony feel unwanted. One day his dad was going to need him way more than Rico was going too. After what seemed like five minutes, Dewayne busted the bedroom open.

"Get y'all asses up! Come on get some clothes on!" Dewayne came in taking everything out the drawers.

"Huh? What's going on?" Tony asked groggily.

"Boy, I didn't ask you to ask questions. I said get up now! We're leaving." Dewayne had black trash bags and began stuffing them with clothes.

"Where are we going?" Rico mistakenly asked. Dewayne looked at him as if he was about to slap the black off him. The boys just did as they were told and began getting dressed.

Bang! Bang! Bang! Tony and Rico wondered who could banging on the door like they were NYPD.

Dewayne froze for a minute because he knew exactly who was on the other side of that door. Dewayne told the boys to stay put. He tiptoed in the living room and looked through the peep hole. He runs back to the bedroom and urges Tony and Rico to go out the fire escape. Feeling a little nervous they both started going through the window.

Boom!

The sound of the door being kicked in made them move a little faster. Once the boys were halfway down Dewayne starts to climb out next. He feels a bullet brush past him barely. He quickly ran down the fire escape behind Tony and Rico.

Pop! Pop! Pop! Pop!

Bullets from the mystery man's gun shot at them while they fled, but each one kept missing. When the three of them made it all the way down, they ran for Dewayne's car and quickly got inside. Dewayne was hoping and praying his car would start. Once it did they sped off. Grateful they got away, Tony and Rico wanted to know who that mystery man was and why he started shooting at them.

"Dad, who the hell was that?" Tony boldly asked.

"First of all, you watch your goddamn mouth boy. And second, that's none of your business."

"Well, it should be. We're your sons. Don't you think you should've told us there's someone after us?"

"They're not after you! They're...after me." Dewayne said.

"But why?" Tony asked.

"Let's just say I owe somebody a lot of money that we don't have."

"So why are we running away? There's three of us and one of him." Tony added on.

"Because Mr. Tough Guy, the nigga had a gun...we don't. And next time, it won't just be one. Next time it will be two, maybe even four. That's why we're leaving New York." Dewayne said.

"What?!!" The boys said together.

"Dad listen, can't we just stay in like a hotel or something. I'm going into my senior year next year." Tony said.

"Yeah and what about our friends? And my girlfriend?" Rico said. His heart felt heavy knowing he abruptly had to leave Akeelah behind after their first kiss. Tony side-eyed him with that last comment.

"Nigga what you know about having a girlfriend? That hoe probably playing you for a sucka."

"Yo, don't talk about her like that!" Rico said getting mad at Tony for disrespecting Akeelah when he didn't even know her.

"Or what?" Tony said trying to challenge him. Rico leaped over at him and they started fighting in the back seat.

Screech!!! Dewayne slammed on the brakes making Tony and Rico stop.

"Stop the bullshit! This is some serious shit and now more than ever you two need to listen to what I say and when I say it. Tony, don't you ever think in this world you need friends. Fuck 'em....Rico, females always going to be there, but right now they ain't fucking important. Understand?!" Dewayne yelled. They both slightly nodded. Dewayne started the car back up and continued driving towards the freeway.

"So, where-"

"Boy, you ask me one more time where the fuck we going and I will wring your fucking neck. You'll find out when we get there." Tony and Rico both remained silent while Dewayne drove like he just robbed a bank. Eventually, they both dozed off.

After hours of driving, Rico could feel the car slowing down. He opened his eyes and looked out the window at a place he'd never seen before.

"Where are we?" He asked Dewayne.

"Baltimore...look, if we gon get to where we going I'm going to need you boys to do something. We're almost out of gas and need food." Tony suddenly sprung up because he wanted to know where this conversation was going.

"Y'all know what panhandling is?" Dewayne asked. Rico didn't but Tony knew all about it because him and Tiago used to do it sometime back in Brazil.

"You want us to beg random strangers for money?" Tony asked.

"Do we have another fucking choice? Now it's either y'all do it or we gon be stuck and hungry." Dewayne said. The boys both looked at each other. This was going to be a long day.

"Excuse me ma'am, can you spare a dollar?" Tony asked. Dewayne heard from some of the locals that Baltimore Street was a good place to start. Tony and Rico had been out there for two hours asking for money as they walked by.

"Excuse me, think you can help me and my brother out with some change?" Rico asked this one lady who was about to walk past.

"Well, aren't you a handsome young boy. How much do you need?" She asked.

"About twenty dollars."

"Twenty dollars?! Uh uh, what kind of scam shit is y'all running? Twenty dollars pshh." She sighed and walked away. Tony walked up behind Rico and bopped him in the back of his head.

"Ouch, what was that for?" He said rubbing the back of his head.

"Why the fuck you say twenty dollars?"

"Well, I figured if we get the whole twenty then we wouldn't have to be out here all day."

"It doesn't matter. None of these people out here are going to just give two teenagers twenty dollars." Rico shrugged his shoulders because he thought it was a good idea.

"Rico look!" Tony said with his mouth wide open. Rico looked in the direction he was looking in and now his mouth was wide open. A lady wearing booty shorts with her entire ass hanging out, a white tank top with no bra, and some platform heels was walking up to this club. Tony didn't know what kind of club it was, but he was interested in finding out.

"Come on, let's go over there." Tony said.

"But what about the money?"

"Relax little bro. There's plenty of people out here and besides we can both use a break." Rico was worried that they wouldn't make enough and Dewayne would be pissed, but he did want to see what was inside of that building.

They both crossed the street and saw it was a line of people outside waiting to get in. Tony needed the security guard distracted so him and Rico could sneak past.

"Aye nigga, you cut in front of me." One guy said that was standing in line.

"Man no I didn't." The other guy said and turned around. Next thing you know the dude behind him grabs him by his shirt causing a ruckus and grabbing the attention of the bouncer, who immediately walked over to break it up.

Tony hurried and pulled Rico's arm and inside they went without anyone noticing. Once they were inside the strip club the room was covered in a bunch of neon and fluorescent lights. There was half naked women walking around either on stage dancing or at the bar talking men to death.

"Damn. I ain't never seen so much ass in one room." Tony said. Suddenly, he feels a hand caress his shoulder.

"Hey there cutie, you want a lap dance?" The girl asked. She had on a green and pink two piece, some jet-black hair, and some platform heel boots. Her face was full of make-up, but her ass and titties were poking out.

"Shit don't mind if I do." Tony said as if he was in a daze, until Rico elbowed him telling him not to go.

"What? Nigga you better go grab you a handful of ass and have some fun. Shit I know I am." Tony walked off with the girl leaving Rico all alone. This was Rico's first time in a strip club and he was fascinated at how well some of the girls could do circus tricks on the pole to all the money falling on the ground.

"Alright coming to the stage is one of Norma Jeans finest, straight out of West Baltimore we have Candy." The DJ announced.

"Beautiful" by Snoop Dogg begin playing and the same woman that they saw enter the club came out on stage. Instantly, Rico was drawn in by how huge her ass was and how full and perky her boobs looked. She had long, red hair and nothing but a one-piece lingerie set on. She began shaking her ass in a circular motion making Rico's dick start to rise. He tried to hold it down but when she started doing flips and making her booty clap, it was difficult. When she turned Rico's direction they locked eyes. She swayed over to him while walking across the bar top. She squatted down in front of him and began grinding in slow motion. At this point, Rico was pretty sure he had pre-cum on himself. The aroma of her sweet-smelling perfume put him in a daze, making him feel like they were the only two in the room.

"What's your name sweet cheeks?" She asked him.

"Ri...Ri...Rico." He managed to let out.

"Well Rico, you gon tip me for my dance." She said rubbing her hand through his hair.

"I...I wish I could. But I don't have any money."

"What?! Whatchu mean you don't have any money? What type of nigga come in here with no money?" She asked in a disgusted tone. All Rico could do was shrug his shoulders and that made her even more pissed off.

"Oh hell no! Carl!" She yelled. This tall, buff security guy came up behind him holding Tony with one hand and grabbed Rico with the other. He dragged them both to the door and pushed them out.

"Don't let me catch you two in here again." He said and closed the door.

"Well it was fun while it lasted right?" Tony said. Rico just looked him and shook his head.

After spending the rest of the evening panhandling, the boys managed to come up with $40. Although Dewayne wasn't too pleased and felt that the boys could have did better, he decided to use half for food and the other half to make it to Atlanta.

Chapter 5

At every other city, they would stop to either rest or panhandle for more money. Since they didn't have enough money for a hotel, all three of them slept in the car. Rico often thought about his mother to keep him going. Sometimes he would think about Akeelah and how she must hate him by now for abandoning her. He figured it would be easier to accept it as a loss.

A few days later, they finally make it to Atlanta. Rico and Tony couldn't be more relieved that they wouldn't have to sleep in the car anymore, but they still worried where they would stay. Dewayne pulled up in front of a run-down looking house. Tony and Rico both wore confused looks on their faces.

"What is this place?" Tony asked.

"My great aunt left it to me after she passed about ten years ago. It needs some work but it's still livable. Come on, let's go." Dewayne gets out the car. Tony and Rico do the same and walk up to the house.

Inside, it was really dusty and still had furniture that looked like it was from the Victorian period covered in plastic. The house had two bedrooms and two bathrooms, a dining area and an outdated kitchen.

"Here, take this and go to the nearest store. Get any cleaning supplies you can find." Dewayne said giving Them. Tony and Rico do as they're told and find a little family-owned corner store at the end of the block. They buy bleach, some sponges, and some antibacterial spray. Once they came back, Dewayne made it clear the only thing he was interested in doing was getting the TV set up. That evening, the house was half clean along with the bathrooms. Since there was no beds for them to sleep on, Tony and Rico just made pallets on the floor out of clothing and old towels, while Dewayne slept on the couch.

One week later....

Tony and Rico both enroll in the local high school and this time are both in the same building. They actually liked going because it gave them time to be away from that run-down house and Dewayne. Since moving he has been drinking heavily and took his anger out on the boys. The other night he almost practically burned Tony with an iron. On the way to school, they both talked about what they'd do after graduation. While talking, they walk past a group of drug dealers. Rico tried to pay them no mind, but Tony was a little intrigued.

"Hey!" A guy named Shawty called out to them. Tony and Rico stopped in their tracks as the guy wearing all types of jewelry and a fresh Adidas sweat suit came up to them.

"Where you two from? I ain't never seen y'all around here before." He said with a thick accent.

"We uhh...just moved around here." Tony said.

"Oh ight, going to school and shit I see. I like that. Young black boys making something out of yourselves. Just one thing....don't let a diploma fool you. Real money is made out here on these streets every day." He said in a low tone. Rico felt a little nervous, but Tony was distracted by all the shiny jewelry he was wearing.

"Well get on to school now. Need your education." He said and walked away. They both kept walking towards school.

"Man, did you see the type of jewelry that guy had on. Damn, I wish I had chains like that." Tony said.

"But how do you think he gets those chains?" Rico said back.

"It doesn't matter. The point is he got them." Tony said giving the Grinch smile.

"Come on, let's just get to school." Rico said. The rest of the way, Tony brags about how he's going to be able to buy expensive jewelry and clothes one day. Once they made it to school they went their separate ways to class. Unfortunately, Rico had an oral report due on the benefits of the solar system that day.

"Last but not least, another huge benefit that we get from the solar system is the sun. The sun provides Vitamin D from its ultraviolet rays giving us the energy we need. The end." Rico said.

"Good job Rico." The teacher said.

"Ahem, dork." His classmate Reggie mocked him. Since his first day there, him and Reggie had bumped heads a lot. It was mostly because Reggie secretly saw Rico as a threat because all the girls liked him.

"That's enough Reginald." The teacher warned him.

"Right...besides you wouldn't be able to give your report no way without stopping to figure out the words on the paper." Rico fired back. The class whole cracked up laughing making Reggie mad that they found him funny.

Lunch time had finally come but Rico had always found himself sitting alone. He hadn't made any friends yet, and Tony always went off campus for lunch. Rico figured it was better to be a lone wolf than be surrounded by people who meant nothing....until today.

"Hey." A soft voice said to him. When he looked up he locked eyes with Leah. She was in his English class and was a top student.

"Oh, hey Leah." Rico admitted that he did like her but wanted to see where things could possibly go before he made her his girl. So for now he would play it cool.

"Mind if I sit?" She asked him.

"Sure. It's a free country." Rico said biting his sandwich.

"So I heard you did great on your oral report today."

"Who told you that?"

"Nikki Roxben. She sits in the front and wears glasses."

"Oh yeah...her." Nikki tried flirting with Rico his second day there. For her to look like such a geek, she had a deep, freaky side to her. But Rico turned her down flat.

"You know she really likes you."

"Yeah well...the geeky freak ain't really my type."

"So then what is your type?" She asked flirtatiously.

"Well...I would say a girl who is smart, funny, has ambition, wants more than what life has to offer her. Straight up, I like a go getter. Only time will tell when I meet a female like that."

"How do you know you haven't already." She asked. There was a mild silence between them. Rico could tell Leah was really feeling him.

"Leah!" A loud voice came out of nowhere. Reggie walked up to their table. He didn't like the fact that Leah was now associating with the new kid and not him.

"What Reggie?" Leah asked being annoyed.

"What are you doing over here? I told you to sit at my table." Reggie said.

"You don't control me Reggie. I can sit where I want." Leah

snapped back.

"Oh yeah? So you would rather sit with the nerdy, new kid, than the cool crew. That's funny. Stop playing games and let's go!" Reggie said as he snatched her up from the table.

"Ow! Get off of me!" Leah yelled. Hearing the despair in her voice, Rico decided enough was enough with this Reggie person.

"Yo! She said let her go." Rico said getting up from the table.

"And what are you going to do about it?" Reggie asked him letting Leah go and now focusing on Rico standing up to him.

Reggie pushes him, making Rico react and push him back. Reggie tries punching him but Rico blocks him. He puts Reggie into a headlock like how Dewayne taught him, and the whole cafeteria got in a uproar. Everyone was either yelling fight or rooting for someone to win. Rico was holding Reggie in a choke-hold so tight that eventually he passed out.

"Oh my God! I think he killed him!" Someone yelled. Rico looked down at Reggie hoping he didn't kill him by accident. He had never been to jail before but knew it was a place he didn't want to go. The principal appeared and kneeled down next to Reggie to feel his pulse and luckily he was still breathing.

Later that evening after spending all day in the office, the principal decided to only give Rico detention due to the fact that Reggie was the one who started the fight. However, that didn't stop Dewayne from ranting.

"I am getting so tired of this bullshit from you! Don't you know every time you fight I have to take time out my busy day and go talk to these stupid people!" He yelled at Rico.

"So. It's not like you have anything important to do other than drink all day." Rico said.

"What'd you say?...Huh boy?" Dewayne got close to Rico.

Rico stood his ground as he prepared himself.

Wham!

Dewayne slaps Rico to the floor. Rico had to admit it felt a little painful, but he still pretended like it didn't faze him. Looking up at Dewayne, he had a look of anger and resentment. Dewayne took off his belt ready to continue.

"I think you need to learn who's the child and who's the parent here." Dewayne said. He lifted the hand with the belt in it ready to strike Rico again, but Tony appeared and rammed into Dewayne knocking him on the floor.

"You good bro!" Tony asked Rico.

"Yeah." Tony helped Rico up and glared at Dewayne who stood back up.

"You stay out of this Tony." Dewayne said.

"No. I'm not gon to stand here and let you hurt my brother. We had enough."

"Hahaha, well if I can't beat his ass. I guess I'll have to just beat yours." Dewayne swung at Tony but missed because of he was off balance.

"Come on old man," Tony taunted him while holding his fists up. Dewayne lunged at him again, but Tony moved out the way making Dewayne hit the wall.

"Just give up. You're drunk as usual and can't even fight." Tony said and turned his back. As soon as he did, Dewayne grabbed him by his shirt and threw him into the glass coffee table.

Crash! Tony was a little dazed but now had blood trailing down his face from the pieces of glass stuck in his skin.

"Tony? You ok?" Rico asked coming to his aide.

"Ah!... yeah....at least I will be when this bastards finally dead." Tony said glaring at Dewayne.

"You know what, I am getting sick and tired of your little ungrateful ass. I take you, I feed, clothe you...this is the thanks I get?!" Tony remained silent.

"You know what? Get out." Dewayne said. Tony and Rico both looked with confusion.

"You heard me! Get the fuck out my house!" Dewayne yelled while gulping down another beer.

"Cool...you ain't got to tell me twice." Tony hopped up like his skin didn't have pieces of glass still stuck in him.

Tony rushes upstairs and starts packing the stuff he did have. Rico slowly followed behind. He didn't want Tony to go because he had always been there. Without his brother he didn't know what he would do.

"I'm coming with you." Rico said. He didn't care where they went. He just wanted to be with Rico and away from Dewayne.

"No. He didn't tell you to leave. He told me." Tony said throwing clothes in his backpack.

"I don't care. You can't just leave me here with him. Come on Tony please." Rico begged. Tony turned around and gave a contemplating look.

"Ight fine. But you gotta do what I say Rico." Tony said. Rico nods his head in agreement.

Once the boys packed all they could carry in their bags and they headed for the door. When they reached the bottom of the steps, Dewayne was knocked out with an empty beer can. They both just shook their heads and left out.

The rest of that night, Rico and Tony walked around trying to find a place to lay their heads. The night air was cold and their feet felt sore. At one point they even thought about maybe going back, but decided being outside was way better than being abused by their drunken father. After hours of walking around they found an old, abandoned building that used to house apartments. When they walked inside it was a few homeless people and dope fiends laying around on the bottom floor. When they walked up the almost torn apart stairs and found the upstairs part empty, they decided that it would make do for now. Tomorrow was a whole new day and a whole new plan.

The next morning, Tony and Rico walked down to the gas station to shower and headed on their way to school. On the way there they passed them same guys from the day before slinging dope. Tony then had an idea.

"Hey bro!" Tony called out to Shawty.

"What are you doing?" Rico became nervous because Shawty looked like the type of guy that would shoot now and ask questions later. Shawty turned around with a confused look on his face and quickly walked over to them.

"Excuse me? What the fuck did you just call me?!" He asked in an angry tone.

"Nothing I-"

"Let me tell you something youngin'. Around these parts we don't call each other bro. You ain't my blood and damn sure don't look like you came out my momma pussy. Show some motherfucking respect, you got that?" Shawty asked.

"Yes." Tony said. Rico had to admit if Shawty had his brother damn near scared then he had to be feared by the other niggas around him.

"What's your name anyway little nigga?" Shawty asked.

"Tony...and this my little brother Rico." Tony replied back.

"Tony huh? So, what's so important that you had to interrupt my conversation I was having? And it better be good."

"Well we was....well I-" Tony stuttered.

"Spit it out. I ain't got all day." Shawty said lighting up a cigarette.

"I...I want in," Tony said.

"What?" Shawty asked confused.

"How can I start...you know selling?" Tony asked. At first Shawty laughed a little bit, but when he saw Tony was serious he switched up his tone.

"You serious?" He asked. Tony nodded his head yes. He had been up all-night thinking of a plan on how to make him and Rico's life better than being homeless on the streets. He made a promise to his mother and he intended on keeping that promise.

"So, you wanna slang some dope huh?...How about you start right now?" Shawty said.

"Seriously?" Tony asked.

"Yeah little nigga. Let's see what you got. You want in too Mr. Silent?" Shawty asked Tony.

"No, he has school." Tony said answering for Rico. He'd be damned if he got Rico involved in this type of game so soon. He pulls Rico to the side.

"Look, go to school and I'll meet up with you later." Tony says to him.

"Tony, what are you doing?" Rico didn't understand half of what was going on right now.

"Look, do you want to eat tonight or starve?" Tony asked him.

"Eat but-"

"No buts, Rico. Go 'head to school. If anybody looking for me just tell them...I got the flu or something." Rico looked in his brother's eyes and nodded his head in agreement. Rico heads on to school but not without giving his big brother another look. Shawty slap handed him two vials of white stuff. Rico just hoped Tony knew what he was doing.

~

After school, Rico waited for Tony to show up but there was no sign of him. It was almost 5:30 and school had let out at three. Rico was praying nothing happened to his big brother.

"Hi Rico." A soft, familiar voice said. Rico turned around and locked eyes with Leah.

"Hey, what's up Leah? What you still doing here?" Rico asked.

"Oh, we had a scholar's meeting. How about you? You and your brother usually gone by now."

"I know. I was trying to wait for him but...I think he ditched me." Rico said hoping Tony was really ok.

"Well, if you want, you can come with me to my mom and dad's restaurant downtown." She said.

"Oh, I shouldn't. I have to-"

"It's ok. You don't have to. I just thought you might be hungry." She said making these cute puppy dog eyes that made Rico feel weak.

"Uh...actually, you know what? I am feeling a little hungry." He said.

"Great! My mom is making her special tonight. Fried pork chops, mac and cheese, and peach cobbler. Come on, let's go." Leah pulled Rico by the hand and they made their way to the MARTA station.

About an hour later, Rico was stuffing his face with some of the best peach cobbler he ever had. He hadn't had a good home-cooked meal like this since they were back in Rio.

"So what are things like where you from?" Leah asked.

"It's cool...I guess. There's beaches, good music, nice food."

"Did you have a girlfriend back home?" Leah asked. This caught Rico off guard because he liked Leah and didn't want to answer wrong.

"Uh...naw it was mostly me and my brother." Rico scooped up some more peach cobbler into his mouth.

"Oh well...that's good to know." Leah flashed her big smile and it warmed Rico's heart. He hadn't felt this way about a girl since first seeing Akeelah.

"Ok, baby me and your father are just about done with our last round of customers." Leah's mother said. "Rico, did you need a ride home?" She asked.

"Oh um...no thank you, I'm fine." Rico said. He knew if Leah saw where he was living, there was no way in hell she would be interested in him anymore.

"Are you sure? If it's on the way I don't mind."

"Yeah, I'm sure. I'll be fine." Rico insisted.

"Ok, well Leah, honey, can you come help me count the inventory for tomorrow." She asked and walked away.

"Sorry, I gotta go now." Leah said being annoyed that her mother kind of ruined the moment.

"It's all good. I gotta meet up with my brother anyway, so I'll catch you at school tomorrow."

"Ok." She said smiling. Rico had some thoughts going through his head about Leah. Even though he hadn't done it to a girl yet, he watched plenty of porn and got a lot of advice from Tony to have an idea.

~

Later that evening, Rico decides to just head back to the abandoned building. The only light they had was from the street lights outside and there was no working bathroom. The halls smelled of urine and feces. Rico found an old bucket that him and Tony have been using. It wasn't the best but at least he didn't have to deal with Dewayne and his drinking.

"Aye, what up bro?" Tony said walking into the little space they made themselves.

"What up? Nigga, you left me hanging after school." Rico said.

"My bad, but look. This is what I made today." Tony pulls out a wad of money.

"Damn! How much is that?"

"Only 200, but Shawty said if I work harder at it then I can make triple this in a day."

"Cool...but what about school?"

"What about it? School isn't important to me. Only thing that's important is chasing this paper and getting us the fuck out of this hellhole. Move us into one of those nice ass apartments downtown."

"I feel you. Well, can I get on it?"

"Naw, you too young. Besides, I don't want you wrapped up

in this type of shit. You keep ya head in them books."

Rico listened to what his brother was saying, but didn't truly understand why he had to focus on school and Tony wasn't. He figured that was something else he wouldn't understand. He'd just have to see it play out for himself.

Back to reality....

The feds are still trying to get as much information out of Rico as they can. Jamil wasn't interested in hearing about his whole childhood, but he figured if it was going to eventually give him the answers he was looking for then he would play along.

"So...how close are you and Leah exactly?" Jamil asked him. Rico looked at him blankly and tried to think of a quick, made up answer.

"What do you mean?" Rico asked.

"You know exactly what I mean? I know all about you and Leah being married. And I also know she helped you." Jamil said slamming his hand down on the table.

"I don't know what you're talking about." Rico would be a fool to tell these federal agent jokers anything about Leah. He made a promise to protect her.

"Oh, you don't do you? Well, I got six police cars outside yall's house right now. Ready to arrest her and take your two kids into child custody."

"You leave her out of this!" Rico yelled. He would've gotten up but they had him chained to the table like an animal.

"In order for me to do that I need the truth, Mr. Mitchell. Like I told you, I'm here to help you." Jamil gave a devilish looking smile.

"Yeah right. Since when you motherfuckers ever want to start helping me?"

"Well, if you tell me what I need to know we can work out a deal."

"Tell you something like what?" Rico asked. He was getting tired of playing Jamil's game and just wanted this to stop.

"Tell me....everything." Jamil said taking out a notepad and pen. Rico glared at him.

"Everything huh? I don't know about everything but I'll tell this much..." Rico begins talking about his teen years again and how he officially got started in the game.

Da' bluff, Atlanta Georgia....A few years later

After being homeless and struggling for a while, Tony managed to save up and did exactly as he said he would do. He copped him and Rico a two-bedroom apartment in the downtown area. Rico was now in the 12th grade and doing pretty well in school. Tony had become one of Shawty's top hustlers and went from being a corner boy to Shawty's right-hand man. Everything was going good for the two brothers.

BAAAAAAAAAAAAAA!!!! Tony pressed the button on the noise maker, making Rico jump up and fall out his bed.

"Rise and shine." Tony said. Today was Tony's 19th birthday and Rico couldn't wait to celebrate later.

"What the fuck Tony? Just because it's your birthday don't mean you gotta try to make a nigga deaf." Rico said rubbing his ear lobe.

"Nigga I can do whatever I want." Tony helped Rico off the floor giving him a manly hug.

"Happy birthday bro." Rico said.

"Thanks. Still just feels like another day."

"That's because you haven't gotten your day started yet. So we celebrating later or what?"

"Aye, don't worry about all that. Now get dressed. You don't want to be late." Tony said leaving out the room.

After showering and enjoying a birthday breakfast, Tony drops Rico off at school in his brand-new BMW. He sees his friend Anthony outside waiting for him. Tony gave Anthony a mean mug because for some reason he didn't trust Anthony. Rico couldn't figure out if it was because he told him that Anthony and his family snuck out of Guatemala or if it was just Tony being Tony. Rico shrugged his shoulders and went about his way.

"Damn man, why your brother don't like me?" Anthony asked as they walked inside school.

"I don't know. Probably trust issues or something." Rico said as they stopped at their lockers.

"So you going to tryouts today?" Anthony asked.

"You know it. I may not have made the football team last year but this year is mine for sho." Rico said.

"I don't know, man. That new senior Thomas looks pretty rough."

"Well, we'll see how tough he is once we get out on that field. One main thing Tony always taught Rico was to never think someone else was better than him, and if they thought they were then it had to be proved.

"Uh oh. Look who's coming." Anthony said. When Rico turned around he saw Angela Pearson coming down the hallway swaying her wide hips from side to side. She transferred a year ago and all the boys been on her since her first date. Rico had to admit she was a bad bitch for real. He just didn't think he had much of a chance with her.

"Hi Rico." She says flirtatiously.

"What's up Angela?" Rico said trying his best to ignore her.

"Well, what's up is I'm having a few friends over this weekend. Just wanted to know if you would come?" She asked.

"Uhhh...naw I can't. I gotta do this thing with my brother." Rico lied. He was trying his hardest to ignore Angela but her nicely shaped body, light cocoa skin, long natural hair, and hazel colored eyes was making his dick hard.

Last year on his birthday, Tony decided it was time Rico became a man and experience the world a little bit. Tony took Rico to a brothel and paid extra for one of the girls to have sex with him. Rico didn't entirely like the whole idea, but once the girl started giving him head and rode him until the sun came up, Rico had sex regularly after that. Now he had girls from every hood wanting him.

"Well, how about next weekend?" Angela asked. She had her eye on Rico for a minute and had been wanting to see how he got down in the bedroom.

"Ahem." Angela turned around and locked glares with Leah, Rico's now girlfriend. They made things official last summer and it seems like ever since then. Everyone wanted to snatch Rico from her.

Leah had blossomed into a beautiful young lady. Her perfectly chocolate skin, naturally good hair that reached her shoulders, and how thick in the waist she got. Rico had been dying to hit that but for some reason Leah wanted to hold out and not move too fast. Something Rico just wasn't understanding.

When Angela could see that now wasn't a good time to keep

pressing Rico about coming over, she walked off. Angela felt so angered by that he would choose Leah over her, but she definitely was cooking up a plan to make him hers or at least get the dick.

"What was she doing over here? And why were you two talking?" Leah asked.

"Nothing babe, she just...wanted to borrow my textbook." Rico said but from the look on Leah's face he could tell she saw through his lies.

"Mmmhmm, sure." She said poking her lips out.

"Babe, you know she only jealous of you because she can't have me." He said. That seemed to make her smile a little bit. "Keep poking them lips out and I'm gonna bite em off." Rico put his arm around Leah's waist and pulled her closer to him.

"Haha, stop Rico." She said.

"Why? Everyone here already knows you my girl."

Riiiiiing! The first period bell rung.

"I gotta get to class. You still trying out today right?" Leah asked.

"For sho." Rico replied.

"Ok, I'll meet you later." Leah said and walked down the hall to her class, as Rico and Anthony did the same.

~

Later that day, football tryouts were about to take place. Rico and Leah sat over on the bleachers until the coach called for him.

"So you nervous?" Leah asked.

"A little but this ain't nothing I can handle." Rico said. As soon as he said that Thomas Floyd went speeding across the field and caught the football effortlessly. Leah could see the worry in Rico's face.

"Don't worry about him. Just focus on what you got to do." She said.

"Mitchell! Let's go!" The coach yells out for Rico's turn on the field.

Rico could feel his heart pumping a mile a minute.

"Muwah, good luck." Leah said pecking him on the cheek. Rico smiled and felt recharged. He was confident he would get out there and dominate.

He went out on the field and got some quick instructions. Rico was going to show how good he was at throwing, catching, and blocking. When the coach instructed one of the guys to throw the ball, Rico ran half a yard and caught it. Already he could see the angry, jealous look on Thomas' face. Next, it was Rico's turn to throw the ball. Rico got in stance, pulled back and threw the ball. When he hit the field goal, the coach was very impressed. Lastly, he had to block a player from getting the ball from the quarterback.

"Ready, set, hike!" The coach blew his whistle. When one of the players tried to tackle Thomas, Rico blocked him and slammed him to the ground.

"Ha! Haaaa! Good job Mitchell. Can you come to practice tomorrow after school?" Coach asked.

"Sure thing, Coach. Does this mean I'm on the team?"

"Hell yeah it does. I haven't seen talent like yours since I played college ball. As a matter of fact, I want you to be on varsity." The coach said.

"Aww, Coach come on. You're not going to really let this

amateur be on varsity are you?" Thomas said with an attitude.

"Excuse me Thomas, but I do believe I can do what I want since I am the coach. Now you are the Captain, you have the right to express your opinion, but in the end...I have the final say so. Do I make myself clear?"

"Yes, Coach." Thomas mumbled.

"Good. Now hit the showers. Mitchell, I'll see you at practice tomorrow." The coach said. Rico was ecstatic and couldn't wait to get home and tell Tony.

When Rico got home, he heard weird noises as soon as he opened the door. He already knew what was going on.

"Oh yeah, Daddy! Just like that!"

"Yeah, you like that?! You like this dick don't you?!"

Rico could've almost thrown up at that last comment. He knew better than to walk in on Tony when he had company over, so he went into the kitchen instead to make him a sandwich. First, he walked over to the couch to put down his book bag, but something caught his attention. It was a huge duffle bag with pounds and pounds of weed in it. The wheels in Rico's head began turning. He knew quite a handful of people at school who smoked weed. If he could somehow sell it, he could have his own little money on the side instead of always asking Tony for money. Rico could hear his brother almost finishing up and decided to go for it. He started stuffing his backpack full of weed until he couldn't anymore. He quickly took it to his room and hid it under his bed. When he walked back out, Tony was coming out his room with no shirt on and sweating.

"Damn, little bro. I didn't even know you was here. Did you hear-"

"Nigga by now the whole building probably heard y'all." Rico laughed.

It seemed almost every other night Tony had some girl over. He just hoped Tony was smart enough to use protection. Last thing both of them needed was to be taking care of kids or end up with something.

"Well, you know how your big brother gets down." Tony joked. Tony liked the relationship he had with the string of girls in his phone. Sex any time he wanted, and no strings attached.

"So look, check this out. Go get dressed because tonight is going to be lit. Shawty throwing me a party at the Hilton." Tony said.

"Ight, but what about ole girl?"

"Who her? She fine. She in there knocked out." Tony said. Rico just shook his head and went to change his clothes.

~

An hour later, Tony and Rico were on their way to the party. This would be Rico's first official party, and it would be some fine ass women there. He just kept a mental note to behave himself.

"Man, I'm telling you, if I don't fuck something tonight, I'm punching the air." Tony joked.

"Good luck with that. Because I'm not fucking on anything at this party."

"What?! Man, so what you gon do? Hold up the wall? Nah Rico, you can't be hanging with me if that's all you're going to do."

"Then take me back home then." Rico said.

"Yo loosen up. It's not like you and that bi…I mean girl married or something." Rico gave Tony a glare just as he was about call Leah a bitch. Tony knew Rico was gon have nobody disrespecting her.

They hit a speed bump, making Tony's glove compartment open. When Rico saw the gun laying there, he looked at Tony. Tony noticed he had seen it and closed it back up.

"Why do you have a gun in your car?" Rico asked.

"Look, you never know when you might need to use that shit." Tony answered.

"Tony, what if the cops pull you over?"

"They can pull me over, but they got to have a search warrant to search my car. Something you learn, especially when you're a Black man driving a nice-looking car."

Rico admired his brothers advice. He wished Tony would just give him a chance and teach him the game.

"What? What's on your mind little bro?" Tony asked.

"Why can't you teach me the game?"

"Yo really? We gotta talk about this again for the thousandth time?"

"Because I just don't understand why." Rico said.

"You're too young Rico."

"Well, so was you when you started." Rico knew he would be able to learn and pick up on things quickly if Tony gave him a shot at it.

"Let me break something down to you little brother. Out here on these streets you see and do things you never thought was possible. Especially when it comes to selling dope. Now if you want to sell lollipops and candy bars to your friends at school, fine, but this right here is grown man shit." Tony said.

"But Tony-"

"No more buts Rico. Now the answer is no, ok? End of discussion. Only thing you need to do is focus on school and graduate. That's it."

Rico sighed and gave up on trying to convince Tony he was ready. He knew right now wasn't probably the best time to ask, but he damn sure was going to keep pressing the issue, even if he had to do the shit himself.

When they pulled up at the hotel, Tony could see everyone lining up to go inside. They even had a bouncer at the door. Once they got out the car, he and Tony walked straight to the front. The bouncer let them straight in without asking any questions. Inside, the music blasted, people danced, and smoke filled the air. It was a good thing Shawty rented out the residential suite or otherwise it would've been overcrowded.

"I'll be right back! I'mma go see what they got at the bar!" Tony yelled over the loud music. Rico shook his head and stood off to the side. Rico wasn't much of a dancer at parties, so he just hung back and watched the hotties on the floor do their thing.

"Well, if it isn't baby brother." Shawty said coming up to Rico. Rico remained silent. He didn't really like Shawty because it was just something about him that seemed off. Off the strength of his brother was why he was even at this party to begin with.

"So what's up? You decided to put the video games down and hang with the big dogs huh?" Shawty asked. Rico shook his head and pretended like Shawty wasn't there.

"Well you should be fucking celebrating. Go on. Get you one of those hoes on the floor."

"Nahh thanks, I'm good." Rico said. And just in the nick of time, Tony was walking back with two cups in his hand.

"What up Shawty?" Tony greeted Shawty giving him an

elbow tap.

"I was just telling your brother here he need to loosen up a bit. Go bend ova one of these hoes."

"Oh, don't worry, he will. After drinking this, he gon wanna do all that and more." Tony said.

"Alright, well y'all enjoy the rest of the party. And happy birthday man." Shawty said and walked away. Rico looked at him with an untrusting look. He could tell Shawty wasn't the person Tony believed him to be.

"Here, try some of this." Tony gave Rico the shot glass. Rico gulped it to the head but not without making a sour face from the taste of it.

"Ughh, what is that?" Rico asked.

"Pineapple Amsterdam, Cîroc, and a splash of rum. Your seventeen now, you gotta learn to drink like the big boys do." Tony laughed. "Here, have another." Tony gave him another one, and another one after that.

Soon before Rico knew it, the room was spinning. He couldn't tell which way was up or down.

"Hey Rico." A familiar voice said. Rico turned around and saw it was Angela from school. *What is she doing here?*

"Hey, wassup Angela? What you doing here?" Rico asked.

"Well Shawty is my older cousin. He said I could come as long as I don't tell my momma about the smoking and drinking." Angela held her red cup to her lips sipping on some Remy Martin.

"Oh ok, that's cool." Rico had to admit that Angela was looking real good right now. She had on some jean booty shorts, with a red tube top, and you could see her nipples poking through.

"Yeah...so I see your little girlfriend ain't here." Angela said looking him up and down.

"Nah. She probably at home studying or doing something boring." Rico joked. He had no idea why he just talked about Leah like that, but it had something to do with all the liquor he consumed.

"Ohh well, that's too bad. Because if you was my nigga...I'd be sitting on your face until the sun came up." She stood close whispering in his ear.

Rico's dick instantly got hard at the sound of that.

"Uhh...I'll catch up with you later ma. I gotta go drain the pipe." He said and quickly made his way to the bathroom.

Rico walked into the restroom and closed the door behind him. He unzipped his jeans and whipped out to handle his business. After he dribbled off he went to go pull his zipper back up, until he heard the bathroom door open.

"Whoa somebody..." There stood Angela in the doorway eye fucking him.

She closed the door and locked it. She slowly walked up to Rico feeling on his muscles. Rico wanted to stop her, but for some reason he just couldn't. Suddenly, like she read his mind, Angela dropped down to her knees and was eye level with Rico's penis. She stuck out her tongue and circled the tip making it wet. Inch by inch, she eased it into her mouth, until it was all the way to the back of her throat. Rico felt like he was in heaven right now and couldn't stop even if he tried. She bobbed her head up and down all while making slurping noises. Angela has had her share of giving head. Otherwise Rico wouldn't be feeling like his knees was going to buckle.

Ready to see what the other end of her felt like, Rico pulled her up and turned her around to the bathroom sink. He bent her over, pulled down her shorts, and searched for the hole to her honey pot. When he found it, he eased it in not wanting to hurt her too much. For him to be only seventeen, he was glad to be blessed with a monster in his boxers.

"Ohh fuck!" Angela moaned. He had her feeling like she was cumming already.

"Shit, this pussy good." Rico went in and out, slapping against her ass cheeks. For Angela to be rumored to sleep with so many niggas, her pussy was just right. Not too loose and not too tight like a virgin either.

"Fuck, I think I'm cumming." Rico said. He didn't want to cum and would rather stay in this pussy all night, but he knew if he didn't get back out there Tony would be looking for him.

"Ughaaah!" Just in time, Rico pulled out and shot his sperm right on the bathroom floor.

He tried laboring his breath, while getting the last drips of cum to come out. Angela pulled up her shorts and turned to Rico. She kissed him on the cheek with a wide smile on her face. In Rico's mind, reality had just set in. *Fuck, I cheated on Leah.* While he straightened himself up, he hoped and prayed this wouldn't get back to Leah somehow. Exiting the bathroom, Rico is met with admiring eyes from Tony who heard the whole thing.

"Bro….how long were you-" Rico began to ask.

"Haaaahaaaa! That's my little brother! Bussing down bitches in the bathroom! Hahaha!" Tony joked. Rico managed to smile, but he still worried in his head if Leah would find out.

~

The next day while in class Rico could hardly stay awake. It was bad enough he had a terrible hangover from all the drinking and now he could barely keep his eyes open.

"Yo Ric, you good?" Anthony whispered while their teacher lectured.

"Huh? Yeah, I'm straight. Just tired is all." Rico said.

"Oh, from that party last night huh?"

"What...how you know?" Rico asked.

"Yo everyone knew about that party Shawty threw last night. Said it was the party to rival all parties. But it was invitation only. I know you had to be there to celebrate with your brother."

"Yeah, I ain't gon lie. I did get a little fucked up." Rico says rubbing his temples.

"Did you....you know...get some?" Anthony asked. Rico had almost completely forgot about him and Angela's little encounter last night.

"Uhh...I plead the fifth." Rico said.

"What?! Nigga you got some pussy at the party last night? Who was it? Was it an older woman? Was her ass fat?"

"Whoa, whoa...pump the brakes Anthony. We can play ask a thousand questions later. Right now, I got a migraine."

The bell rang signaling class was over. On the way to Rico's locker Athony still continued to ask questions about who he fucked last night at the party.

"Was her pussy wet? Aww man, I bet that shit was wetter than a waterfall."

"Anthony, enough ok." Rico stuffed his history book into his locker and got out his algebra book for his next class.

"Come on, I'm ya boy. Why can't you tell me?"

"I will tell you later. Not right now ok." Rico closed his

locker only to be startled by Leah standing on the other side.

"Oh shit! Babe, you scared me." He leaned in to kiss her, but she quickly snatched away. "What's wrong?" Rico asked her.

"Rico...did you fuck Angela last night at some party?" Leah asked. As those words escaped her mouth, Rico started to sweat trying to come up with an answer.

"I...I..."

"Well did you?" Leah asked louder.

"Hughh...yes but...how do you even know this?"

"Because that bitch been bragging about it to the whole fucking school Rico! Talking about how big you were and how you was all over her." Leah said as a few lone tears started to come down her face.

"That's a lie. That bitch was on me...babe look, that's beside the point, it was an accident ok?"

"Accident my ass!" She said louder this time attracting people's attention.

"Leah, keep your voice down. Listen, I'm sorry ok. I was fucked up and I wasn't thinking clearly. Please forgive me." Rico pleaded but Leah wasn't looking too convincing.

"Forgive you? You want me to forgive you after fucking the school slut?! You can forget it! We are done! Good-bye Rico." Leah stomps off in the other direction. Rico wanted to go after her and just hold her saying how sorry he was, but he decided to just let her cool off a bit first.

"Aye, look man, don't worry about her. She'll probably be over it by tomorrow...oh yeah what was it you wanted to tell me?" Instantly, Rico remembered about the weed he took out of Tony's stash. Rico pulled out his backpack and showed Anthony what was inside.

"Damn nigga, what'd you do rob a dispensary?"

"I got it from my brother...or well borrowed it. If we can sell all this we can make the same amount of money Tony makes and plus some."

"Ight, well I can spread the word around and see who's interested."

"Ok, sounds like a plan." Rico put his bookbag back in his locker for safe keeping. Luckily this was one of those schools that didn't have metal detectors or drug sniffing dogs. Rico was going to get his share of the pie.

~

Later at Rico's first practice, he and all the newbies ran laps around the field.

"Come on new guys, let's move it!" Since the Coach was out sick, the team's captain was taking over practice today. When Rico was out of breath, he stopped for a moment. As soon as he did that he heard footsteps coming towards him. Of course, it was Thomas.

"And just what do you think you doing? There are no breaks." Thomas yelled.

"Well...y'all need to...enforce some breaks. A nigga over here dying." Rico said sweating and trying to catch his breath.

"Well if you can't handle it then maybe you shouldn't be here." Thomas said.

"What?" Rico was confused at first as to why Thomas had such a problem with him, but now it was clear as day that it was because Thomas was jealous.

"You heard me. Coach might think you're all that, but I don't."

"Well, I didn't ask for your opinion motherfucka." Rico got close to his face ready for any and everything. Thomas might have thought he was hot shit on the field, but Rico knew he could take him on in a fight.

"You know what, you not even worth it." Thomas said walking away.

"Yeah thought so." Rico decided he had enough practice for one day. He grabbed his duffle bag and headed home.

Later, when Rico returned home, he opened the door to see the apartment looking a mess as if a tornado had hit.

"What the fuck?" Rico said. He immediately thought the worse assuming someone had broken in.

"Tony? Bro, where you at? I think we've been robbed!" Rico yelled. Tony comes out his bedroom.

"What do you mean we? You mean me." Tony said.

"What the fuck are you doing?"

"Nigga half of my weed is missing. I can't find it anywhere." When Tony said that Rico could feel his nerves starting to shake. He felt bad for stealing from his brother, but he needed a come up too.

"Fuck! I bet it was that bitch I fucked last night that took off with my shit. Maaaan Shawty is going to shit bricks when he finds out."

"Right...well I'm going to umm...start my homework now." Rico said trying to not look suspicious. Tony just ignored him and went back to tearing the house apart looking for his missing bags of weed.

When he got to his room, he flipped open his phone and dialed Leah's number. It rung a few times until it went to voicemail. He tried again but got the same result. He figured she was still mad about him having a quickie with Angela, but hopefully she would get over it.

The next morning, before the first bell rang, Anthony had a line of at least 10 people ready to buy weed from him. One person even bought two bags. Before lunch he made a good $200 and still had more to sell. At lunch, he sees Leah's sitting alone. He walked over to her and sat down, but she ignored him.

"So you still not talking to me huh?" Rico said.

"Sorry, I don't talk to boys that cheat." She said twirling her fork around.

"Babe, I said I was sorry. It was an accident. I was drunk and-"

"That's what you all say. You don't just accidentally have sex with somebody." She said now looking at him dead in his eyes. He could see that she was hurt, and it did something to him.

"You know what...you're right. It wasn't an accident but I will say I fucked up. I fucked up bad. Can you forgive me?" Rico asked. Leah was the girl of his dreams and he didn't want to lose her.

"I don't know. Give me a reason why I should."

"Well...um...how about if I promise to never ever cheat on you again. My dick belongs to you and only you." Rico said. He know it wasn't the best thing to make up for what he did, but he hoped it would be good enough for now.

"You promise?" Leah asked.

"Yes babe. I promise." Rico reached out and held her hand. Leah couldn't help but flash a slight smile although she didn't halfway believe him. His promise would do for now.

Chapter 6

"Rico, would your simple ass stand still so I can take the picture." Tony said.

It was homecoming night, and Rico was on his way to pick up Leah for the dance. Tony bought him a $1,200 Tom Ford suit and wanted to send a picture to their mother.

"Ok, one more, then I got to hurry up and pick Leah up." Rico poses while Tony clicks the camera.

"Ight prefect. Oh, I almost forgot, you got another letter from mom." Tony gives him an envelope. It had been weeks since Rico heard from her.

Rico meu filho,

I am so proud of you for making the soccer, or as they call it, football team. Every day that passes I regret more and more about letting you go with your father. I never should have trusted him. I just wanted to keep you and Tony safe, and I failed. Please forgive me. Keep going and succeeding.

I love you. Mom.

Rico could have almost shed a tear at reading the letter. The fact that Serafina thought Dewayne's bullshit was her fault made him feel sad. It was bad enough their mother mentioned having health problems the last time he called her long distance, but the last thing he wanted was her stressing.

"Hey little bro. Got something for ya." Tony held out a pair of keys.

"Is that....to the Mustang? Really?" Rico said. Tony had a whole bunch of foreign cars he owned but kept them at a private garage on the other side of town.

"Mhmm, but only for the night." He tossed Rico the keys. Rico looked at the set of keys like it was rare diamonds. "Hey, don't fuck up my car, and have fun." Tony said.

"Oh, you know I will. I might not be home tonight because uhh...me and Leah getting a room."

"Word? Look at my little brother finally becoming a man. You want some condoms or you straight?" Tony said.

"Nahh, I'm good. Besides, I don't think your condoms would fit me. I'm too big." Rico laughed and rushed out the door as Tony reached for something to throw at him.

Rico raced down the highway doing at least 80 mph. He loved the way the engine roared every time he hit the gas pedal. When he pulled up to Leah's house, he saw her sitting on the front step and could tell by the look on her face she wasn't happy. Even with the sight of what they would be riding in to-night.

"Hey babe, you ready to go?" He said walking up to her. She had a coral-colored halter top dress on that was hugging every curve of her body. Her hair was curled up into a ponytail and her make-up was to die for. Rico's dick started to get hard. He couldn't wait until later when they were alone.

"You're late Rico. The dance is halfway over." She said standing up and crossing her arms.

"I know. Look, the first suit I had didn't fit, so we had to drive way up College Park on some last-minute shit to get this one. But check it, my brother let me borrow his car for the night, and

I got us a room at the Hilton...you know, for later." Since making up, Rico and Leah had many times discussed about having sex and even experimented over the phone a few times. Tonight, Leah finally decided she was going to let Rico be her first.

"You still look handsome." Leah said smiling.

"Thanks babe. You look beautiful as well. I know all the guys and the girls at school going to be jealous with you on my arm."

"Oh yeah? Well, let them be. Come on, let's go." She took his arm as they went to the car and rode to the dance.

Meet me in the trap, it's goin down
Meet me in the mall, it's goin down
Meet me in the club, it's goin down
Anywhere you meet me, guaranteed it's goin down...

"Alright y'all, it's going down up in here on homecoming night. Let's congratulate our varsity football team on their win!" The DJ announced and everyone started cheering. Even though Rico didn't get to play the homecoming game, he still supported his team on winning. Even Thomas non-catching ass.

As soon as Rico and Leah walked through all eyes were on them. Anthony couldn't make it because he had to babysit but told Rico around 11:00 that it would be potential customers waiting for him in the boys' bathroom to cop weed from him.

"There's Jolie. I'm going to go say hi to her." Leah released Rico and ran over to her friends, who complimented her on her dress.

Rico looked at his watch and saw it was 10:50. Without being seen, he slipped back out the door to the car to get his backpack. He didn't want to tell Leah he had weed in the car because she might freak out about it. When he went back inside, he went straight to the bathroom, and just like clockwork, the same boys that copped from him before were there. Rico locked the bathroom door so that none of the chaperones would walk in. Everyone got in a single file line and exchanged their dollar bills for dime bags of weed.

Bang! Bang! Bang!

Someone knocked hard at the bathroom door.

"Uh...sorry bathroom's full." Rico said as he hurried to try and put his backpack away.

"It's me." Thomas' voice said from the other side. Rico looked in confusion as he unlocked the door.

"What do you want?" Rico asked cracking the door.

"I...look can you just let me in?" Thomas said. Rico eye-balled him suspiciously. *How did he know I was even in here?* Rico opened the door even wider to let him inside the bathroom.

"What? Are you here to snitch on me to Coach?" Rico said.

"Naw man I...look, I'm sorry about being hard on you all the time. It's just...football is my life you know. And over these past few weeks I been under a lot of stress from doing college interviews to trying to get recruited. And then you come in and...I guess I got a little jealous. No hard feelings though right?" Rico let his mind wander for a minute. He never thought he would see the day where Thomas was not being a asshole. Nevertheless, he didn't see why they shouldn't squash their beef.

"Naw, no hard feelings." They gave each other a handshake.

"So...listen man, I was wondering do you have enough weed left to sell?" Thomas said.

"Hell yeah I do." Rico opened his back pack up ready to make another sale.

Once he's done handling business and got back to the dance to slow grind with Leah on the dance floor, they left around 1 am on their way to the hotel. All kinds of thoughts was running through Leah's mind.

What if I'm too tight for him?
What if he decides to leave after getting some?
Will he even like me the same?

Meanwhile, Rico had some thoughts of his own.

Damn, that pussy probably wetter than the Nile.
I wonder if she got on something sexy under that dress.
What if she into being rough, like pull her hair or choke her type of sex? Ohhhh yeah. Tonight is going to be epic.

BLOP! BLOP!

Suddenly, Rico sees police lights flash in the car mirror. *Fuck!* He thought to himself. He began getting nervous because he knew how the police was. He had marijuana in his backpack, and he was driving without a license.

Rico pulled over and looked over at Leah who had a worried look on her face as well. He could see the cop coming up to the side of the car, so he rolled down the window.

"Uhh hi Officer. Is there a problem?" Rico said.

"License and registration." The cop said. Rico bit his bottom lip as he went into his jacket pocket and pulled out his school ID.

"Son, I need license and registration. Not a high school ID."

"I uhh...don't have that." Rico admitted. Leah sucked her teeth at the bullshit unfolding in front of her. She wondered why he would have the nerve to be driving around with her in the car with no driver's license.

"Well...see Officer me and my girl just came from the dance and my brother let me borrow his car." Rico told honestly but the officer wasn't buying it.

"Ok you two, step out of the car for me please." He said.

"But why-"

"Step out of the car now! Don't make me ask you again." Tony had always told Rico to be very careful around cops. They were always quick to shoot first and ask questions later.

Rico and Leah did as they were told and got out the car. The police officer motioned for the other officer in the patrol car to come over. Instantly, the officer leaned Rico up against the hood and the other one searched the car.

"Yo, come on man, is all of this necessary?" Rico said. He looked back over at Leah who now had tears coming out her eyes.

"Just tell me where you stole the car from." The officer said.

"Stole? Look man, I told you this is my brother's car." Rico said as the officer patted him down.

"Is this also your brother's?" The other cop held up a bag of weed from his backpack. Leah's eyes grew wide and she looked at Rico in confusion.

"Well, well looks like we're taking you in. Cuff the girl."

"What?! No!" Leah said screaming.

"Yo, just let her go! She don't got nothing to do with this." Rico said. He now was starting to regret taking that weed from his brother.

"Yeah, yeah tell it to the judge." The cops dragged Leah and Rico to the patrol car and put them inside. Rico tried to keep his cool, but Leah couldn't help but kick and scream.

"Leah baby, we gon be alright. You'll see."

"Drugs Rico? This whole time you had drugs in the car?!"

"Leah, once we're out I can explain-"

"Save it. Who's to say we won't be in jail for God knows how long." Leah said.

The entire ride to the police station was silent between them. Once they got there they were fingerprinted and processed. The sheriff decided to let them go on $500 bail since both of their records were clean.

Rico spent his time in his cell worried about Leah. They had took her to a different cell and he felt like shit dragging her into this. He tried calling Tony but just got his voicemail. Hopefully he would decide to listen to the message he left him, because if not, only God could save him now.

"Mitchell! Let's go. You made bail." The guard said. He opened the cell door and walked him up front. When he locked eyes with Tony, he felt his heart drop into his stomach.

He caught a glimpse of Leah too leaving with her parents. Her father gave Rico the death stare before they walked out the station. After being processed, Rico was free to go.

"You lucky I ain't have to work at the trap tonight. Otherwise, your ass would've sat in there until Monday." Tony said while they walked out the station.

"Tony I-"

"Shut up Rico! What the fuck were you thinking?! This whole time I'm thinking some hoe stole my weed, not knowing it was my own brother. Get ya ass in the car." Tony got into the driver's side slamming the door, while Rico got into the passenger's side. He could tell this ride home would be a long one.

"Tony, look I'm sorry I stole the weed, but I felt...left out. You slanging and making all this money and I wanted to be a part of it...actually I still do."

"What part of no do you not fucking understand?! Huh? You're not ready to become no hustler."

"But I am Tony. If you could just talk to Shawty and give me a chance to prove myself. I already made close to $500 tonight from selling at the dance."

"You just don't get it do you. I said the answer is no mother-fucka. Now you keep this shit up and I'm going to tell ma." Tony said. Rico just threw his head back and let Tony win the fight this time. What was supposed to be an epic night ended in disaster.

Three days later at school, Rico looked everywhere for Leah to apologize to her. He tried calling her last night, but her dad picked up the phone, and before cussing him out, he told Rico Leah couldn't talk to him anymore. But he was still determined to try.

"Leah!" He said running over to her locker but she ignored him. "Hey, babe I just wanted to say sorry about the other night." Leah closed her locker door and walked away from Rico like he was invisible. Rico wore this confused look but ran after her. "Leah? Leah?! Hello you there?" He said walking next to her. "Leah stop, ok. What is going on?"

"You! You're what's going on! If we never would have gotten arrested I wouldn't have gotten in trouble and forbidden by my parents to talk to you!" Rico chuckled a little bit because it sounded silly that Leah would actually even say that.

"Yeah, but I mean come on. This isn't the dark ages. You're not actually going to listen to them are you?" He asked. The look on her face told it all; she was serious.

"Rico, you...been keeping shit from me. You cheated on me with Angela, you're selling weed at school.... I think we need to take a break."

"A break? But-"

Riiiiiiing!

"I have to go." Leah said and walked away. The fact that she was actually not going to talk to him anymore made him angry, more so at himself. In his mind, he prayed that this would blow over and Leah would come to her senses.

Later on, at practice, Rico was a little off his game because of what Leah said to him. He kept missing catches and having a bunch of fumbles.

"Mitchell! Come here, let me talk to you for a sec." The coach said. Rico runs over towards him ready for the coach to get on him about the way he was practicing.

"Hey Coach, listen. I know I'm messing up, but I promise I'll do better-"

"It's not that son. I just got word from one of your teachers that you're failing algebra."

"Oh…I mean yeah but it's no big deal. I only got a D."

"Rico, grades are a very big deal. In order for college recruiters to choose you as their number one draft pick, your grades need to be up. I'm sorry but you're off the team until you bring your grades up."

"Off the team? But Coach-"

"I'm sorry Rico. But I can't let you play until your grades are up. Now get your stuff and go home." The coach said and walked off. Rico felt like whole world was falling apart. First Leah and now this. Who knew being in high school would be this stressful.

When he got home, he saw Tony on the couch watching TV as he rolled up a joint. He figured now would be the perfect time to try and convince him to sell. Rico plopped down on the couch next to him and stared at him waiting to say something.

"The answer is still no Rico." Tony said.

"Aww, come on Tony. I need this, especially now because...I got kicked off the team today."

"You what?!" Tony asked.

"Just because of my grades, but in the meantime, I need something to depend on. Me getting recruited is up in the air right now." Tony sucked his teeth and went back to rolling. He was definitely going to roll another one after Rico told him he was no longer on the team.

"Please Tony....I need this." Rico pleaded. Tony just sat there silently as he lit the end of his joint and exhaled.

"There's some rules to this shit you need to know. Rule number one don't get fucking caught. I guess you learned that from the police. Rule number two don't get high on your own supply. Unless you want your head chopped off by yo supplier. And rule number three always make sure your shit is top of the line. That weed you stole was some shit straight out of Jamaica. I'm talking about some shit Bob Marley would smoke."

"Damn, that's why them niggas at school kept coming back."

"Damn right. For right now, you can start off with the small stuff, which is weed. You not ready for the big stuff yet."

"Shit, that's cool with me." Rico was happy Tony was finally going to let him sell. This would be the start of his new side hustle.

Before leaving for school the next morning, Rico stuffed the pound of weed into his backpack to sell at school. Once he met up with Anthony, they lined up their usual crowd of customers and new ones, and made a good $1,000 before lunch. Everyone around school called them the weed plugs. They both split it down the middle and Rico knew exactly what he wanted to do with his hard-earned money.

Rico waited outside the school for Leah to come out. He knew she had book club meetings around this time and wanted this to be the perfect time for him to talk to her.

"Leah!" He called out to her. She stopped in her tracks with an unwelcoming expression on her face. Only thing that did was turn Rico on even more. It was something sexy about when Leah got mad.

"What Rico?" She asked crossing her arms.

"Hey uh...look I just wanted to apologize for getting you in trouble. I didn't want it to go down like that. And to show you how sorry I am...I was thinking maybe we could go out on a date tonight."

"I don't know." If it was one thing Leah knew how to do, it was playing hard to get. But Rico saw right through all of that.

"Don't you know that new seafood restaurant they built downtown? We could go there. Come on, babe. Just give me another chance to make this right."

"Well.... ok fine. You lucky my parents are out of town anyway. Be at my house around nine."

"Ight then forsho'." Rico smiled from ear to ear. Things were starting to look back up.

Back at home, Rico was trying to find something to wear for his date with Leah, until Tony barges in.

"What the-bro have you ever heard of knocking?" Rico said.

"Listen you wanna prove yourself now is the time. Throw something on. We got a hit to do."

"A hit? What do you mean a hit?"

"Nigga, you know what I mean. We gotta go light somebody up right quick for Shawty."

"Uhh...I would but see I got a date-"

"Rico, damn the date. You begged me to teach you the game and this is part of it. Now do you want to prove yourself or don't you?"

"I mean yeah more than anything, but-"

"Then it's settled. Come on, let's go." Tony said heading for the door.

Rico looked at his watch and it read a quarter to eight. *Oh Leah, please don't be mad.* Rico hurried along hoping he would still make it on time for his date.

Twenty minutes later, Tony and Rico pulled up to the location Shawty told them to go to.

"Ight, this bitch ass nigga should be walking out any minute now." Tony said turning the head lights off.

Rico was listening but the only thing that was on his mind was getting this over with and getting to Leah. He sneakily was texting her while Tony had his head turned.

Be there soon I promise. Xoxo.

As soon as their target walked out the store, Tony's eyes lit up. This nigga had been snitching to the cops about Shawty and his operation for months. Little did he know Shawty knew each and every police officer very well and nothing got past him. As soon as someone told him what was being done, Shawty gave Tony the order to put an end to it.

"You ready Rico?" When he didn't get no answer, Tony turned his head and saw Rico texting away on his phone.

"Rico!" Tony yelled.

"Huh? What? Yeah ok. Let's do this." Tony curled his upper lip up which usually meant he was getting pissed off.

"Look, we are on a mission right now. Pay attention. Stay alert. Don't make me regret bringing you here tonight." Tony said in a serious tone. Rico just nodded his head in agreement.

"Come on, let's go do what needs to be done." He and Tony got out the car and walked up to the target of interest.

"What's up Loc?" Tony said.

"Oh....hey what's up Tony?" he said back shakily.

"What's up is word on the street is you been running your mouth." Tony said back. Loc looked at Tony for a moment before he took off running.

Tony and Rico ran after him. Loc dipped into an alley way, and Tony pulled his gun out ready to shoot.

POP! POP! POP!

Tony shot at him, but he missed.

"Fuck!" Tony kept running behind him, with Rico in tow, until suddenly Rico slipped and fell. He slowly got up and could feel a drop of blood dripping from his eyebrow.

"Come on Rico!" Tony yelled. Rico shook it off and went back to running.

When their target got to the end of the alley, there was a metal gate blocking his way. He started to climb up the gate, but Tony caught up with him and pulled him back down throwing him on the ground.

"Come on man. Please don't kill me." Loc started crying.

"That's not my call Loc." Tony said pulling out his gun.

"Please man!" Loc began shaking. Rico had finally caught up out of breath. Tony pauses and thinks of a good idea.

"Actually, you know what...I'm not going to kill you. He is." Tony put the gun in Rico's hand.

"Me?"

"Yeah you. Shoot his ass Rico." Tony said. Rico looked at the gun in his hand and had a nervous feeling he never felt before. He had never used a gun before, let alone kill somebody.

"Come on man! Don't do this to me man." Loc continued pleading.

"Tony I...I can't."

"What the fuck you mean you can't? You asked me to show you the game...to teach you. Killing no good ass snakes is a part of the game. It's either you kill them or they gon kill you. That same fire I saw in your eyes about selling some fucking weed, I need to see that same fire in your eyes when these bullets start flying. When a nigga cross you, you shoot that motherfucka. I need you to pretend that he's that nigga." Tony said getting inside Rico's head.

Rico held the gun slightly up, with Tony's guidance, and aimed it at Loc who by now shitted on himself.

"Now shoot." Tony whispered in his ear. Rico did a big gulp and counted inside his head.

Three...two...one

Pop! Pop! Pop!

Rico closed his eyes as he shot Loc. When he opened them Loc was slumped over with blood gushing out his chest.

"Good job, but next time don't count to yourself. Just shoot. Come on, let's go." Tony said walking back towards the car.

Rico looked on in amazement at how Tony even knew he was counting in his head. He looked back at the dead body and felt a rush go through him. As of today, he had his first body.

Racing back home and borrowing Tony's car, Rico rushed over to Leah's house. Judging by all the missed calls and text messages he had, he knew she was probably pissed. It was already after ten and the restaurant they planned on going to was closed by now. That still didn't stop Rico from trying to win her back.

Ding dong!

Rico waited patiently for Leah to answer the door. At first, he heard nothing, and just as he went to ring the bell again, Leah opens the door. If looks could kill, Rico would be laid out right now.

"Babe...I can explain."

"I don't want to hear it." She starts to close the door, but he stops her.

"Listen, if you let me come inside I can explain everything." He said. Leah went from looking him in his face and noticed his eyebrow was bleeding.

"What happened to your eyebrow?" Rico touched above his

eye and almost forgot about the fact that he fell.

"I uhh...I fell."

"...Come in. My mom has a first aid kit upstairs." Leah opens the door to let Rico in.

While tending to his wound, Rico told her everything. About the weed, about what Tony does for a living, and about the shooting. He thought he would regret telling her, but in a way he felt good about getting everything off his chest and didn't have to lie anymore.

"Wow...I can't believe you kept all of this from me." Leah said.

"I know. I guess I did it because...I thought you wouldn't understand."

"Rico, I understand more than you think. But I think you need to leave the street life alone. That shit is not for you."

"I'm not in the streets Leah. I just sell the product ok; it's a difference." He said. There was a long pause between them.

"You know...I never told you this, but I have an older brother." Leah said.

"For real?" All this time Leah had never mentioned having an older brother, so now he was wondering where she was going with this conversation.

"Well...had an older brother. He used to sell drugs and hang out in the streets around the same guys you and your brother hang around. Until one night he got shot." Leah said with sadness in her voice. It was hard for her to talk about her brother and what happened, which is why she declined her parents trying to make her go to therapy.

"Damn. I'm sorry to hear that ma."

"It's ok, but something my father always used to tell me was...dealing with a street boy will only get you heartbreak because of death or jail. I just don't want that to happen to you Rico." Leah said making deep eye contact with him. Rico moved a piece of hair out her perfectly round face.

"I will never break your heart Leah." He said holding her chin making her lean closer to him. Before you knew it their lips touched. Rico loved how soft Leah's lips were and it had him hot and ready. They separated their lips and stared at each other for a moment. Rico could read a different expression on her face. One that looked more passionate.

"Umm...well if you want, we can go catch a late-night movie. I heard that new Martin Lawrence movie is good." Rico said, but Leah remained silent just staring at him.

"You ok Leah?" he asked her.

"Yeah I'm fine, but I don't want to go to the movies."

"Well whatever you feel like doing we can do." Rico said. Leah started biting her bottom lip.

"I uhh...I want you to take my virginity tonight Rico." Leah said. Rico's eyes grew large out of shock.

"You...I...for real?" Rico couldn't believe after months and month of Leah saying she wasn't ready, and other bumps in the road, he had finally gotten the green light.

"Come on. My bedroom is up here." She grabbed his arm leading to her bedroom.

Once they got there Leah turned her lights off and opened the blinds to let the moonlight peek in.

"Leah, you sure you want to do this? You don't have to if you not ready." Rico said.

"Yeah.... I'm sure." She said. Rico didn't know if she was really ready or she was just making herself ready because of the whole Angela situation. Either way, he wasn't going to turn down the chance to have sex with the only girl he really loved.

Leah starts undressing until she is fully naked. She had double D cup sized breasts, and her hips and butt gave her that perfect hourglass shape. Rico was in awe staring at his girl naked in front of him. He pulled his shirt off and his sweat pants down to his boxers. He had sent pictures of his dick to Leah before, but this would be the first time she seen it in person. When he whipped it out, he could tell by her expression she didn't think it would be that big. It kind of reminded him of that scene from *Love & Basketball* when Quincy and Monica first had sex.

Leah was in shock but turned on at the same time. She could feel the middle of her getting moist as Rico walked over to her. The sunlight was glistening on his smooth skin, and for him to only be sixteen he was built like he already was twenty. He caressed Leah's face and kissed her like it was his last.

Pushing her softly onto the bed, Rico was ready to give baby girl something she would remember. Especially since this was her first time. Leah laid on her back and Rico hovered over her. He could feel her start to tense up as he rubbed the tip against her opening.

"Relax ma. I'm not going to hurt you." He whispered and kissed her neck.

Leah relaxed her legs as Rico made his way inside. At first, it was a little painful only because she was so tight from not getting any. She grabbed onto his back trying to brace herself. When she felt something pop, she tried to hold her scream in because she didn't want Rico to think he was hurting her and stop.

"You ight shawty?" Rico asked. Leah nodded her head yes and they kept going.

The way Leah's pussy felt around his dick had Rico's mind blown. Before even making things official with Leah, he had some encounters with girls who had some ok pussy and some that would make you slap your mamma. But this right here made him feel more connected to Leah because she trusted him with her body.

"Mmmm." A soft moan slipped from Leah's lips, letting Rico know to only go deeper and remain gentle.

Rico breathed hard into her neck. For her to be a virgin, her pussy felt like a warm jacuzzi. He could feel his nut coming on but didn't want to pull out yet. He wanted to savor this moment. He sped up a little and could tell by Leah's expression that she was enjoying it.

"Mmmm.... ohhh Rico baby." Leah yelled out. He went faster and deeper knowing he was hitting that spot. When it came time for him to nut, Rico quickly thought to himself.

Should I nut in her?

She might kill me for doing that though.

I don't even know if she on birth control.

Having a little Rico Jr. don't sound too bad...but she might still kill me though.

"Fuck!" Rico pulled out and quickly nutted all in his hand. He walked to the bathroom and washed his hand, wiping the last remaining drips off of him.

He came back into the room and saw Leah still in the same position staring up at the ceiling. *Ha ha my poor baby. This dick got her worn out.*

"You ok?" Rico asked laying down next to her.

"I feel...amazing. My legs feel stuck but...it was wonderful."

Leah said turning over to her side facing him.

"Well, what can I say. This dick isn't nothing to play with." Rico said.

"Can I ask you something?" Leah asked.

"What's up?"

"When you had sex with Angela...did you...like it?" Leah asked. Rico should have known that question would eventually come up.

"Honestly...no I didn't. I was tipsy, I didn't know what I was doing...I wish I never even went to that stupid party." Rico said. Leah's eyes was fixed on him, but deep down inside she still thought about it and just needed to know the truth.

"Leah, I want to never hurt you like that again. Ever." He said holding her caressing her hand. They started kissing again and just like before Rico's dick got rock hard.

"Look at you, just getting started and don't know how to stop." Rico joked.

"Shut up." Leah said. Just as they were about to get in to it again, Leah heard a familiar noise.

"Wait...you hear that?" Leah asked.

"Hear what?"

"Leah! Sweetheart, we're back!" Leah's mom called.

"Oh shit!" They both hopped up trying to put their clothes on.

"I thought you said they was out of town." Rico said in a low tone.

"They were." Leah could hear her mother's footsteps coming up the stairs.

"Quick uh...hide under the bed." Leah said.

"What?" Rico said wondering why did shit like this always have to result in hiding in closets or under beds.

"Just do it!" Leah said getting nervous and hoping her mother does not walk in on them.

Rico quickly dived under the bed. Leah had all kinds of shit under there. Mostly shoes, stuffed animals, and a clean pair of pink lace underwear that he would now stuff in his pocket. He heard the bedroom door open and made sure he didn't make a sound. It was bad enough her parents were trying to keep her from talking to him. Imagine what would happen if they knew they had sex and he was now hiding under the bed.

"Oh, hey momma. I was just...reading a book." Leah quickly put a robe on and was laying across her bed pretending to read a book. "What are you guys doing back so early?" she asked.

"Oh that hardheaded father of yours got food poisoning at some restaurant we stopped at on the way to visit your grandmother. So, we had to turn back around and continually make stops along the way for him to vomit on the side of the road.

"Ohhh,, well I hope he's ok."

"He will be. Well goodnight baby."

"Goodnight mom." Leah said.

"Oh, and one more thing, whose car is that parked outside?" Her asked referring to Rico's car.

"Oh umm...I don't know. Maybe the neighbors."

"Hmm, probably their son Kenneth's car. Oh well, goodnight sweetie."

"Goodnight." As soon as Leah's mother left the room, Rico climbed from under the bed.

"Actor of the year award goes to Leah Goodson." Rico said giving her praise.

"So how you plan on sneaking me out of here?" Rico said.

"Well, there's only one way out." Leah said and looked at her bedroom window.

"Oh hell no. What? Are you trying to kill me?"

"There isn't another way Rico."

"Like hell there is. You better wait until your parents fall asleep and sneak me out of here." Rico said. There was no way he was going to jump from Leah's window and end up with broken bones.

"Rico, my dad has food poisoning. I don't think he's going to sleep anytime soon with him running back and forth to the bathroom." Rico sighed but realized she had a point. The only way out would be through the window.

"Ight, help me climb out." Rico opened the window and looked down. It didn't look like too far of a jump, but still Rico didn't want to take any chances.

He climbed on to the window sill and put his legs out first. Once his whole body was over the edge, he counted to three and made a jump for it.

One...two...three. Thankfully the bushes at the bottom broke his fall. He got up and brushed himself off. He looked back up at the window to see Leah was still there.

"Call me when you get home." She said.

"I will....aye Leah?" He said before she shut the window.

"I love you." For the first time, Rico could admit that he loved Leah with all his heart. Any female that was so willing to forgive a nigga who constantly messed up, was ride or die. Leah was the kind of girl he needed and was glad to have her in his life.

A few days later....

Today was Rico's eighteenth birthday. He felt like he was becoming more and more of a man, especially since Tony let him sell weed, and him and Leah had finally had sex. Life couldn't get any better.

"Wake up birthday boy." Tony said barging into his room.

"Ya ass still don't know how to knock." Rico said rubbing his eyes.

"Fuck knocking. I came in here to tell you that I am throwing you the biggest birthday party ever later."

"I don't really want a party."

"What?! Why not?" Tony asked confused.

"Because that's kiddie stuff. Birthday parties are played out anyway."

"Well, fuck what you saying. I'm going to throw a party anyway and ya ass just not invited." They both laughed at Tony's humor. Rico finally got out the bed and went to shower.

At school, he met Leah by her locker who brings him a gift. After chatting it up about the upcoming holidays, he met Anthony behind the school to do their usual selling spot. By lunchtime, they were sold out of weed.

"Damn we all out?" Anthony asked him.

"Yeah, looks like it."

"Damn...so what are we going to do now?"

"Just have to get more. Maybe I can call Tony and ask him to bring us another pound."

Just as the boys were discussing a plan, a group of older guys walked up to them.

"Hey little homies, this here our territory." They said. Rico and Anthony both looked at each other and began laughing.

"Yeah right. This is our turf. We were here first." Rico said. One of the boys grabbed Rico by the collar.

"You're a little big mouth aren't you?"

"Hey man, let him go." Anthony said trying to get the boy off of Rico.

"Oh yeah, and what are you going to do about it?" Anthony looks at Rico's face and watched him do a head nod.

"Now!" Rico kneed the boy holding him right in the crotch and they break out into a brawl.

Rico swung left and right trying his best to fight back. Anthony would help him out by blocking anyone who came near him. It was like a game of football but without the ball.

"Hey! Hey! Break it up!" Rico could hear the principal's voice but that didn't stop him from trying to fight.

Once the principal and school security were able to break up the fight, all five of the boys ended up getting suspended. When Rico went home and told Tony what happened, he was grateful that Rico stood up for himself, but that still didn't stop him from fussing at him about getting suspended.

"Who in their right fucking mind gets suspended on their birthday Rico?" Tony said as they were riding in his Audi A4. Tony had a surprise party planned for Rico and couldn't wait to see the look on his face.

"What was I supposed to do? Let them punk us?" Rico said.

"No, that's the last thing you want to do, but damn, you

couldn't wait until after your birthday and then fight? Shit, I practically had to bribe the principal to not expel you."

"Well, look. I had to do what needed to be done."

"Then you don't it. Another rule to this game, always have your goons do your dirty work like fighting and all that other shit. Only time you do shit yourself is when you have to dead a nigga." Tony said. Rico nodded his head and understood what his brother was saying. Over the past few weeks, Tony had been giving Rico tip and tricks on different things. He was coming to realize the game wasn't just about selling weed or dope, but included a whole different lifestyle.

"Now I'm not going to rag on you all night due to the fact it's your birthday, but just remember what I said." Tony said pulling up to this huge mansion.

"I will...whose house is this?" Rico asked. He was mesmerized by the beauty of the mansion. It had to be at least six bedrooms and four bathrooms in there. Rico knew whoever house this was had to be big time. Tony remained silent as he opened the door and had Rico behind him.

"SURPRISE!!!" Rico almost turned white until he saw everyone from school shouting happy birthday at him.

"You sneaky ass nigga. I told you I ain't want no party." Rico laughed trying to catch his breath from being startled.

"I know but you know I don't listen. Everybody, let's get this shit jumping!!" Tony yelled and signaled the DJ to start the music.

It seemed like everyone from school was there. Rico even recognized some of the guys Tony hanged with from the trap. Only two people that was missing. Anthony, but he figured it only because his dad grounded him, and Leah. Either way he knew she had to have heard about the party and was going to be there. Rico started looking for her until Tony walked up beside him with some shot glasses.

"To being...two young ass niggas getting it." Tony said and they clinked their shots glasses. Rico swallows the glass full of fire tasting liquid.

"Do you know if Leah is here?" Rico shouted over the loud music.

"Nigga how am I supposed know? That's yo girl. I'm sure she gon show up, but in the meantime, go enjoy yourself. There's plenty of other pretty girls here."

"Naw I think I'm going to just wait for Leah." Tony didn't all the way understand why Rico was so sprung over one girl.

"I thought you might say that. That's why I invited my friends here tonight. Aye Sky! Peaches!" Rico turned around to where Tony was shouting to and his eyes almost fell out of his head.

There before him stood two fine ass exotic dancers, half naked, and had everyone's full attention.

"Is this the birthday boy?" The one named Peaches said.

"Sure is." Tony replied back. Rico was stuck and didn't know what to say. He had never seen such beautiful bodies up close and personal before.

"Ohhh, he is so cute. I can dance with him all night." The other dancer named Sky said. She caressed Rico's shoulders while Peaches bent over in-front of him shaking everything her mother gave her. The DJ started spinning "Back That Thing Up" by Juvenile. Rico figured he could maybe have a little fun. After all, it was his birthday.

Rico went from looking like a deer in headlights to making it look like he was in the actual strip club. Everyone surrounded them cheering Rico on as him and Tony broke out some one-dollar bills and made it rain. The liquor from the shots had started to sink in and made Rico feel like he was on cloud nine. All up until he locked eyes with Leah watching from afar.

"Oh shit." Rico said to himself. When Leah saw he noticed her she quickly walked back out the door of the mansion. Rico cut the lap dance short and ran after her.

"Leah! Leah! Leah wait!" He grabbed her arm but she snatched away.

"Don't touch me!"

"Leah, I'm...I was looking for you."

"Oh yeah, all while you were getting assed down by your two hoe friends."

"No, my brother...look Leah just come back inside and we can talk about this."

"There's nothing to talk about Rico. As matter of fact, I don't want to talk to you ever again!" Leah got inside the all-white Chevrolet her dad let her borrow for the night and sped off with tears in her eyes.

Rico once again felt like shit. Here he was trying to prove he really loved Leah and wanted to be with her but still kept fucking up. He decided to go back to the party, but tomorrow he was going to do whatever he could to get Leah back...again.

Chapter 7

One month later....

Hey mom,

Hope everything back home is going well.. I know in your last letter you were worried about Tony and me, but I can assure you we have been doing fine. I know you also wanted to know about dad...me or Tony haven't seen or heard from him in years. Honestly it's probably best. As far as how me and Leah, the girl I told you about, she's still mad at me. I really messed up big time, but hopefully things will work out. I miss you mom and pretty soon I'll have enough money to come visit you for Christmas this year.

Amar,
De'Rico.

P.S. Happy Thanksgiving.

It was Thanksgiving Day and Rico was just finishing up the letter to Serafina. When the aroma of food filled his nose, he went out into the kitchen area to see if dinner was done yet. Tony and him decided to have dinner with just the two of them. Rico did want to invite Leah, but she was still ignoring him after what happened at his birthday party. So the only upside was the good tasting food. Tony might have been a street nigga but he knew how to throw down.

"Damn, that smell good. Is that the pie?" Rico asked.

"Yup, I just took out the rolls and the mac and cheese. We gon be feasting like kings tonight." Rico loved it when he got to spend time with his brother. He was either at the trap day in and day out or making runs. But being as though it was a holiday today, Tony decided all of that could wait.

An hour later, they were both eating the food Tony had made. He learned from his mother and a little bit from some of the hoes he messed around with how to cook. Rico thought it would be the perfect time to tell him the good news.

"So guess what?" Rico said.

"Nigga you know I hate guessing...but what is it?"

"My grades are going up. Coach said if I can stay at a B, he'll let me back on the team." Rico said. He kind of missed being on the team even though he got kicked off before his first game.

"You know I'm happy for you, bro, but check this out, I was finally able to convince Shawty to meet with us. I told him let me put you on to some real product."

"Yo for real?" Rico could jump across the table and hug Tony, but he knew that would be doing too much.

"Yeah, but...the only thing is you gotta do one or the other. Either football or trapping." Just that quick Rico's excitement went down the drain. *Give up football?* He thought long and hard about it and didn't know what to choose.

"Ahhh, I'm full. If you'll excuse me I gotta go take a shit." Tony said getting up from the table.

Rico just sat there not knowing which direction to go in. With football, he knew he had the potential to go to college and even earn a scholarship. But it wasn't a guarantee. On the flip side, hustling weed was making him a good profit, but if he could go much higher than weed he knew that would be double the money he made on a daily. Even with that there was still the risk of getting killed or going to jail. The next day at school Rico met up with Anthony to tell him what his brother said.

"Yo what?! He gon let you sell some dope?" Anthony said.

"Shhh. Yo man, keep your voice down."

"Sorry, but damn. You know much bread we gon be making."

"Yeah that's the catch. Tony said I have to give up being back on the football team."

"Damn...you can't just do both?" Rico shook his head no. "So what are you going to do?"

"I don't know but I need to figure it out but the meeting this evening." With wandering eyes Anthony noticed something he knew was going to make Rico upset.

"Looks like that ain't the only thing you need to get figured out." Rico had a confused look until Rico turned around and saw Leah and their classmate Jamal.

"Man, aw hell naw. Out all the niggas she could've left me for, she choose this pussy ass nigga!" Rico yelled. It had been a while since Rico and Leah talked. Leah was still in her feelings, even after Rico said he was sorry. At end of the day though he missed his baby and wanted to prove he wouldn't fuck up again.

"Yeah...I heard they dating now."

"Man ,fuck that." Rico walked over to where they was sitting across the courtyard. As soon as they locked eyes, Leah instantly got nervous. If it was one person who knew what Rico was capable it was Leah.

"Leah?! What the fuck is going on?!" Rico asked aggressively.

"None of your business Rico." Leah snapped back.

"Oh yeah? What? Are you fucking him too?" Rico asked but not meaning to say. He vowed to get back on Leah's good side and he knew this wasn't the way. But seeing Leah on the arm of someone other than him was painful.

"Come on, let's go Jamal." Leah grabbed Jamal's arm and walked away. Rico wanted to run after her and kick Jamal in the face. He decided not to because he wanted Leah to come to him willingly. So right now, he decided to let it go and prepare himself for this meeting with Shawty.

Later that evening, Tony and Rico arrived at the warehouse that Shawty owned. They both had to do security checks at the door. Rico wasn't fond of being patted down, but Tony told him it was necessary for everyone, even the workers. When they reached Shawty's office, they entered to see him with his feet up on the desk, while smoking a cigar.

"Well, if it isn't the rio brothers." Shawty said with a wide, fake smile.

"What's up Shawty." Tony said but Rico remained silent.

"So what's this I hear about you wanting to be recruited into the drug game." Tony said to Rico.

"Yeah...I want in."

"Hahahahah...little nigga you should want in those textbooks. I heard through the grapevine you failed your classes. Now what would I look like taking a child away from his education."

"Come on Shawty. Can't you see that he's ready." Tony added in. Shawty had a real problem with trusting people. And right now he didn't trust Rico. He didn't care if he was kin to Tony or not.

"Shawty...with all due respect, I think I'm ready. I have already sold hundreds maybe thousands of bags of weed at school. If I can do that imagine how much I can sell on the street."

"Hmm you got a point youngin'. But you need to understand this is ain't no weed we are talking about."

"...I know that." Rico said. Shawty looked back and forth between Tony and Rico still feeling a little unsure.

"He's your responsibility Tony. Show him what you know without just throwing him to the wolves." Shawty said.

"I got you big dawg."

"Good. Now get out of my office. I have shit to do." Shawty said side-eyeing Rico.

On the way out, Shawty's henchmen gave Tony and Rico a key of cocaine to start off with. Rico felt like from this point on, his life was never going to be the same.

The next morning, Tony got Rico up early so they could both hit the block. Tony figured now would be a good time to train him so Rico could get a good idea of what he was going to endure.

"Why are we sitting in the car?" Rico asked.

"Because this is what you do. You see those corner boys? They do all the exchanging and we are the link between it." Tony pulled out his phone and holds it in his hand.

"Man, when are we-"

"Shhh, just look." Tony said. They both looked out the window at a black Camry pulling up to the block. One of the corner boys approached the car and appeared to be talking to the person in the driver's seat. The boy then goes over to the pay phone and dials a number.

Bzzzzz! Bzzzz! Tony's phone began to vibrate as he picked it up.

"Yeah...tell him we ain't got that today. We only got blue tops and green tops." Tony hangs up the phone.

"Make a mental note that these customers can get a little demanding. Also always wait for the corner boy to call you. Never call them first."

"Why?" Rico asked. This trapping stuff looked much more complex than he thought.

"In case you get caught that's why, but that's another rule... never get caught. Stay on your P's and Q's." Tony explained.

"What does P and Q stand for?" Rico was now full blown confused.

"We have a lot of work to do." Tony sighed.

Tony's phone rang again. This time after Tony gave the green light to make the sale, the corner boy came walking by the car and got the vials from Tony. The boy made the sale and quickly stuffed the money in his pocket.

"So how do we get paid if the corner boys taking all the money?" Rico asked.

"They don't take anything. They get a percentage and if any of them try to short me...well let's just say the next time anyone sees them is at the funeral home." Tony said showing his piece tucked at his side. Tony's phone rang again for another sale. He let Rico answer the phone to get the hang of things and after a few hours Rico would answer the phone, tell the corner boys what they had, how much the customer wanted to pay, and Tony would make the transaction. By the end of the day, Tony and Rico went home with 3,000 in their pockets. Thus the start of Rico getting into the drug game.

A few weeks later....

Over the next few weeks, Tony shows Rico how to trap, how

to make drops, and even how to cook a little product if he ever needed to. Eventually Rico was able to buy his first car; a BMW Z4. With Christmas right around the corner Rico felt on top of the world. He decided playing football would probably never make him this much money within weeks. Only thing missing was...Leah. She still wouldn't return his phone calls and on the days when he would go to school she acted like he was invisible, but Rico had an idea.

"Uhh excuse me...excuse me?" Rico said trying to get the sales lady attention. It was Christmas Eve and he was just about done shopping for everyone, and he wanted to get Leah something special. He spotted a diamond necklace he figured she would like. It cost a pretty penny, but he felt like it was worth it.

"Hello? Can I get some help over here?" Rico said for what felt like the hundredth time. The sales lady turned around with an attitude and walked over towards him.

"Yes, can I help you?" She said snobbery.

"Uh yeah, I want to purchase that necklace right there." Rico said.

"Well, I don't see how being as though that necklace is worth a thousand dollars."

"I know. I have money I can-"

"Listen, why don't you just save yourself the trouble and leave before I call security."

"Security? But why I'm-"

"I said leave ok, just leave. I will not be intimidated by you thugs today." Rico looked at the lady in confusion, until he fully understood what was going on. He was engaging in his first racial profiling.

"Is everything ok over here?" A Black guy dressed in a plaid button down and khaki pants walked over to them.

"Uhm, I don't know. All I asked this lady was could I buy a necklace and she threatened to call security on me." Rico said.

"Listen, you and...your dad need to leave." The sales lady said again.

"Excuse me? Kathern is it?" The guy said.

"Yes, and who are you?" The lady asked.

"I'm actually the new superintendent of this store." He said. The sales lady's face suddenly flushed when he said that.

"Oh, well uhh...I wasn't aware-"

"You wasn't aware of your bad customer service skills or the fact that you're being a racist?" The guy said.

"I'm sorry; it's just....we get so many young kids who come in here stealing, I...I just thought-"

"You just thought nothing. Now here is what I think, I think you should take the rest of the day off. Permanently." When he said that, the lady's face turned red with embarrassment as she walked away from the counter.

"I apologize for that young man. Hey Justin, can you come assist this young man in whatever he needs and give him my discount while you're at it." He called out to another sales associate.

"Sure thing." Rico had never experienced racism before, but now that he knew what it was like, he would know how to respond next time.

After getting the necklace wrapped up, he made his way over to Leah's house.

He pulled up in front of her house, dreading to ring the bell.

Ding-dong!

It took a good five minutes before Leah finally came to the door. When she snatched the door open, Leah stood there shocked at Rico being on her doorstep.

"Rico, what are you doing here?" She asked looking over her shoulder making sure her dad didn't notice.

"I uhh...Leah look, I know I fucked up. But that don't change how I feel about you."

"Rico-"

"Just listen...the strippers weren't my idea. They were Tony's...but not saying that's an excuse. Leah...I love you. I knew since I saw you, you just had to be mine. I know you may not forgive me right now but...hopefully this will show you how sorry I am." Rico pulled out the wrapped gift box.

Leah wasn't at first interested in Rico's sorry apology but was now intrigued by the small gift box. She quickly unwrapped it and gasped when she saw the shiny diamond necklace.

"Rico...are these real?" She asked.

"Of course, they're real. You didn't think I was gon' have you rocking anything fake did you?"

"They're-" Suddenly Leah felt a presence behind her.

"Young man what are you doing at my house?" Leah's dad asked.

"I umm...came to see Leah." Rico said boldly. He figured now would be good as any time to show Leah's father how mature he was to stand up to him.

"Well she cannot be seen right now. Especially by the likes of you." He pushed Leah inside the house and now stood in the doorway.

"With all due respect sir...I love Leah and...I don't think it's right you're trying to control her life like she's two years old." Rico said. Leah smiled on the inside at how Rico was standing up to her father.

"Love? You or her don't have a clue about love. Now I'm only going to say this once...stay away from my house and stay away from my daughter." He shut the door right in Rico's face. He knew in his heart Leah's father telling him to stay away would only make him want her even more.

Tap! Tap!

Rico turned around and saw Leah in the upstairs window. She used the frost on the window to draw a heart. Rico returned the gesture by making a heart with his fingers. Nothing was going to stand in his way now that he had his other half back.

Chapter 8

Christmas Day....

"Thanks G." The corner boy said grabbing the last vial of coke out of Rico's hand through his car window. He watched as he ran back over to the customer and completed the transaction. He was flying solo today only because Tony didn't work on certain holidays like today, but to Rico it was just another day.

Celebrating Christmas was never really a thing they did growing up, due to them being so poor. Only thing they did was fast, pray, and be thankful to have each other. But now that things were different, Rico knew the perfect gift to get his brother.

As far as Leah, they went back to communicating shortly after he showed up at her house. He could only call or page her at a certain time so her father wouldn't suspect nothing. He ordered some flowers to be delivered to her today and hoped she got them. If not, he would just keep sending them until she did.

"5-0! 5-0!" Rico immediately lifted his head up and saw police lights.

"Aww shit!" Rico started the car up and drove off.

At first, he thought the police didn't notice him, until he saw them in his rearview mirror. He sped through a traffic light and hopped on the highway. The police chased after him, but was no match for Rico's engine. He began doing 100 mph and tried to think of a way to lose them. When he reached a point where the highway didn't have a barrier wall, Rico swerved over to the other side, almost crashing into other cars and began going the other way.

He got off at the closest exit and dipped into a nearby alleyway. Taking a minute to catch his breath, Rico flipped open his sidekick phone and sent a text to Tony. Once he didn't hear any sirens and it was safe, he started home while avoiding the freeway to stay low-key.

Thirty minutes later, he made it back home and couldn't wait to tell Tony how he dodged the police.

"Tony, you won't believe-"

"I already know. Little Tay Tay told me about the police rolling up on y'all."

"Man, they chased me down the highway, but I shook them though."

"Yeah, well next time lose them and the car. Just in case they took pictures."

"What?! So I was supposed to just leave my brand-new Audi on the side of the road?"

"Nigga it don't matter. You're a fucking drug dealer. You can buy a new one. Now get your ass over here and open your gift."

They both walked over to the tree and Tony hands him a gift wrapped in blue wrapping paper. Rico excitingly opened it and once he finished he was holding a .45 caliber gun in his hand.

"A gun?" Rico asked feeling a little nervous. The last time he held a gun was when Tony made him shoot someone.

"Yeah. It's about time you really learn how to use one. You never know if a nigga will try to short you, rob you, or if the police show up again and you can start bussing." Tony said. Rico just held the gun in his hand in amazement. *Wow my own gun. Definitely gotta keep this from Leah.*

"Ight where my gift at? And it better not be no bullshit." Tony asked. Rico dug in his backpack and pulled out a special edition Superman action figure.

"Sorry I ain't have time to wrap it." Rico said handing him the gift. Tony just stared at him with a disappointing look.

"What?" Rico asked.

"Nigga do I look five?....sike naw, I'm just fucking with you!" Tony laughed. Actually, he loved the gift. Growing up, Tony loved Superman and Rico remembered always begging their mom for one.

"Damn special edition?!....Thanks Rico. I appreciate this." Tony really admired the young man his little brother was becoming.

"Come on. Let's put that gun to the test."

A few hours later, Tony takes Rico on a desolate back road for target practice. He figured it would be no good if Rico walked around with a gun and didn't know how to use one.

Bang! Bang!

Rico shot the two soda cans down that Tony had set up.

"Good, but try not to stand like that. Go 'head try it again." Tony instructed.

Bang! Bang!

"Good...you know I saw dad the other day." Tony said. It caught Rico's attention because they hadn't seen their dad since leaving his house.

"He looked pretty bad...I think he might be using. Also I did

123

some digging and...remember those guys that were after him when we left New York? They were after him because he owed them money for drugs." Rico felt a little disappointed that his dad decided to go down that road. He thought about his dad from time to time and always thought they might could rekindle one day...but now those thoughts were down the drain.

"Rico? You ight?" Rico snapped out of his thoughts and focused on what Tony said.

"Let's just change the subject." Rico said. As of now, he was no longer interested in his father or anything involving him. Dewayne was dead to him.

Chapter 9

Later on, Tony finishes teaching Rico how to use his new gun and takes him to a brothel, which is also owned by Shawty. They pick out a few girls and get private lap dances.

"Damn Skylar, what'd you get? New implants or something?" Tony said talking to one of the girls. "Hey, bro how you liking this shit? This is the life huh?" he asked Rico who was more in a daze from thought.

"It's cool." Rico had other shit on his mind that didn't concern naked women right now.

"What's on your mind Rico? I know it's something bothering you." Tony could sense there was something eating at Rico and wanted to know what it was.

"Nothing, it's just…you ain't never think about starting our own business instead of working for Shawty?" Rico asked. This caught Tony off guard because he had never once thought about becoming competition for Shawty.

"Ladies, can you give us a minute?" Tony asked. The women did as they were told and left out the private room they were in.

"Rico, what are you saying?" Tony asked.

"I'm saying working for Shawty is…it's aight but it's not gon get us nowhere. We need to start thinking about doing this shit ourselves."

"Check this out. You ain't been in this game nothing but a minute. Working with Shawty is how we got a roof over our head, designer on our backs, and some fly ass cars to drive in."

"Yeah, but imagine what running our own drug empire could do. We could have mansions, more fly ass whips; I'm talking so much money we could go swimming in it."

"See, that is exactly why that imagination shit is for niggas who do the corner work. Not us because we already living their dream. That's exactly why I put you on as more than just some scruffy corner boy, because you're my brother and we both know what we came from."

"Tony, I hear you, but you have to think outside the box for once."

"I am and I'm also thinking how this could end if we go against Shawty. Lesson number one Rico…in this game you have to stay in your lane. That's how you make it. Now this conversation is over. I'm about to get some pussy." Tony said and left out the room.

Rico sighed at his brother's poor thinking. He would have thought Tony would be onboard with starting their own empire, but apparently he was too stuck in the lifestyle they was living. Rico wanted more and felt in his gut he was destined to have more. If Tony wasn't going to join him, then Rico would do the shit on his own.

"Wait a minute…run that by me again? We should what?" Anthony asked Rico the next day after class. Rico had started going back gradually to the point they wouldn't contact child services from him being absent so many times.

"We should start our own drug empire. Go into business for ourselves and you be my right-hand man." Rico said.

"What about Tony? Does he know about this?"

"Forget Tony. If he wants to continue working for another

nigga for the rest of his life then that's him. What we need to do is start building this shit ourselves from the ground up."

"And how are we supposed to do that?" Anthony asked. He thought Rico was crazy about this whole idea of becoming drug lords.

"Well, first we need a supplier. Someone who trusts us enough to let us sell their product. I heard from one of the corner boys I fucks with that Eduardo Domingo was looking for a new seller."

"Eduardo Domingo? Isn't he in like the Mexican Mafia or something?" Anthony asked.

"Nigga, he is the mafia. He's the leader of that shit."

"And how we gon' get him to sell to us instead of Shawty?"

"I uhh…I got it. We can have one of those sit downs at his restaurant over on Peachtree. It's called El Chupacabra."

"Rico, I don't know about this. Eduardo and his goons are dangerous and…we going against Shawty. This whole neighborhood pretty much fucks with him."

"Not if somebody new steps on the scene. Now are you with me or not?" Rico glared at Anthony and could tell he was scared, but he wanted his best friend to join him in this money-making plan.

"Alright fine."

"Good. Ok, let's meet up after school and drive over there."

Rico wasn't playing no games when he said he was going to talk to Eduardo and not leave until he did. He felt crazy about having to go behind his brother's back, but if that was what it took then so be it. After school, Rico and Anthony drove to the restaurant Eduardo owned. When they pulled up, it was two guards standing out front. Anthony got a little nervous, but Rico saw it as a piece of cake.

"Excuse me but...we're here to see Eduardo." Rico said walking up to the guard.

"Yeah right. Get lost kid." He said back to him.

"Not until we see Eduardo Domingo." Rico pressed on.

"I said get lost kid!" The guard said stepping closer to Rico standing almost six feet tall.

"Come on, Rico, let's just go." Anthony whispered to him, but Rico wasn't about giving up.

"Look, tell him...tell him Shawty sent us." Rico said hoping his lie would work. The two guards looked at each other and was starting to be convinced at the mention of Shawty's name.

"Wait here." One of the guards went inside, as Rico sighed relief that he might get in to talk to Eduardo. If that didn't work, there was always plan B; sneak in through the back door. After waiting about five minutes the guard came back out, this time holding the door open for Rico and Anthony.

"He says he'll see you, but be brief." The guard said.

Rico and Anthony walked in and could instantly smell the good cooking in the air. The place was decorated with all kinds of balloons and Mexican colors. They walked to the back where the guard told them to go and reached a door at the end of the hallway.

"Remember, just let me do all the talking." Rico said and knocked on the door.

"Come in, come in." Eduardo said. Rico and Tony entered right in the middle of Eduardo getting his tie fixed by his seamstress. He was an older Spanish guy, with black and gray hair.

"Who are you? What do you want?" Eduardo said in a hostile tone.

"If you don't mind, Mr. Eduardo sir, we would like to discuss some very important business matters." Rico said.

"Well, it's going to have to be quick. My granddaughter's wedding reception will be starting in thirty minutes."

"We promise this won't take long, but....I'll just come out and say it. We want you to sell to us."

"Haha what is this? I thought you boys where sent by Shawty? Now you're saying you want me to sell to you?"

"Yes sir. You see...working for Shawty is alright, but it ain't nothing like having your own."

"Hey...wait a minute. I know you. You're Tony's little brother."

"Yeah, I am."

"Right...so how do you think they would feel hearing about you coming in here demanding I sell to you and I already sell to them. I can assure you they would not be pleased."

"I know that, but quite frankly...I don't give a fuck. This is business."

"Haha...you know what, I like you. I like your boldness and fearlessness. Tell you boys what...I'll sell to you but you have to do something for me."

"Cool, what is it?" Rico was overjoyed that Eduardo was agreeing to this.

"Take out Shawty." Rico's smile, now turned into a frown.

"Uhh...come again?"

"You heard me. I want you to take him out."

"But uhh...but why? Why can't you just take him out your-self?"

"Hahaha, why do that and I have you two. That little piece of shit is becoming too much of a threat. Only reason I even deal with him is because his father and me were like brothers. Until that punta fucked my wife."

Anthony chuckled a little bit at the thought.

"Oh, you think that's funny?!" Eduardo said angrily.

"No, no- he doesn't." Rico said giving Anthony the look to be quiet, which he quickly did.

"Look...if you want Shawty gone, then it's done." Rico said.

"Good. Glad we could talk business. Now out, the both of you."

Back in the car, Rico and Anthony discussed the task they now had to carry out in order for this to work.

"Rico, how in the hell are we going to pull this off?" Anthony asked.

"What do you mean we? Ain't you flying to Miami for two weeks to visit your auntie."

"Well fine. How are you going to pull this off?"

"Easy. My brother ain't give me that gun for it to be just sit-ting in my closet. If Eduardo wants Shawty gone for him to sell to me, then so be it. Less competition anyway."

"But it's a lot of people who fuck with Shawty. A lot of hoods, drug dealers, mob bosses-"

"So. What that mean? Who said anyone was going to find out it was me anyway. Besides I already figured out the perfect time and place to do it. Killing Shawty will be like killing an ant at a picnic."

New Year's Day....

It was almost a new year and almost time for Rico to unfold his plan. Since Anthony was out of town, he would he doing this whole thing solo. Shawty was throwing his annual New Year's Eve bash at Club 2000. It seemed like the whole entire 404 area code was there. Strippers dancing everywhere, confetti falling, and bottles popping as everyone anxiously waited for the ball to drop. Tony and Rico had their own section along with some of Tony's homeboys.

As everyone else around him was having fun, Rico sat there letting his tunnel vision set in. He zeroed in on Shawty, whose section was across from his. He was dancing around, while popping bottles of expensive champagne. Rico stayed focused on his target so he could make his move. He knew he needed to get him alone without Tony seeing the two of them.

"Yo little brother you aight?!" Tony said snapping him back to reality.

"Yeah bro, I'm good."

"Aight well get up. Dance, drink...smack some ass." Tony said palming a bottle girl walking past him.

"I am. I'm just...tired that's all."

"Aww, there you go sounding like an old man. Well, I'm about to head back to one of these private rooms and get my balls licked before the ball drops."

"Haha ok. Go handle ya business." Rico said as he watched Tony walk to the back.

At that same given time, Rico saw out the corner of his eye that his target was moving. He looked over and saw Shawty headed for the bathroom. He thought now would be the perfect time to run up on him. He got up and unsuspectingly made his way towards the bathroom area too. When he got in the men's room there was a line, but Shawty was right in front of him.

"Hey uhh...Shawty can I talk to you for a moment?" Rico asked.

"What's up?" Shawty replied back dryly.

"No, I mean...outside." Rico said. He had to admit he was a little nervous, but the shit had to be done.

"Outside? Young blood, whatever you got to say to me..." Shawty turned around to face Rico, who was now flashing his gun at his waist. Shawty started surprisingly smiling and chuckling. He'd be lying to himself if he said Rico hadn't grown no balls over the past year.

"Fine little man...let's take this outside." Shawty said. They both leave out the bathroom and out a side door that leads to an alley. The brisk, cold air hit their faces as they stood silent.

"So tell me Rico...what's this really about?" Shawty asked. Without saying a word, Rico drew his gun from his waist and pointed it at Shawty.

"You know what the fuck is up nigga." Rico said trying to sound tough.

"No. I don't. Now why don't you explain to me what the fuck is going on and why you stupid enough to have a gun pointed in my face."

"Well, it's like this...see me and Tony been talking and we decided to go into business for ourselves. I paid a visit to Eduardo yesterday and-"

"You what?" Shawty said stepping closer to him. "Hmm... you ain't man enough to shoot me. Kill me and you'll be dead by morning."

"You got a lot to say for someone with a gun in his face."

"Listen, I understand you young. You hungry. You want your own empire, but the sad thing is you just don't have what it takes. You or ya bitch ass brother. Now why don't you give me the gun and we can pretend this never happened." Shawty said.

"...No."

"No?!"

"You heard what I said, I said no."

"You little-" Shawty charges at Rico trying to knock the gun out his hand.

Bang! Bang! Bang!

Rico sends three shots into Shawty. When Shawty falls down and is unresponsive Rico begins shaking. This was his second time killing somebody in cold blood. Suddenly, the side door busts open and coincidentally it's Tony. When he sees Shawty laying on the ground he quickly checks his pulse.

"Yo! Shawty!" Tony yells but doesn't get an answer back. "What did you do?!" Tony yells.

"Nothing I-"

"Well, this sure as hell don't look like nothing Rico!"

"Look Tony he....he was playing us."

"What?"

"He was playing us. He was going to sell us out." Rico said making up a reason why he killed Shawty.

"That's bullshit Rico! For as long as I've known Shawty he would never have done no shit like that!"

"Well, you didn't know him that well then."

"Yo, I swear if you wasn't my brother I would-"

"You would what? Kill me?!" Rico asked. There was a long pause between them.

"Look...I'm pretty sure somebody's called the police by now. You need to get the fuck out of here and I'll handle this. Give me the gun."

Rico glared at him, left wondering would Tony really kill him. He reluctantly gives Tony the gun back and starts to walk down the alley, until he is suddenly met with Atlanta police.

"Oh shit!"

"Run Rico!"

Rico starts to run the other way, until there are some more police cars coming down the opposite end. Two cops get out the car and point their guns at Rico.

"Freeze! Put your hands up." One of them shouted. Rico looked back at Tony, who was already leaned up against the wall being handcuffed. Rico just decided to surrender and put his hands behind his head. How will they get out of this?

Chapter 10

"Look you two can play stupid with me all you want, but I know the truth about you guy's little drug game."

After being booked and processed, Rico and Tony now had to be interrogated on illegal gun charges, drug charges, and Shawty's murder. Detective Brunson had been trying for hours to get answers out of Tony and Rico, but so far both of them stuck to the code to remain silent.

"The DEA has been trying to track down Shawty aka Shawn Harris for months...but now that he's dead, I guess we can call it a favor. Bad news is one of you still has to go down for his murder and the rest of these charges." Tony and Rico looked at each other. Tony was still feeling some type of way for Rico getting them into this. He loved his little brother, but hated when he made stupid decisions.

"Now from the looks of your records that we pulled up, you two aren't even from here. You're both originally from Brazil and your Visas expired almost three years ago. So here's the deal, one of you leaves this room free. The other one gets fifteen years and after that deportation back to Brazil. Whichever one of you decide I don't care, but the both of you aren't leaving this room together...I'll give you some time to decide." The detective leaves the room and now the two brothers sat in silence.

"I should go....I got us into this." Rico says finally.

"I would agree with you...if I didn't see the real reason why you did what you did." Tony said. Rico looked over at him confused.

"Little brother you always been...ambitious. When you came to me about the whole going solo thing...I said no because I forgot how much potential you have. You got the potential to be someone great. If you think for one second I'm going to let you throw that away, then not only have you let me down... but you let mom down...you let yourself down." Tony said. Rico usually tuned out when Tony started preaching, but this time was different.

"I been in this game for a while and you know that...maybe this is a sign telling me to sit my ass down and think. Think about life, think about more than just slanging. I've had my chance...now it's your turn." Rico couldn't believe Tony was going to take the blame for Shawty's murder. Before Rico could say anything, Detective Brunson came back in.

"So boys...have we reached an agreement?" He asked. Tony took one last look at his little brother before he went into confinement.

"I killed Shawty. The gun was mine." Tony said still looking at Rico and could almost feel a tear coming out his eye. The detective looked back at Rico and knew Tony was covering for him. In his mind, he thought Tony was actually brave for taking the blame for Shawty's murder. Had it been his little brother's life in jeopardy, he would've done the same thing.

"Alright...Tony Mitchell you're under arrest for the murder of Shawn Harris." Two police officers came into take Tony away. They uncuffed him from the chair and took him back to his cell.

Rico was at a loss for words. Everything was happening so fast and there was nothing he could say or do about it. He couldn't imagine what his life was going to be like without Tony.

"Hey kid...stay here. Somebody from child welfare wants to talk to you." The detective said. Hearing those words alerted Rico. He knew child welfare weren't good people. He remembers them coming by the house a few times trying to get Tony to sign over his guardianship rights but he would always bribe them with money to leave them alone. Already Rico's world was turning upside down.

A moment later, a White lady with red hair walks in. She sits across from Rico who is still handcuffed to the table.

"Hi De'Rico, my name is Marla with The Department of family and child services. I'm here because since your brother is going to be incarcerated and you have no next of kin that live here, and you're still a minor, the police are going to release you in our custody. Does that make sense?" Rico stared off into space with tears forming in his eyes, but still shook his head yes. "Ok, give me about an hour to get your release papers and we can go." She said and got up to leave. Rico looked over at the clock and saw it was midnight. It was now a whole new year.

Some hours later, Rico was released and getting into the back of Marla's car. As he drove away from the station, he thought about Tony. He was going to miss his brother, but now was the time to buckle down and become a man. Snapping back to reality, he realized he couldn't go with child welfare. They would throw him into the system and he would never get where he was trying to go.

When they pulled up to a red light, Rico saw it as his chance to make a run for it. He opened the back door and ran out.

"Hey! Hey!" Marla yells. She gets out the car and starts to chase after him, but realizes he's too fast.

After chasing him for a few blocks, Marla eventually gives up and lets him go. Rico ducks off into an alley and hides out behind a dumpster. He digs in his pocket for his keys and decides to go back to his and Tony's condo to grab some stuff. He knew by now they had towed his car, so the only other option was to walk.

He walked for what seemed like hours, but Rico finally made it to the apartment. Once inside he quickly grabbed some clothes, whatever money Rico had left in his safe, and the last brick of cocaine Tony had. He knew he couldn't stay in the apartment because child welfare would probably come searching for him with the cops. He only had $78 left and was pretty certain all the hotels were booked for the night. He was now out on the street with nowhere to go.

Finally tired of walking, Rico found a lonely bus stop and decided to rest there for the night. It went from chilly to now ice cold. Times like this Rico wished he could be back in Brazil where it's mostly warm year-round.

Just as he was about to lean his head back and go to sleep, he saw two bright headlights pulling up to where he sat. It was a classic red 1996 Cadillac Deville coupe. Rico squint his eyes to try to see the driver and could tell it was a lady driver.

"Hi there." She said. She was an older lady in her mid 40's, with red hair, and favored Pam Grier a little bit. "You lost or something?" She asked Rico.

"Uhh naw...just waiting for the bus." Rico lied.

"Hahaha...honey there ain't no buses running this time of night. Especially on New Year's." She said. "Do you...need a place to stay?" She asked but Rico shook his head no. It was bad enough everything that happened tonight had ruined half his life. He didn't need some strange lady in his business too. "You sure? It's fucking freezing out there and like I said it ain't gon be no buses until morning." Rico thought long and hard about what he could do. Either freeze on the bus stop or go with this strange lady and he had no gun.

"Naw...I don't have no place to stay." Rico finally admitted.

"Well, I got a three-bedroom house thirty minutes from here. If you want you can come stay with me." She said smirking. Rico got a bad feeling about all this but the thought of having a warm bed to sleep in sounded nice.

"Come on, get in...I won't bite." She said flirtatiously. Rico hesitantly gets up grabbing his duffle bag and gets inside the strange lady's car. "And what might your name be cutie?" She asked.

"Rico."

"Ok, I'm Lady Shonda but you just call me Shonda." She said. Rico looked Shonda up and down. She had on a tie up crop top that exposed the top half of her breasts and surprisingly flat tummy, and had on some white booty shorts. For her to be in her 40's, she was built like a Cowboy's cheerleader. Rico wasn't sure what this would lead to, but he made a promise to himself to use everything that Tony had taught him in order to survive.

When they arrived at Shonda's house, some people might have mistaken it for a trap house. It was a run down one level house, one of the windows was boarded up, and needed a serious paint job. They both got out the car and walked inside. To Rico it was pretty decent inside. It could be a little clean and not reek of cigarettes, but it was better than the bus stop.

"You'll have to excuse the mess. My maid's on vacation." Shonda said plopping down on the couch and lighting a cigarette.

"Oh naw it's cool." Rico sat his bag down and sat on the other chair.

"So what is it that you do Rico?" Shonda said blowing smoke out the side of her mouth.

"What do you mean?"

"I'm just saying...judging by the expensive tennis shoes on your feet, I can tell either you do something, or your parents."

"Well...my mom lives in Brazil and...I don't really know my dad." Rico said. In a sense he didn't feel like he was lying because he really didn't know Dewayne that well, even after living with him all that time.

"Well around here you got to pull your weight. I got bills to pay just like everybody else." Rico nodded his head and started to dig in his bag. He pulled out a brick of cocaine and put it on the coffee table.

"I think I got that covered." Rico said. He looks over at Shonda whose eyes lit up over the drugs.

"So you say-" Shonda reaches out to touch it but Rico snatches it back.

"This the last brick I got left."

"Ok, ok...I can respect it." Shonda sat back and began eye-balling Rico like a piece of meat.

"Umm...look I'm a little tired so...where can I sleep?" Rico asked feeling uncomfortable.

"You can take the back room. There's no bed in there though...just a mattress." She said continuing to look him up and down.

Rico grabbed his bag and brick and went to the room. It was a small room with a stained-up mattress in the middle of the floor and no windows. To go from the top back to the bottom was hitting really hard, but Rico was going to stop at nothing to get back up.

Once Rico was about to go to sleep Shonda knocks at his

door.

"Come in." He says. When the door opens, Shonda is standing there in nothing but a bra and thong. Rico didn't know whether to be turned on or weirded out.

"Let me ask you something Rico...have you ever had sex with an older woman before?" Shonda asked. Rico shook his head no. He couldn't even find the words for how he was feeling right now, but his dick was starting to rise.

"Well, here's the deal...you don't have to pay rent, but you have to please me sexually. I ain't had a fine young thing like you in a long time."

Rico stared at her silently and didn't know what to say. Him and Leah was still technically together, but lately her focus had shifted more on going away to college. Nowadays Rico worried about if they would even stay together after they graduate.

"But you know if you don't want to then there's plenty of room still left on that bus stop I picked you up from." If Rico could slap Shonda right now for even threatening the roof over his head, he would.

"So what's it gonna be Rico?" Shonda asked again. Rico had always heard stories about niggas having sex with older women. He was a little curious what it was like.

Before Rico could answer, Shonda gets up and walks over to him. "Maybe you just need a little more convincing." She gets in between his legs and starts to unzip his pants. Rico's brain was telling him to stop this, but the bulge in his underwear was saying something else.

Shonda pulls his dick out and begins to stroke it. She takes the tip and put it in her mouth. Rico starts to moan a little bit from the moisture of Shonda's mouth. She started to go down some more, taking him in deeper. She had head skills Rico has never experienced before. He felt semi bad for secretly cheating on Leah again, but if this was how Rico was going to survive then so be it. The rest of the night, Shonda kept Rico busy and even taught him some new things.

The next day, after a long night, Rico wakes up early to start selling his last brick. Once he got the re-up money he was going to pay Eduardo another visit. After walking along for a few hours, Rico finds a lonely block with mostly vacant houses on it. There was no other corner boys or competition. Rico was going to be the first to start selling here.

"Hey youngblood, you got a little something something? The other blocks are all out man." A crackhead says walking up to Rico.

"I sure do. $10 a hit."

"$10?! Damn man that's a lot." The crackhead said scratching his neck.

"Either $10 or you can hold out until the other blocks get some. Which probably won't be until tomorrow."

"Fuck! Alright fine." He gives Rico a ten-dollar bill. Rico takes out one of the mini plastic bags with dope in it and hands it over. He officially just made his first customer.

Over the next few weeks, Rico continues selling on his own block. Eventually Anthony joins in and a few other boys from school. They steadily buy from Eduardo while paying him 40% of what they make. After a while three more guys join them. This was the start of Rico's empire.

"Excuse me, I'm looking for my boyfriend Rico?" Rico heard a familiar voice while he was chatting it up with one of his corner boys. He turns around and sees Leah.

"Leah? What are you doing here? How did you find me?" Rico asked.

"I asked Anthony where you were. What are you doing? Why haven't you been to school?"

"Leah I'm-"

"Hey Rico, Connie from up the block says she wants two hits." A boy name Brandon interrupted.

"Ok go over there and there should be some underneath that loose brick. Tell her its $20 and an extra $10 from last time." Rico said. Brandon nodded and ran off.

"You're still selling drugs?" Leah asked.

"Leah look, I got to survive. This is what I have to do. Besides you wouldn't know nothing about that anyway. Your parents take care of you."

"What did you say?" Leah asked feeling hurt at his comment.

"I..I didn't meant it like that. I'm just saying you...you wouldn't understand."

"Then help me understand Rico. Come back to school. Prom and graduation are coming up...I just want to see you do great." Leah said.

"Ok, fine I'll...I'll find time too."

"Ok...I gotta go. I'm meeting with some people from Spelman." Leah said walking away.

Rico wanted to be a better man for Leah, but he also wanted her to be understanding. His lifestyle was about to change.

Chapter 11

Prom night...

Tonight was the biggest night of every high school senior's life. Prom. Between running the block and trying to keep a roof over his head, Rico finally decided to go back to school and has been doing exceptionally well. He and Leah started going out more and her father even loosened up and let her go out with him. Everything was going good and tonight he was going to share a dance with the love of his life.

"So who you going to the prom with?" Shonda asked Rico standing in his doorway while smoking a cigarette. Him and Shonda have had multiple sexual encounters over the past few months he'd been there. At first, Rico liked having sex with an older woman, but then it started to just flat out disgust him. Some nights he would have to bribe her off with a hit of cocaine just so he could get some sleep.

"Nobody, just me." Rico answered. He knew if he would have said he was taking Leah Shonda would bitch and complain. She might even threaten to put him out. Rico could tell Shonda started to develop feelings for him, but he for sure didn't want to go there. Once he really made a come up, he was leaving Shonda's house and never looking back.

"Mhmm. I know you lying. I know you got a girlfriend Rico. I be hearing you two up talking on the phone all night....who is she?" Shonda asked.

"....Leah. We been together for some time."

"Oh...do you love her?" Shonda asked. Rico fiddled with his bowtie getting annoyed with Shonda's questions.

"Look, I gotta go or I'm going to be late." Rico picked up the corsage he had for Leah and quickly by-passed Shonda. She never thought she would develop feelings for such a young boy, but to her Rico was special.

When he gets to the dance, everything was in full effect. People dancing, eating, drinking, taking pictures; this was going to be the best night ever.

"Hey, you made it." Leah said. She was standing with Anthony and his date Tina. Leah had on a hot pink gown with gold trimmings and her hair up in a sleek bun. Her make-up was beautifully done, but Rico thought she was beautiful with or without it.

"Yeah, sorry I'm late. Bad traffic. So you ready to get out there and dance?" Rico asked.

"Oh, you know it." Leah said.

"Yeah uhh...y'all go ahead. Me and Tina llfinna'...go smoke a bit." Anthony said taking out a sandwich bag with weed in it.

"Aight man." Rico takes Leah's hand and leads her to the dance floor. "Crank That Soulja Boy" was playing and had everybody following the dance moves.

After a few more fast songs, the DJ started playing a slow jam by Jamie Foxx. Rico gently grabbed Leah and they slow danced back and forth along with everyone else.

"I'm glad you came tonight Rico. I'm glad you came back to school period." Leah said.

"Yeah well...I couldn't have your parents thinking I'm completely stupid."

"They don't think you're stupid...well at least my mom doesn't. They just don't understand your lifestyle that's all."

"I don't care about them not understanding. I just need my girl to understand."

"I...at first I didn't. But now I do." Leah said. She knew Rico's new drug dealing habits would consist of him missing school and sometimes not answering the phone whenever she called him. On the inside, she hoped it wouldn't last forever.

"You sure about that? I know you plan on going to college and all that, but....one day when the time is right I want to marry you. I love you Leah."

"I love you too." They both share a kiss as they continued slow dancing.

After prom, Anthony surprises everyone with two suites at the hotel his father works at. Rico was definitely ready to get some pussy from his baby instead of Shonda for once.

When they got up to the hotel room, Rico and Leah began making out. He unzips her dress stripping her down to her bra and panties. Leah crawls slowly on the bed feeling already wet in between. Just as Rico was about to unbutton his pants, his phone started ringing. He let it go to voicemail, but then it rang again. When he looked at the caller ID, he saw it was Shonda calling him.

"Hold on babe...Hello?....What?...right now?!....I'm in...I'm in the middle of something....hugh, ok.....ok! Fuck!"

"What's wrong?" Leah asked. Rico knew he couldn't tell her about the situation between him and Shonda, so he made up a quick lie.

"I uhh...I have a issue I have to go handle on the block. So I'm going to have to drop you off home."

"What? Are you serious Rico? It's our prom night. I don't even have to be home until one."

"I know Leah but...look I promise I'll make it up to you."

"Rico, come on. You cannot do this. You're going to choose drugs over me now?"

"I'm not choosing anything over you. It's just...complicated ok. I thought you said you understand?"

"Well, apparently I don't. You know what, just take me home." Leah jumps up from the bed and snatches her dress off the floor.

"Leah-" Rico reaches out to grab her arm.

"Don't touch me! Just take me home." Leah snatches away and quickly gets dressed.

The ride home felt like the longest. They were both quiet and Leah couldn't even look at him. Once they arrived at her house, she quickly got out and practically ran inside the house. Rico felt bad about having to cut the night short, but if Leah really understood, then maybe she would get over it.

A few weeks later...

Over the next few weeks, Leah didn't speak to Rico at all. She didn't return any of his calls or texts, and completely tried to avoid him when he was at school. It actually started to bother Rico that Leah was giving him the cold shoulder. He began feeling depressed and it showed.

"Boy, what you in here moping about?" Shonda says walking out of the kitchen.

"Nothing." Rico said not wanting to talk about it.

"I know what it is...It's that girl isn't it?" She asked. Rico remained silent. "Child you better get over her. Hoes come a dime a dozen, you'll be aight."

"What?" When Rico heard the word hoe he instantly got mad.

"Hoes come and go. It's life. Get over it." She said lighting another cigarette.

"Leah's not a hoe. We go through shit all the time, this is nothing."

"I'm just saying you shouldn't be sitting here crying over some little stuck-up bitch." Shonda said. That was the last straw for Rico.

"You know what, that's it. I don't have to stand her here and listen to you talk shit about Leah." Rico rushes in his room and starts snatching some clothes out his closet. He throws them in a duffle bag and heads for the door.

"And where the hell do you think you going?"

"Away from you. You ain't nothing but a low-down dirty cocaine sniffing whore!" Rico slams the door and gets as far away from Shonda's house as he could.

Not wanting to spend money on an expensive motel, he decides to crash at Anthony's house for a while. Just when things seemed like they were going good, they were back upside down.

Graduation Day....

"Ladies and gentlemen, I give you our senior graduating class." Everyone applauded as the seniors jumped up and down and threw their caps in the air at another milestone.

Rico honestly didn't think he would see the day where he would be graduating with everything going on. If only Tony could have been there to celebrate his glory. He had been staying with Anthony and his parents for the past few months now. He refused to go back to Shonda's after she disrespected Leah. Now all he had to figure out was where to go from here. He hadn't applied to any colleges, let alone give much thought into going to one.

"Yo man, I can't believe we fucking made it bro." Anthony said as he and Rico walked away from the ceremony stage.

"I know; it's unbelievable." Rico said.

"Oh, hey man and check this out...I got accepted into Georgia Tech."

"What? Yo Anthony that's great man."

"Yeah, I haven't told my parents yet. I was going to wait and surprise them at the graduation party. You coming right?"

"Yeah man I-" Rico paused when he saw Leah walking across the yard.

"Hey, I'll uhh...I'll catch up with you later." He rushed over to Leah. They still weren't talking, but Rico wanted to try and make things right now that they were officially out of school and could possibly start a life together.

"Leah! Leah!" Rico said running after her. Leah turned around with a unpromising look. She decided to finally hear Rico out and get some closure.

"Hey." Rico said.

"Hey." Leah said back.

"I uhh...I just wanted to say....Leah, I'm sorry. For everything. Listen I love you but I can't help the lifestyle I live. At least not right now. But just be assured that when I'm out here doing what I'm doing...Leah I'm doing this for us."

"It's...ok Rico. I understand now." Leah said.

"Good…so does that mean we're back together?"

"Um-"

"There you are! I been looking all over for you!" Rico heard Shonda's voice behind him. She walked over to him and Leah wearing a tight-fitting blue dress, with blue heels, a blue church hat, and an umbrella. Her hair was in its usual bushy state and she of course was showing a lot of cleavage. Rico of course was not pleased that she decided to even show up here.

"Congrats on graduating, I'm so proud of you." Shonda said pinching his cheek. Rico tried his best to keep his cool in front of Leah.

"Oh Rico, this must be Leah. The one I heard so much about."

"Right…Leah this is my umm…my-"

"I'm his aunt Shonda. I flew all the way from Miami just to see my favorite nephew graduate." She said as she pinched his cheek again, but this time Rico moved his face away. Even though her presence was upsetting him on the inside, he was glad Shonda didn't expose who she really was.

"Nice to meet you." Leah said.

"Uhh Leah…Anthony is having a party at his house to celebrate. Do you wanna go? Together?"

"I wish I could but…I have to go home and pack."

"Pack? What are you- wait, did you get accepted into Spelmen? Baby that's great-"

"No Rico. My dad got a new job…in Dallas." When she said that Rico's face completely dropped. *Dallas? What the fuck she mean Dallas?*

"Umm, ok I mean…we're still going to see each other right? Maybe I can catch a plane out there once a month or something."

"Rico...I think this is the end for us. We're both...going two separate ways and...it's just not going to work." Right now, Rico went from celebrating the happiest day of his life to feeling heartbroken. He couldn't believe he would never see Leah again.

"I gotta go. My parents are waiting." Leah said and walked away. She was a little sad too that she and Rico would never get to work things out, but she figured it was for the better.

As she walked away, Rico just stood there with sadness. He felt Shonda's arm slowly go around his shoulder to try and comfort him.

"Come on. You can come back to my house. I'll make you something to eat." Since Rico wasn't much in the celebrating mood anymore he decided to just go with Shonda.

Rico would always love Leah but knew that life goes on. He didn't know where the road ahead would lead to, but he did know he would stop at nothing to make it to the top.

Adulthood

Chapter 12

Rico pulls up to the block to see everything is hustling and bustling as usual. He gets out his all-white Mercedes-Benz and walks over to Anthony who was watching over everything while he was gone.

"Yo, what's up man? I was in the middle of something." Rico said.

"One of the new workers hasn't turned in his percentage for the week. " Anthony said.

"Aight, I'll handle it. Come on, let's walk around to old Betty's and get a chicken box." Rico said. He figured Anthony could use a break after being on the block all day.

"Oh fo'sho." After graduating, Anthony actually ended up dropping out his freshman year due to stress. He decided just to come work for Rico and help grow his empire.

"Oh, by the way happy birthday." Anthony said to Rico.

"Thanks' man but honestly today is just another day. I'm more excited about Tony getting out of prison later." After going back and forth to court, paying for lawyers, and bribing a few judges Tony's case was ruled self-defense and he was being released early from what could have been a life sentence. Rico was just glad to see him again, and this time without a glass window.

"Well I think you should at least throw a party at Shonda house. It can be a birthday and welcome home party."

Rico had told Anthony the truth about Shonda a few years ago. Him and Tony was the only two who knew the truth about his living situation. After going back to live with her, they continued to keep their deal on the table and have sex in exchange for Rico paying rent. But nowadays since Rico was making a little more money than he was when he first started, he would have rather paid all of Shonda's bill's than to continue pounding on her middle-aged pussy. Especially now that he was getting pussy thrown at him left and right.

"I guess so. Hey, let me stop in the post office real quick. I'll catch up with you." Rico said.

He stops inside to grab his weekly mail out his P.O. Box and sifts through until he finds a letter from his mom.

Filho,

Happy birthday. I am blessed to know you have grown into a handsome young man. You and your brother. I hope this letter reaches you well because I have some sad news. My doctor has said I have become very sick with Malaria. There is treatment but no cure. Some days are good and some bad. What keeps me going is knowing that you and your brother are both still alive. Come and visit me when you can Filho.

Te amo. Mom.

Reading the letter from his mother Rico became worried. After grabbing something to eat and telling Anthony to tell everyone to be over Shonda's house at eight, he drove back to her house to clear his mind.

When he gets there, Shonda is sitting on the couch smoking a cigarette as usual watching reruns of *Sanford and Son*. He takes his shoes off and doesn't say much to her. He plops down on the other couch and takes a bag of weed out his pocket. He begins breaking it down to roll it up.

"You got any for me?" Shonda asked.

"What you mean? I'm the birthday boy."

"So you are. Damn time has flown by. I remember you was just a scrawny little thing when I picked you up off that bus stop."

"Yeah whatever. Look, I'm having some friends over later for drinks and food."

"Ha...who the hell you think you talking to? Do this look like a goddamn party house?"

"I pay the bills in here don't I? So I can call the shots."

"Last time I checked this was my house."

"Like I said I pay the bills in here. So if I want to have a party, then I can. Now why don't you get off your ass and straighten up or something." Rico hopped up with his weed and walks to his room locking the door.

He lit his blunt and let the weed take over. He pulled out a sheet of paper and a pencil and begins writing a letter to his mother. He makes a promise to come over there as soon as possible.

Later that night, the house was filled with some of Rico's closest friends and some associates to celebrate his birthday.

"Go! Go! Go! Go! Go!" Everyone cheered on Rico and Anthony as they threw back shots of bourbon. They cheered when they both finished. The music was blasting, and everyone was either high or drunk. Rico tried calling the prison that Tony was supposed to be released from but got no answer. He started to get a bad feeling but brushed it off and hoped for the best.

"Hey Rico." Rico turned around and saw it was the hoe from around the way Lameeka.

"Oh, what's up Meeka?" He said. He had to admit she was turning him on with her cropped tube top, pierced belly button, and tight-fitting jeans showing off her curves.

"Happy birthday." She said eyeballing him up and down. She had been trying to get at him for the longest, but so was every other broad in the hood.

"Thanks. I see you looking good as usual."

"Oh really? I...didn't know you noticed."

They flirted back and forth for about an hour, until Rico felt the alcohol starting to kick in. He began to feel his dick rise and decided to get a birthday quickie in. He took Lameeka by the hand and led her to his bedroom without anybody noticing. All except for Shonda.

They got to his room and were like two dogs in heat. Rico practically ripped her clothes off until she was butt ass naked. He swiftly whips his dick out, bends her over, and starts drilling her. It wasn't as good as he expected only due to her being a little loose, but it was good enough for this moment.

Ohhuhhh Rico!" She screamed out. Rico just roughly kept going while smacking her on her ass and watching it jiggle. Every time he did it made him harder.

Boom!

Rico jumped when he heard his bedroom door swing open.

"What the-" He turned around to see who would be dumb enough to bust in on him and Lameeka. Of course, he wasn't surprised to see Shonda standing there.

"Now Rico, why do you waste your time up here when you

have a house full of guest? Especially with this hoe." Shonda scold.

"What?! Rico what the hell is this?!" Lameeka said.

"Nothing, nothing it's-"

"You know what fuck this!" Lameeka pulls up her pants and storms out the room. Rico stands there and glares at Shonda with so much hate.

"Why would you do that?" Rico asked her. She just stared at his half naked body, which made him start getting dressed.

"Quick question...was her pussy better than mine?" Shonda asked. Rico hissed in disgust and brushed past her.

Before going back out into the party, Rico's phone started to ring. He saw it was from the jail and automatically answered. He was hoping it was Tony calling him to come pick him up.

"Hello?" Rico answers.

"Yes is this De'Rico Mitchell?" said an unfamiliar voice.

"Uhh yeah...who's asking?"

"My name is Robert Conwell I'm the warden here at the correctional facility. Is um...Tony Mitchell your brother?"

"Yeah, do you know what time he is supposed to be released? I been trying to call all day and-"

"That's what I'm calling you about...he uh...will not be released today."

"What? What do you mean? His lawyer said the judge was letting him off."

"...Mr. Mitchell there was a prison riot today...in which he was killed." Suddenly, Rico got silent. His throat tightened as he tried to comprehend what he was saying.

"Naw...naw you're not telling me my brother is dead."

"Listen, we need you to come here and identify his body."

"No! no! You're not telling me my brother is dead! That's....yo go get my brother on the phone. Now! Right now!"

"I'm sorry Mr. Mitchell." The warden hangs up leaving Rico with nothing but a dial tone.

Rico's head started spinning as he felt tears coming out of his eyes. He never imagined living in a world without his brother. Even when Tony got locked up it was hard for him to deal with, but now his one and only partner in crime was gone permanently.

When his mind zeroed back in on the music coming from the party, Rico sucked up his tears and walked back out into the living room. Everyone was dancing having a good time, while Rico went over to the stereo and unplugged the cord catching everyone's attention.

"Everyone get the fuck out! Now!" Rico yells.

At first everybody just looked at him crazy, but when Rico pulled his gun from his waist they started moving like cockroaches. Once they were all out, Rico just sat on the couch and sulked trying to gather his thoughts. He hears Shonda slowly walk into the room, but he was too deep in thought to pay her any attention.

"I heard what happened...I'm so sorry." She rubs his shoulder but he snatches away.

"Come on, Shonda. Not right now."

"Ugh...all I'm trying to do is comfort you. Something that little fast tail hoe you had in here fucking can't do." Rico snaps and jumps up pointing his gun in Shonda's face. She holds her hands up. "So what you gonna shoot me now?" She said. Rico stared at her contemplating if he should or not. Then he decided Shonda wasn't even worth taking his anger out on.

"You know what...fuck this." Rico tucked his gun back and headed for the door.

"Where the hell you going?"

"Away from you." Rico slammed the door, hopped in his car, and peeled off.

After hours of driving around all night, Rico decided to get a hotel room instead of going back to Shonda's house. Lighting up his fifth blunt for the night, he stood out on his hotel room balcony, and looked out on the view. Everything in him wanted to just jump over the edge, until he started thinking about what his brother had said to him before he got locked up....

"I been in this game for a while and you know that...maybe this is a sign telling me to sit my ass down and think. Think about life, think about more than just slanging. I've had my chance...now it's your turn."

As Rico reminisced about what Tony told him, he knew if he jumped he would be breaking the promise he made to Tony and his legacy would never live on. Rico knew in order for Tony to live on he had to continue living. He inhaled the weed smoke and exhaled.

As the weeks rolled by, Rico falls into a deep depression. He has a private memorial for Tony by himself. He knew the time was now to make the trip to Rio to break the news to his mother. He planned on leaving first thing in the morning, but first there was something he had to take care of.

"Never thought I'd come back here again." Rico said to himself. He parked his car and got out. He stared at the house that

Dewayne first brought them to when they moved to Atlanta. He still remembered how badly Dewayne treated them, especially Tony. The night Dewayne threw them out the house still replayed in his mind. The house was more run down than it first was and was even bordered up with a condemned sign on it. He took the Hennessey bottle he had been drinking out of and threw it at the house. Rico could feel there was a lot of anger still built up inside and Tony's death only ignited it even more. As he stood there, tears began coming down his face from feeling overwhelmed.

Having enough of walking down memory lane, he leaves and goes to pack for his trip to Rio.

The next day...Rio De Janerio

Spending hours flying in first class, Rico's plane landed in Rio. He catches a cab to his old neighborhood of Santa Teresa. As he rides through what used to be his childhood home, he reminisces on all the good times he and Tony had together. When he started feeling sad again, he focused his mind on seeing his mother again for the first time since leaving. When he gets out the cab, he walks up the long hill that led up to their home.

"Hello? Anybody home?" Rico shouted. He rounded the corner and saw their neighbor was taking care of Serafina, while she was resting in the chair.

"De'Rico!"

"How you doing Mrs. Ditrele." Rico greeted their long time next door neighbor.

"She just went to sleep." She said.

"How's she doing?" Rico asked.

"Not too well. In fact....the doctor says she doesn't have too much longer." When Rico heard those words he wanted to break down, but he had to stay strong at the moment.

He slowly walked over and kneeled next to his mother. He gently took her hand starting to awake her. She slowly opened her eyes and turned her head towards Rico. She was overjoyed to see her youngest son again.

"Rico." She caressed his face, but starts coughing. Rico pours her a cup of water and gives it to her. She sips it while trying to catch her breath.

"How are you my son?"

"I'm good mom. I missed you."

"I can only imagine." She sat up a little bit.

"Where is Tony? I thought he was coming with you." Rico sat silent for a minute trying to find the right words to say.

"Mom umm...Tony...he's...he's...he's dead." Rico held his head down in sadness after telling his mother Tony was gone. She hugged his head and sobbed along with him. They both just sat there and mourned their loss together.

Later that day, Rico takes a walk on the beach while his mother rests. She had got herself worked up and started having problems breathing. He was deep in thought about why God was taking people out his life left and right. First Tony and now his mother might have been next.

"Rico!" Someone called out. Rico turns around and sees his childhood friends Joaquim and Abel.

"Well I'll be damned. Look at y'all, what's up?" Rico said giving them a man hug.

"Nothing much. Heard you was back in town." Joaquim said.

"Yeah, you know word around here travels fast." Abel said.

"I see. Damn man, I missed y'all for real though. Me and Tony both."

"Yeah...look we're sorry to hear about your brother. Like he said word travels fast." Joaquim said.

"Yeah..." Rico said looking out at the sunset.

"But hey, how long you here for?" Abel asked.

"Only for a week." Rico said.

"Ok well let's try to hang out before you go back to the states."

"Aight bet. I'll see y'all later. I gotta get back to mom's." They gave each other one last hug, and Rico headed back to Serafina.

One week later...

Over the next week, Serafina gets weaker and weaker. Rico wants to bring her over to the states and get her the best care, but because she doesn't have a Visa it would be difficult. He had been trying to help nurse her back to health, but so far nothing was working. She had lost her appetite, was losing weight, and some days she didn't even know who Rico was. To clear his mind, Rico invited Joaquim and Abel out to dinner to catch up with each other.

"Hahaha, wow man. I can't believe you getting pussy now Joaquim. I remember you couldn't even get a bitch to talk to you." Rico said.

"Hey, hey...I had some play back in the day. And not only am I getting pussy but I also have a daughter."

"What? What's her name?" Rico said.

"Angel. Here's a picture of her." Joaquim showed a wallet sized picture of his daughter. Sometimes Rico wondered what it would be like to have children of his own.

"She's beautiful man. So that makes you an uncle now?" Rico says to Abel.

"Yeah, this one here, he ain't getting no pussy. I tried to hook him up with a bad ass woman from my job and he turned her down."

"First of all she was a total psycho...and she just wasn't my type." Abel said twiddling his fingers. Rico squinted his eyes at him.

"Whatever. So Rico what's it like over in the states?"

"Aw man it's cool. More to see, more money, and the women...well I'll let y'all see that for yourself."

"Damn. So what do you do over there?" Abel asked. Rico paused while eating his food and pondered on if he wanted to tell the twins what he did for a living.

"Ok look...if I tell you two you got to promise not to tell anybody else. Especially y'all nosey ass auntie."

"We promise." They both said.

"Ok...I sell drugs. I started out small but now I'm building an empire." Joaquim and Abel were actually impressed to hear Rico had got into the drug game. Growing up they would always see how the drug dealers drove around in fancy cars, wore nice clothes, and lived in big houses.

"For real?....you think we could get in on that?" Joaquim said.

"I don't know about all of that." Rico said.

"Come on Rico. Look I'm just trying to have more money so I can take care of my daughter." Joaquim said.

"And I want to buy me a mansion and have a harem." Abel added in. They both looked at him and bust out laughing.

"Ok, ok look...y'all my boys so tell you what. I'll get y'all some Visa's and passports, but it's going to take a while. It's not an overnight thing. I'm trying to get one for my mother but...by the time she gets one she might not even be able to travel." Rico said with sadness.

"Sorry to hear that man." Joaquim said.

"It's cool, but listen I'll give y'all my cell and keep y'all updated on everything."

"Cool." The twins said together. They finished up dinner and went home afterwards. Rico sat up with Serafina all night nursing her fever worried about going back to the states tomorrow and leaving her like this.

The next day, Rico said his good-byes to his mother and old friends and boarded a flight back to Atlanta. He knew he probably had some business to take care of when he got back.

Atlanta, Georgia...

"Yeah, you already know what I'm saying though. Big money big stacks." One of Rico's closet friends and partner was posted up on the block filling in while Rico was gone.

"What up Pop?" Rico said rounding the corner.

"Damn nigga, you came back quick." They gave each other some dap.

"Nigga, I was only gone for a week."

"Aye, I'm going to hit you back later though." Pop said into the phone and hung it up.

"Mom's says hi." Pop said.

"Tell her I said what's up and when she coming back over." Pop jabbed at him as they both laughed.

"So what's up? What you text me for? Said it was important."

"Oh man....so you know that new nigga Jayon right?"

"Yeah. What about him?"

"Well that nigga been missing for the past five days and he got the count for this week."

"Ain't nobody heard from him?" Rico asked.

"Naw. We went by his mom's crib and questioned her but you know how that goes. She ain't know nothing and neither did his sister."

"Ok, find out some more information. Talk to some people, shoot somebody if you have to but I want his whereabouts. And when you find them I'm paying him a visit myself. Nigga think he just ready to play with my money, he got another thing coming."

"Aight, I will boss."

"Ok, I'm going to head home and rest for a bit." They dapped each other up and Rico went about his way.

Early the next morning, Rico receives a text from Pop saying he got Jayon's whereabout and sent him the address. He fucked with Pop because he always got the job done, unlike these young niggas like Jayon. Rico tried to be understanding and give everyone a chance to eat because he remembered at one point he was hungry too. But when it came to fucking with his money, all bets were off.

Rico drove to the address Pop sent to him and parked a block down the street. He loaded up his Glock 45 and made his way to the home Jayon was in. He found a side window open, and quietly sneaks through. The house was quiet and smelled of corn chips and sex. He made his way upstairs to one of the bedrooms and the first one he came to was empty. The next one he went too was decorated in all pink with kid furniture. Rico figured this must be his girlfriend's house. He was just glad there was no kids anywhere in sight because what he was about to do will fuck any child up.

He came to the last bedroom, and found Jayon sleep next to some lines of coke, a wad of money, and some girl who was butt naked. Rico just chuckled to himself how this nigga could get caught slipping like this. Rico puts the gun to Jayon's temple and cocks it making him open his eyes.

"Good morning motherfucka." Rico whispered.

"Ahhh!" Jayon's girlfriend screamed and jumped up.

"Yo...Rico come on man. What you doing?" Jayon said shaking.

"Nigga shut the fuck up. Where is my money at?"

"Look man I...just needed to borrow it, but I promise to put it back ok? Please man don't kill me!" Jayon cried.

"Begging and pleading ain't gon help you little nigga." Rico said. When he looked up he noticed for a split second how Jayon's girl had a really nice body.

"You...turn around for a second." Rico says pointing the gun at her. She scarily turns in a circle with her hands up.

"Mmm...all that ass and you wasting it on this piece of shit." Rico says. Jayon begins whining hoping Rico will reconsider blowing his brains out.

"Nigga stop whining and be a man. Shit, while I'm at I might just fuck ya bitch and make you watch before you die." But Jayon just kept crying and begging Rico.

Bang! Bang! Bang!

Rico sends three shots to Jayon's skull, making blood splatter all on the walls.

"Fuck...and you, I swear on everything you run your mouth I will find you. You hear me?!" Rico said to Jayon's girl who shook her head. With that, Rico left just as swiftly as he came in.

Chapter 13

"So what's up with me and you later?" Rico asked talking on the phone to a girl name Keisha.

"I don't know. You be acting like you so busy." She said.

"Because I do be busy...but I'm saying though you gon let me slide up in that thing or what?"

"Boy that's all you want is some pussy huh?"

"Naw, that's not all I want...I want some head too." Rico laughed.

While talking on the phone, Shonda appears in his doorway dressed in some tight-fitting lingerie. Rico looked with disgust because over the years Shonda's body started to catch up with her age.

"I been thinking it's time we get back on track with our agreement." Shonda says.

"Rico who is that?" Keisha asks.

"Uhh...nobody. I gotta go." Rico hung up and put his phone in his pocket. Shonda positions herself between his legs and begins to unzip his pants to give him some head, but he pushes her away.

"Come on Shonda. Go somewhere with that shit."

"Oh, what you think you too good now that you came up?"

"I don't know what you talking about."

"You know exactly what I'm talking about. You look at me now like I disgust you, but need I remind you motherfucka that this same pussy was the one who taught you everything you doing out here with these little sluts."

"You really gon start this shit right now?"

"We made a deal Rico. Now either come fuck on this pussy or get out because ya ass sure as hell ain't giving me none of that drug money you making." Rico was tired of hearing the same thing from Shonda every day. He figured he had enough money saved up to get his own shit by now.

"You know what? I'm out. I don't need this shit." Rico begins packing some clothes, some money, and a few of his guns.

"What do you mean you done? After I took your ungrateful ass in and you gonna leave me like this?!"

"Look thanks for all of that but this ain't working for me no more. I'll send somebody to get the rest of my shit tomorrow." Rico threw his duffle bag over his shoulder and headed for the door.

Before leaving out the front door, a glass bottle almost hits him but misses. Rico looks back at Shonda who is in tears and on her knees.

"Listen, if it will do you any good, I'll send you a hit every now and then for your troubles Shonda." Rico said. Shonda slowly gets up off her knees. She pulls a loose cigarette from her bra and lights it.

"Get the hell out of my house." She says. Rico shrugs his shoulders and leaves.

Before hitting the block, Rico stops and closes on a furnished condo he had been eyeing. He did truly appreciate

Shonda for giving him shelter but had enough of her always wanting dick from him. Especially since she was one pack of cigarettes away from lung cancer.

Later on, Rico pulls up to the block and notices some commotion going on. He gets out and sees everyone standing around in a circle. Rico pushes through the crowd and notices it's one of his top corner boy's Zell beating up some crackhead.

"You trying to play me nigga? You trying to play me?" Zell picked him up by his collar and when Rico saw his face, his stomach dropped.

"Yo Zell....let him go man." Rico said.

"What? Man hell naw. This druggie gon get what he deserve."

"Zell...let him go. I'm not gonna say it again." Rico said. Zell glared at him wondering why he was taking a crackhead's side.

"Man, fuck!" Zell throws him to the ground and walks off. Everyone else dispersed.

"Haha well, well...if it ain't the little runt I call my son."

"What do you want Dewayne?" Rico asked.

"I was just trying to get a hit and ya boy over there decided to play Mr. Tough Guy. Wow....I almost didn't recognize you. When was the last time I saw you?"

"That night you threw me and Tony out of the house."

"Ohhh yeah. That damn Tony. Always talking back and never taking direction."

"Yeah well Tony's dead. So you better watch what you say before I tell Zell to come finish you off."

"Look man, I'm just trying to get a hit, that's all." Dewayne said getting up off the ground.

"And why should I serve you a hit?"

"Well...I'm your dad. I love the fact you own your own corner and shit son. Makes me real proud. I just really need a hit right now." Rico glared at the man he used to call father and just shook his head in disbelief.

"New product just came in. Maybe you can be the first to try it." Rico pulls a small vial from his pocket. Dewayne reaches for it but Rico closes his hand back.

"$5." Rico says.

"$5?! Come man I'm... I'm your pops."

"You're right....$10 ." Rico was enjoying taunting Dewayne after thinking about all the shit he put him through.

"Aight fine. Ain't gon be able to eat tonight." Dewayne put the $10 in his hand, took the vial, and hurried along. Rico feels disappointed about his father, but crying over spilled milk was pointless.

Later that night, after getting the rest of his stuff from Shonda's house, Rico decides to take everyone out to Magic City. Him, Pop, Zell, Chris, and Anthony arrive there and don't even have to wait in line. They're instantly let in and get a VIP section. The club had its usual crowd and choice of strippers. The DJ was spinning some Three Six Mafia, while bottles popped everywhere.

"Hey y'all, I'll be back." Rico said and got up to leave.

"Nigga where you going?" Pop asked.

"None of ya damn business. Just save me some Patron and don't smoke up all the weed." Rico said.

Rico didn't mind hanging with his boys, but right now he needed some alone time and something to relax his mind. He went over to the bar and ordered some time in a private room and two of the best strippers they had. The bartender walked him to a room with neon pink lights, a comfortable velvet couch, and a pole in the middle of the floor. He gave the bartender an extra $200 and lounged on the couch while he waited for his entertainment. Rico sparks up a blunt he had in his pocket and sat back to relax.

Tap! Tap!

"Come in." He said when he heard a slight knock at the door.

Two nicely thick women walked in, one dark skin and the other light skin. Rico's dick started getting hard staring at their bodacious hips and plump breasts.

"We heard you wanted some private entertainment." The dark skin stripper said.

"You heard right." Rico said.

"I'm Star and this is Remy." The light skin one said.

"Nice to meet y'all." Suddenly some slow music starts playing. Star and Remy head towards the pole and begin winding and grinding next to each other. Star took off her top as Remy seductively felt on her breasts, all while never breaking eye contact with Rico. He was amused but wanted to see what else they could do.

"I like y'all style. I really do, but uhh...what else can y'all do?" Rico asked.

"What do you mean?" Remy asks.

"I'm saying y'all tryna hop on this dick or what?"

"Well...technically we not supposed to do that." Star hesitated.

"What if I throw in...a few extra dead presidents." Rico pulls out a wad of money and lays it on the couch. Star and Remy look at each other and say fuck it. They both get undressed, and walk over to Rico to give the best threesome he ever had.

Ten minutes later, Rico has Remy bent over throwing it back on his dick, while she ate out Star's pussy. He could tell by the way they was enjoying it that this wasn't their first time doing this. Rico slapped Remy on the ass, as he felt himself reaching his climax. He quickly pulled out and came, but he wasn't finished. He ordered Star to get down on her knees and deep throat his dick. Without hesitation, she got down on her knees and stuffed Rico in her mouth. She bobbed her head up and down while making it hit the back of her throat. Remy just stood behind him and caressed his back. This had to be one of the best nights of his life.

"Hey, if y'all tryna make some more money, me and my boys got a section over by the bar." Rico says.

"Yeah, sure we down." Remy says.

"Just give me a minute, I gotta change my outfit and fix my make-up." Star says.

Rico nods and opens the door with Remy in tow. They walk back to the section where they are on their fifth bottle of Patron.

"I'd like y'all to meet a special friend of mine. This is Remy." Rico says introducing her.

"How y'all doing?" Remy says.

"Damn, you looking good ma. How you doing? My name is Pop." Pop said shaking her hand. Remy went and sat next to him and they begin flirting. Rico threw back a shot and danced to the music playing. He spotted Star walking over and got turned back on. Next time he thinks he might take her pussy for a spin.

"Yo, this my other special friend right here." Rico announced as Star walked in the section. Everybody was eyeballing her with lust, all except Zell who had a look of anger. Star looked back at him like a deer in headlights. Rico could tell this was about to get interesting.

"Oh hell naw! Doniesha?!" Zell yelled. Pop, Chris, and Anthony stopped and looked at what was about to go down.

"Zellton?....I-"

"What the fuck are you doing here?! Don't tell me this is where you been working night shift at?!" Zell hollered.

"You know what yes Zell! I been working here since you don't seem to want to help me take care of your son!" She blurted out. Rico started low-key chuckling at the drama unfolding before him.

"Doniesha, you need to go the fuck home right now and stop being a hoe!" Zell yells so loud half the club probably heard him.

Slap! Star slaps Zell and walks away upset. Everyone started laughing, except Zell who gave Rico the cold look.

"Look Zell, lighten up nigga. She just making her money like the rest of us." Rico said.

"Yeah and I bet you got your money's worth didn't you?" Zell says.

"What? Man I was just having me some fun. How was I supposed to know she was your baby momma? Besides, bitch can't suck dick no way." Rico says throwing back another shot.

"Yo you better take that shit back." Zell says getting closer to Rico. For a moment, Rico thought Zell was joking, but when he saw the fire in his eyes he knew he wasn't.

"Or what?" Rico says. Zell knew better than to try something in the middle of the club. Some of the niggas in the room might have been from different hoods, but they all fucked with

Rico.

Zell got mad and left. Everyone else kept dancing and having a good time, while Rico's brain started turning. He was going to be sure to keep a close eye on Zell.

The next day Rico meets up with a realtor who was selling an old warehouse. He thought it would be the perfect place to start distributing his product.

"So the place has four working belts, five truck ports, two boiler rooms, and two empty rooms you can use for storage or office space or whatever." The realtor tells Rico.

"Good and what did you say it's going for again?" Rico asks.

"Uhh, I say about a fifty grand."

"Fifty grand? But the ad said twenty thousand."

"Yeah but when you add in all the renovations that will have to be done-"

"Man listen, don't worry about all that. I got that part. I got twenty thousand in cash right now, so what's up?" Rico said.

"Well, if you're willing to put in the extra work, we can get the paperwork started."

"We can do all that later." Rico takes his duffle bag off his shoulder and dumps out wads of money. The realtor picks up one of them and sifts through it.

"You're a very...determined young man Rico."

"Yeah whatever. I'll be in contact and let me know when you have those keys ready." Rico's phone started going off. "I gotta go." Rico says walking out.

"Thank you Mr. Rico." The realtor yelled happily. Things

were really looking up for Rico. He felt good about his first major move as an up-and-coming kingpin. Just as things was starting to get better, Rico receives another 911 text from Pop. He knew whatever it was couldn't good.

Later that day, Rico pulls up to the block and Pop walks over to his car and gets inside.

"So what's up man? My junkie father showed up again or something?" Rico asked.

"Naw man...I just saw Zell....talking to Jax." Pop said and it caught Rico's attention.

Jax was a across town rival from Augusta. He figured because he was older than Rico and owned almost half the city that he could disrespect Rico whenever he wanted to. It's been times when Rico and Jax crossed paths, but it was street code to keep it mutual. Now that he's learned of Zell's disloyalty, Rico was disappointed.

"Do you know what for?" Rico asks.

"Who knows man. Probably still in his feeling about last night."

"Hmm...I'll pull up on him."

"Man fuck that. You want me to pop that nigga?" That's how Pop got his name. He was always ready to pop somebody even if they looked at him the wrong way, but it was niggas like him that Rico needed on his team.

"Naw, since he making this so personal I'll do it."

"Ight man, let me go. The block is hot today." They dapped each other up and Pop got out the car. Rico stroked his chin to think of how to carry this out. Zell was cool in his book, but if he wanted to take things personal over some hoe at the club then so be it.

Rico eventually made his way over to Zell's house in East Point. He tucked his gun away in his waist and got out the car.

Knock, knock.

Rico knocked on the door and got ready when he heard Zell coming to the door. The door swung open and Zell wore this confused look on his face.

"Rico, what-" Rico didn't hesitate pointing his gun in Zell's face. Zell backed up.

"Yo what the fuck is going on Rico?"

"Shut up. What's this I hear about you meeting up with Jax?"

"Man, I don't know what you talking about."

"So, you saying I'm a liar?" Rico stuffed his gun right in the middle of Zell's forehead.

"I...ok yeah man. I met up with him, but it wasn't about you I swear."

"Then what was it about? Huh?"

"I...I can't tell you."

"You can't tell me? Me? The nigga who's making sure you get your fair share, making sure you got money in your pocket, and making sure you straight. You meeting up with my arch enemy behind my back and you can't tell me why? You know what I think? I think this is all about me almost fucking your bitch last night at the club. If it's one thing I keep telling you simple ass niggas, it's never get in ya feelings over some bitch. Especially a bitch who pussy is loose."

"Rico man...come on man; it ain't nothing like that."

"Hmm...I find that hard to believe."

Bang! Bang!

Rico put two shots in Zell's head and watched him fall back. Within a few seconds, he was lying in a pool of blood. Rico just shook his head at having to kill off one of his friends, but he figured any nigga who was associating with a nigga like Jax was just as bad.

Pulling up to the two-story safe house that he knew Jax stayed at sometimes, Rico made sure his gun was still loaded just in case things went left. He decided to pay Jax a visit and get to the bottom of why he was talking to Zell.

"Yo Jax in there?" Rico asked the bodyguard at the door.

"No he ain't. And even if he was you need an appointment to see him."

"Yeah, well I got an appointment." Rico said showing his gun.

"Pshh, you act like we ain't got straps too little nigga."

"Oh yeah, what's up then?" Rico said ready to empty his clip.

"Hey, what the fuck is going on out here?" One of Jax's right hand men came out and asked.

"This little bitch ass nigga-"

"Watch who you calling a bitch." Rico said pointing his gun in the bodyguard face.

"Is Jax in there? Tell him Rico Jefe is here to see him." Rico says.

"Aye, let him in. Just let him in." The other guy says and opens the door wider for Rico to enter.

Rico steps in and looks around the house that looked like

someone from the 18th century decorated it. They go upstairs to the first bedroom where Rico see's Jax standing by the window.

"Rico Jefe." Jax says.

"Jax."

"And what do I owe this unexpected visit?" Jax asks sparking a cigar.

"Yeah, what I want to know is why you meeting up with my peoples behind my back."

"Your peoples? You mean Zell? Hahaha, technically speaking he came to me asking me for a job. I simply told him he had to discuss it with you."

"Yeah, well you don't have to worry about him anymore. Let's just say he flying with the angels now."

"Hmmm, you know something Rico. I get a feeling that this is not just about Zell betraying you."

"No. It's not. I also heard you been trying to get a few of your corner boys to sell on my territory and that's stepping on my toes. I thought we had this conversation before."

"See, the thing is, Rico, it is not my fault that your loyalty to your workers is fucked up."

"What did you say?" Rico asks stepping closer to Jax.

"Wait a minute now. I wouldn't do that if I were you. I got shooters just outside that door just in case anything gets funky. So back the hell up."

"Look...Jax....all I'm saying is stick to your part of town and I'll stick to mine." Rico says.

"Fine. You don't gotta repeat yourself."

"Yeah, don't let me have to. Or the next time I come back

here I'm burning this shit down to the ground."

"Hahaha." Jax chuckled but Rico was dead serious. He left the room to a hallway full of men dressed in black with machine guns. Rico smirks and walks downstairs and out the house. While driving away, Rico had a plan in mind. He was going to snatch Jax's territory away from him and take him out if needed.

While driving home that night, Rico's phone starts ringing again. He sees Camela's name pop up on the caller ID. Him and Camela had been messing around for almost a year now, and out of all the girls Rico has messed with Camela seemed to be like the main chick. Her head game was on point and the pussy was even better.

"What's up ma?" Rico asks answering the phone.

"Hey baby, what you up to?"

"Nothing much. Riding around. What's up with you?"

"Well, I just got the rest of my furniture for my new place and wanted you to come over." Camela said seductively into the phone. Rico looked at the time and it was only 7:30 in the evening.

"Yeah I'll swing by. Text me the address." Rico said and hung up.

In twenty minutes, he was pulling up to Camela's house. He knocked on the door and Camela answered dressed in some lingerie.

"Mmmm. Looks like somebody missed me." Rico says stepping in and closing the door behind him.

"I did. Come on. I'll show you the bedroom." Camela takes his hand and leads him upstairs.

They get to the room where Rico sits on the edge of the bed

and takes off his shirt. Camela wastes no time and gets between his legs. Immediately, she pulls out his dick and slides it into her mouth. Rico loved it when Camela took charge a little bit without his command. She sucked and slurped while deep throating his shaft and even managed to lick his ball with his dick still in her mouth.

"Mmmm shit." Rico moaned biting his lip. He grabbed the back of her head and guided her up and down.

When he had enough of that, he was ready to squeeze into her warm pussy. He got her off her knees and laid her back on the bed. He cocked her legs open and started pushing the tip in.

"Ohh fuck. I almost forgot how big you are."

"Oh really?" Rico pushed inside more and more.

H began stroking Camela while sucking on her nipples. Every time he fucked her it felt like a wet puddle. She always kept her shit tight because Camela wasn't the type of female to let every nigga hit. She worked a corporate job at an advertising agency and was on her way to being Assistant Vice President. How did she meet Rico? One-night dancing at the club and a few drinks later, they were laid up in her bed. After that, she was stuck on the young kingpin like glue.

"You love this dick huh?" Rico says.

"Mmm yes daddy." Camela moaned. Rico went harder and harder and could feel Camela's juices covering his dick.

"Fuck, I'm about to cum." Rico says. Usually, Rico would have lasted a lot longer, but since him and Camela haven't fucked in a while, the pressure on his dick had him breaking code and cumming quick.

"Uggghhh fuck!" Rico moaned loudly. He shot a few squirts of cum in the opening of Camela's pussy. While catching their breath, they lay there holding each other.

"Mmm, this feels nice to just lay here on your chest like this Rico." Camela says.

"Yeah. It does." He says kissing her hand. Rico could have easily made Camela his girlfriend but didn't feel like she was ready for the type of lifestyle he was living.

"Rico...there's something I need to tell you."

"What is it?" Rico asks feeling his eyelids starting to close.

"I...I'm...I'm pregnant." Camela says. Rico's eyes shoot back open when he heard what she said.

"What?" Rico asks.

"I'm pregnant. About two months now. I just found out last week...we're going to be parents." Camela said excitedly. Rico sits up in the bed feeling spaced out.

"Wha...what are you talking about?"

"I'm pregnant with your child Rico." Camela says sitting up next to him.

"....Damn." Rico whispers.

"Damn?"

"I mean...not damn like that but....so what are you going to do? Are you going to keep it or what?"

"Yes I'm going to keep it. I'm not killing my child." Rico sat there quiet for a minute and decided he should leave and needed some space. He hopped up out the bed and began to get dressed.

"Rico? Where are you going?"

"I gotta...I gotta go handle some business."

"I just told you I'm carrying your child and this is how you react?"

"Look Camela, it's not like that aight. I gotta go." Rico leaves out the room and hurries to his car.

He had never given much thought to having kids with any-body. The only person he still thought of till this day was... Leah. Even after she left, Rico never stopped thinking about her and wanting to be with her. Camela might have been getting ready to have his first child, but Leah will always be his first love.

Chapter 14

Now that Rico had the warehouse he needed, it was just a matter of getting it fixed up. At first, he thought he had it covered, but now learning that he had a child on the way all of that changed. So he was in need of at least $100,000 to get everything he needed to start distributing. And the only way he would get that kind of money was to rob a bank. Him, Anthony, Pop, and Chris gathered at his house to go over the plan.

"So again...Anthony you're going to watch out for the police, Chris you're going to drive, while me and Pop dismantle the security system and collect all the money." Rico says.

"I don't know Rico, man. This doesn't sound like a good idea." Anthony says.

"Look, if I wanted to have any pussy scary ass niggas in on this then I would have kept Zell's ass alive."

"I'm just saying man...this isn't *Set It Off*. What if we get caught? There's no other way we can come up with the money?" Anthony asks.

"Anthony listen...I know this is something we never done before. But trust me when I say we are capable of doing this. This heist is a must. My mom is sick and I got a kid on the way. This isn't just a come up for me, but for all of us. You can finally buy your parents a bigger house, Chris you can buy that red BMW I always see you looking at, Pop you can finally have enough money to move you and your sister out the hood. This shit is for all of us." Rico says.

"Yeah so stop acting like a little bitch." Chris says.

"Fuck you Chris." Anthony says back.

"Hey! Both of y'all chill. Save that energy for the job....So what's it going to be Anthony? You in or out?" Rico asks. Anthony is silent for a moment and decided if you can't beat them, might as well join them.

"Aight I'm in." Anthony says.

"Good. We meet up downtown tonight at 11. Wear black and Chris make sure your phone is on silent. We all know how Te-Te loves to blow up your phone." They laughed. Rico starts to think this might be one of his best plans yet.

Later that night, they all meet up as planned and man their spots as directed. Rico and Pop go around back with both their guns drawn and kick in the door. The alarm system starts to go off. Rico knew because of that they were on limited time before the cops would show up, so they had to be quick. When Pop managed to dismantle it, they made their way to the safe. Rico pulls out his high-powered laser gun and tries to pry the door open.

"Come on Rico, we only got 15 minutes." Pop says.

"Nigga do you want to try. I told you this shit takes time." A few more minutes later the safe's door pops open.

Rico's mouth could have almost dropped to the floor staring at all the stacks of money.

"Yo! Come on man. Start filling the bag up!" Pop says snapping Rico out his trance.

"Right...right." Rico starts taking the packs of plastic wrapped money and fills up the bag with as much as he could carry.

In less than 10 minutes, Rico and Pop were walking back out the bank with four bags of money and loaded them into the truck.

"Man, this shit was too easy. I could've done this shit in my sleep." Pop says.

"Hey, where's Anthony?" Rico asks Chris but he shrugs his shoulders.

"Little bitch ass probably ran home to mommy." Pop says.

"Hey lay off of him will you." Rico says. They stop when they see Anthony running down the street from the corner and hear police sirens in the distance.

"What did ya ass do?!" Pop yells.

"The police are coming! We gotta go man!" Anthony says out of breath.

"Come on. Get in!" Anthony hops in the truck and they drive off, but not without the police cars on their tail.

"Shit...come on, Chris, drive faster!" Rico yells.

"Fuck this. I ain't going back to jail." Pop loads his gun and starts shooting at the police cars. He hits one of their windshields making the bullet go through the driver's head, and causing the car to swerve to the side.

"Yeah baby!!! Wooooo!!!" Pop yells.

Pop! Pop! Pop!

"Oh shit...these motherfuckas shooting back." Pop says ducking for cover.

"Give me that." Rico says and shoots the police car chasing them busting out one of their tires. The cop still shoots but misses. The car starts swerving out of control and makes him run into a tree.

"Yeah, wooo!!! Now that's what the fuck I'm talking about! Step on it Chris!" Pop yells. Chris goes about 90 mph and they drive off with the money.

Back at the warehouse where they decided to hide out until morning, they all counted up the money. In total, they managed to get away with more than they wanted, which was about one million dollars. They each got 250,000 and was happy Rico's plan worked out for the best despite almost getting caught. Things were about to change for the better.

One month later....

"Thank you so much for your business sir and please enjoy the ride." The car dealer says to Rico.

"Oh, don't worry. I will." Rico says and looks at his new red Viper. He gets in, starts the engine and peels out of the dealership. He figured he could use a little gift to himself since robbing the bank was his idea.

He calls Camela and tells her to get dressed and he was taking her out for dinner. Before going home to change, he stops at the post office to send a letter to his mother.

Ola Mother,

I can't tell you how much I've missed you since my last visit to Rio. I got great news though...you're coming to live with me. It's not official as of yet but I'm almost done getting your citizen paper done. It's still going to take a little bit of time, but I promise to get it done. Also there's more good news...I'm going to be a dad. Not sure what I'm having yet, but whatever it is at least you'll be here to meet them. Don't worry mama. For once everything is finally going to be ok.

Te amo,

De'Rico

Rico put the letter in the envelope and gave it to the mail carrier to take inside. Later that evening, he picks Camela up and takes her to the port for a private yacht ride.

"Wow, this is really nice Rico. Thanks for bringing me out here."

"No problem ma. I can't believe you were born and raised here and never been out to the port."

"Never had a reason to come I guess. Always so busy working." Camela says.

"That's another thing...I don't want you working."

"What?"

"Especially while you're pregnant."

"Rico, I can't just not work."

"Camela...with the kind of money I'm about to make you don't have to work. You can stay home with our baby, get fat, and relax. I told you I got you."

"Wait...you mean like..."

"Yes...I want to make things official." Rico never thought he would reach the day where he would have another girlfriend after Leah, but he figured at least for the sake of his newborn he should give it a try with Camela.

"Oh Rico!" Camela hugs him around his neck. They kiss passionately and ride off into the sunset.

A few more weeks later, Rico bought himself a new home with four bedrooms, three bathrooms, a huge backyard, and swimming pool. He decided since he have been working so hard and his warehouse was almost finished, now was the time for a celebration.

Stop!
Now make that motherfucker hammer time like
Go stupid, go stupid, go stupid

Everybody at Rico's party was dancing to the Big Sean song and either had a drank in their cup or some weed lit up. Every thug, gangster, and hood rat was there helping celebrating his come up. Rico looked at his party guest, but noticed Anthony was missing. Come to think of it, Rico hadn't heard from Anthony ever since they had split the money. It was like he disappeared. He tried calling him again, but got nothing but the voicemail.

Suddenly, he gets a call from a number he didn't recognize. *Maybe Anthony went and bought himself a new phone.*

"Hello?" Rico yelled over the loud music.

"Hey…it's me." Rico recognized the voice as Shonda's.

"What do you want Shonda?" Rico asked.

"Listen, I know you want nothing to do with me, but I was just calling to tell you that you might want to turn on the news. They've been talking about you all morning." Hearing this shocked Rico.

He hung up the phone and ran upstairs to his bedroom where it was quiet. He shut the door and clicked on the news. His gut dropped when he saw camera footage from the night of the robbery and when they got chased down the highway.

"As you can see the suspects broke into the bank, stole what's supposed to be one million dollars, and lead a high-speed chase. The chase resulted in two officers being killed and one seriously injured. Atlanta Police Department now has a warrant out for the arrest of a man named De'Rico Mitchell. Mitchell is believed to have been involved with the robbery and shooting

189

of the officers. Back to you guys at the studio."

Rico turns the TV off and jumped up to go warn Pop and Chris. He gets downstairs and sifts through the crowd, feeling like his heart was pounding. He finally finds them in the kitchen both flirting with some girls.

"Excuse me ladies, I need to borrow these two." Rico says grabbing them both.

"Yo, what's up man? I was just about to go get my freak on in one of your guest rooms." Pop says.

"Forget all that. Look, we got to get these people outta here now." Rico says.

"For what?" Chris asks.

Boom!

The patio door gets kicked in and a bunch of men in SWAT uniforms come in with guns drawn.

"Everybody down now!" They yell.

The crowd of people partying start to scatter like roaches. Pop, Chris, and Rico make a run for it and head towards the front door within the crowd. Rico tries to sneak out without being seen, but is met at the front door with more SWAT men. Rico looks behind him and sees that he is trapped with no way out.

"Put your hands up now!" One of them yell. Rico holds his hands up and put them behind his head. Maybe Anthony was right when he said this would backfire.

~

"So...De'Rico is it? Or do your friends just call you Rico?" A FBI agent asks. After being arrested, Rico was taken to the federal building to be questioned.

"Last time I checked you wasn't my friend." Rico responds.

"But I can be. All I need is for you to tell me everything I need to know about the robbery."

"I don't know what you're talking about." Rico said.

"You don't? Ok, let me ask you this...What do you do for a living Mr. Mitchell?"

"I work for myself."

"Doing what?"

"I'm...I'm an independent investor."

"Haha...I see you're going to make this hard. I have here some of your bank statements within the past month and... I must say you've made quite the come up. You bought a new home, two new cars, expensive jewelry, and a whole bunch of other stuff that people with a six figure salary can't even afford." Rico remained silent as the agent went down the list of things he bought with the money. "Where'd you get the money?" The agent asks.

"Like I said...I don't know what you're talking about."

"Ok. Well, let's just see what the judge thinks." The agent goes to the doorway and motions for two officers to come take Rico back to his cell.

"I want to make a phone call." Rico says before they take him out the room. The agent looks at the two officers and nods his head yes to let Rico use the phone.

The first-person he calls is his lawyer; his bail is at $70,000. Next person he calls is Camela, who was two hours away visiting her aunt.

"Hello?" Camela answers.

"Camela? Hey babe, it's me."

"Rico, what the hell happened? First I hear about some big party you threw at the house and now you're in jail?"

"I know, I know. Baby listen. They not going to let me out of here unless I got $70,000."

"$70,000?...Rico did you really rob that bank?"

"Camela, now is not the time for a bunch of questions. Just post my bail with the money in my savings and meet me down here at the police station." Camela sighed and said she'd do it by tomorrow then hangs up.

That night, Rico spends the night in jail, and he had to admit this was not where he wanted to end up again. Tony had always told him horror stories about jail when he was locked up. Rico was just hoping and praying Camela came through.

The next morning, Rico's bail posts. He still has to face the judge in two days, but he was just glad to be able to go home. When he walks out the station he sees Camela standing there next to the brand-new car he bought her.

"Nice to see you." He says. They kiss and embrace.

"I'm glad you're ok." Camela says.

"Yeah but I'm not off the hook just yet. I have to go to court in two more days to see this bitch-ass judge."

"Don't worry about it babe. You'll get through this."

"Yeah, but how you doing? How's my baby boy in there." He said rubbing Camela's growing stomach."

"Good and how you know it's a boy?"

"Because I can tell."

"Whatever. Come on, let's go." They get inside the car and head home.

"Soo I was thinking since we're official and we have this baby on the way...I thought it would be nice if we have dinner with my parents."

"Your parents? Oh hell no."

"Why not Rico?"

"Your daddy, that's why. Babe, you know that man don't like me."

"That's not true. You two just have to get to know each other."

"Baby, I don't know."

"Please Rico. It's important to me." Camela pleaded. Even though he didn't want to sit down and be interrogated by Camela's parents, if it meant a lot to her, he didn't see why not.

"Fine. I'll go."

"Really? Aww thank you baby." She leans over and kisses him on the cheek.

When they got home the house was still a mess from the party. Rico called a cleanup service to come and fix things. Camela made Rico a nice lunch, and afterwards, they fucked each other to sleep.

The next morning, Rico receives a text from Chris saying it was urgent. He softly gets out the bed from lying next to a sleeping Camela and takes the phone in the other room.

"Yeah, what's up nigga?" Rico answered still feeling groggy.

"Nigga, wake up. I got something to tell you about ya boy Anthony." Chris said.

"I'm listening." Rico says.

"So you know my sister's best friend cousin homegirl Diamond right?"

"What the- nigga just get on with it."

"Well, she told me that ya boy Anthony been flossing all around town spending big money. Last night in the strip club he was throwing big stacks."

"Chris, that still don't explain why the nigga is missing."

"I'm getting there. On top of him not laying low like the rest of us, he's been getting high. And I'm not talking about off no weed either. I'm talking about off of opioids." What Rico was hearing he couldn't believe. He had a feeling Anthony might have been using because of his weight loss after high school, but never questioned it.

"Diamond said she was chilling with him the other night and he was so high and started talking about how the police came to him with questions about the robbery. Anthony said he told them everything and how you planned the whole thing out." Chris says.

"Fuck." Rico says rubbing his goatee. He couldn't believe that Anthony of all people really sold him out. Hearing this disappointed him, but he remembered when Tony was alive, he would always tell him to trust no one in this game. Especially your friends.

"So what are you going to do?" Chris asks.

"You already know. Only one thing to do." Rico says.

"Damn...you sure about this?"

"I don't have a choice but to be sure."

"Aight, you the boss." Chris hangs up.

It was times like this that Rico wished he wasn't in the position he was in. But if he didn't get rid of snakes like Anthony...

then who would?

Once Rico got a location on Anthony, he wasted no time pulling up. It led him to a liquor store on the westside of town. He sat and waited for Anthony to come out for what seemed like forever. After waiting for about 40 minutes, he appeared walking out of the liquor store with a can of beer. Rico made sure his silencer was on his gun and got out the car.

"Long time no see Anthony." Rico says. Anthony jumps dropping his beer.

"Rico uh...look I just been sick, but I promise I was going to call you-"

"Save it man. It's all good." Rico says putting on a fake smile.

"Really? I was...I just been..." Rico could tell by the way Anthony was stuttering that he knew what was to come next.

"You been what?" Rico says sticking his gun in Anthony's side. "You just been snitching on me to the cops? Did you really think I wouldn't find out?"

"Naw Rico it's...it's not even like that-"

"You supposed to be my boy Anthony. We supposed to be partners...you betrayed me."

"Rico...listen, don't kill me man! Please I'm sorry."

"Yeah? I'm sorry too. If it's one thing being in this game has shown me, it's money doesn't change you...it changes the people around you."

Pffft, pfft, pffft!

Rico fires three shots into Anthony and watches him fall to the ground. A lone tear slid down his face as he watched his used to be friend bleed out on the ground. He quickly wiped it away and got back in his car. With Anthony dead, Rico knew there would be no evidence against him. He could face his day in court with confidence.

Two days later....

"You may all rise. The Honorable Judge Simmons presiding." The bailiff said. Everyone in the courtroom stood up as the judge came out. Rico and his lawyer stood up and so did the District Attorney prosecuting him.

"You may be seated."

Everyone sat back down and waited for court to begin.

"Ok, Mr. De'Rico Michell, you are here on charges of conspiracy and the robbery of one million dollars of the downtown federal bank. How do you plea?" The judge asks.

"Innocent your Honor." Rico's lawyer spoke.

"And tell me why is that?" The judge asks.

"Your Grace, there are claims and very false accusations against my client concerning this robbery. I can provide proof of my client's whereabouts the night of the robbery."

"Your Honor, if I may interject. We already have evidence and a witness that can conclude that Mr. Mitchell did indeed orchestrate the heist." Says the DA.

"And what is the evidence that you have counseler?" The judge asks the DA.

"We have bank accounts transactions of Mr. Mitchell's that show a tremendous amount of money being deposited and withdrawn. For example, a purchase for a $9,000 car, another purchase for $11,0000 diamond necklace, and the most recent one for a $100,000 home. I'm pretty sure what the jury wants to know is how does a man with no job make this kind of money?" The DA asks.

"Yes. I would like to know that as well." The judge says looking over the copies of De'Rico's bank account.

"Well, Your Honor, uhh...my client owns his own business." Rico's lawyer says.

"Really? And what business is that?" The judge asks.

"Umm.." Before the lawyer could answer, Rico whispers something in his ear.

"I will be happy to answer that question, but first I would like to know where is this...witness that the DA say they have."

"Object! What does this have to do with Mr. Mitchell's bank transactions?"

"I'm just saying, if you claim to have a witness, wouldn't it make sense to hear what they have to say first?"

"Order!" The judge banged his gravel.

"Counselor, can you present this witness?"

"I...I can't." The DA says and the courtroom gasps.

"And why not?"

"Because...because he's not here."

"Well, where is he?!" The judge angrily asks.

"I don't know. I-"

"Well, you better find out after we take a ten-minute recess or things aren't looking good for the District Attorney's office."

Bang! Bang!

The judge bangs his gravel and releases the court for recess. Ten minutes later, everyone comes back to the courtroom to resume.

"Well, Counselor? Do you have a witness or don't you?" The judge asks.

"I...no, Your Honor." The DA says holding her head down.

"So why would you say you had a witness and you don't?" The judge asks.

"Because...I had just been informed that my witness was killed two nights ago in front of a convenience store." The whole courtroom started whispering in shock.

"Order! Order! Counselor, I cannot proceed with these charges if you don't have any other evidence. I have no choice but to dismiss the case." The judge banged his gravel and court was dismissed.

Rico smirked because he knew this would be the outcome. By Anthony being dead, Rico could go free and continue becoming the south's biggest kingpin.

The next day, Rico keeps his word and has dinner with Camela and her parents. Her mom cooked pot roast, mashed potatoes, and green beans. The dinner was real silent with Camela's dad giving cold stares to Rico every time he looked up.

"Umm...the pot roast tastes really good, Mrs. Cross." Rico says.

"Why thank you Rico. Glad you like it." She says back.

"So Rico...what is it that you do for a living?"

"I uh...own my own business."

"Doing what?"

"Just distributing old car parts and refurbishing them."

"Hmm, well it can't be much business in that. Besides, who would want that? That's...a hand me down." He slyly says. Rico knows that he's trying to be sarcastic, but for Camela's sake, he lets him slide. Though after a while, Rico wasn't going to keep letting it happen.

"I'm sure he makes very good money from it." Mrs. Cross says.

"I'm pretty sure he does...that's why I can't seem to understand why he would rob a bank." Rico drops his fork on his plate and glares at Mr. Cross.

"Look, I ain't have nothing to do with that."

"So you say. But how do we know that?" Mr. Cross asks.

"Daddy, he's already seen a judge and has been acquitted ok."

"Let me ask you a question Rico...what do you want with my daughter? I mean, what can you really do for her and a baby on the way?"

"Dad-"

"Naw baby...let me answer this question. I can do everything and more for your daughter Mr. Cross. Maybe if you focused on actually being her father, she wouldn't look for comfort elsewhere. Maybe you should worry about your own home rather than me and mine." Rico says. Him and Camela's dad have a stare down, until Rico decides he's had enough.

"Thanks again for dinner Mrs. Cross." Rico says and gets up from the table. Camela runs after him.

"Rico, wait-"

"What?!" He says snatching away from her.

"I know my father can be a vulture, but can't you two put aside your egos and get along with each other?"

"...Never. I don't need your father's or anybody else's approval of me. If you can't accept that then that's on you." Rico says and leaves out the door. Camela just stood there disappointed and confused.

Chapter 15

After a lot of back and forth plus some bribing with his connect at The Embassy, Rico was finally able to get his friend Joaquim and Abel and also his mother American Visas. He sent his mother's in the mail almost a week ago and haven't heard back from her. Something in his gut was telling him to worry, but he continued to pray for the best. As far as Joaquim and Abel, Rico thought he could use the extra help since Anthony was out the picture.

Right now, he was at the airport waiting for the twins to arrive. Out the corner of his eye Rico notices something strange. A man in a grey suit and hat kept peeping over at Rico. He noticed that this was the same man who he saw in the parking lot and behind him in line at the information desk. Rico didn't want to over-exaggerate, but didn't want to be too careful either.

He decided to start walking just to see if the man would follow him. When Rico looked behind him, the man was there trying to seem discreet. *Federal Agent,* Rico thought to himself. He sped up a little faster to try and lose him. He had to admit the man was doing a good job trying to keep up, but all the time Rico spent running from the cops when he was younger made him a street bred track star. When he peeped behind him, the man was still following him trying to keep up but started getting lost in the crowd. Rico saw a restroom ahead and started jogging towards it. He ran inside and hid in one of the stalls.

Trying to catch his breath, Rico hides there for five minutes and figures the coast is clear. He opens the stall door and sees the bathroom is empty. Now that he knew that he was being watched he was going to make sure he was extra careful when doing things out in public. He heads back to the waiting area and sees the twins waiting for him.

"Mary-Kate and Ashley, long time no see." Rico greets them.

"Hey fuck you Rico." Joaquim says while they gave each other some dap.

"Took you two long enough. Come on, let's go." Rico says. They go to Rico's all black Cadillac Truck. He only rode in it when either conducting business or trying to keep a low profile.

First stop was where the twins would be staying at. Rico rented them out a two-bedroom condo close to downtown, so they wouldn't be far from all the traps and the new warehouse. Since today was technically Rico's day off, he wanted to show his childhood friends what they'd been missing out on. They went to a Falcon's game, which took the twins some time to understand, and afterwards, went to one of Rico's favorite soul food restaurants.

"So these are called what again?" Abel asks.

"Neckbones fool." Rico says with a mouth full of cornbread.

"Damn Rico, you been over here living it up. Thanks for bringing us over here man. It means a lot."

"Don't even mention it. Tony would be turning over in his grave if he knew I didn't look out for you two or our mother. Speaking of her, I haven't heard her in a while. I told her I got her a Visa but she didn't reply. Have you two heard anything?" Rico asks. The twins suddenly stop eating and both look at each other with sad looks. Rico began getting that worried feeling again.

"Sorry Rico...we meant to tell you but..." Abel began to say.

"What? Meant to tell me what?" Rico asks anxiously.

"Rico...Ms. Serafina died last week from organ failure." Joaquim says. Rico dropped the piece of cornbread he was holding at the news of his mother's passing.

"Wait a minute, wait a minute....you mean you two knew all this time that my mother was dead...and you didn't say anything?!" Rico asks angrily.

"We was going to, but we just didn't know how. We're sorry Rico."

"Sorry?! You're sorry?! Yeah right." Rico quickly gets up from the table and exits the restaurant. The twins felt bad for not telling Rico right away and hoped he forgave them.

Rico drives the twins back to their condo in silence while he was in deep thought. The fact that he didn't even get to say goodbye to his mother pained him. Camela kept blowing up his phone wanting to know where he was, but he wasn't in the mood for her right now. He made a stop to get a bottle of Paul Masson and drove around to clear his mind. By the time he noticed it was almost midnight and he was low on gas, he made his way home.

When he gets home he drunkenly busts the front door open and slams it. Camela comes running down the stairs in her nighttime lingerie with her protruding belly showing.

"Rico, where the hell have you been? Do you see what time it is?" Camela says.

"Camela, fuck off alright!" Rico yells.

"What is wrong with you? Are you...are you drunk?" She says smelling the liquor on him.

"So what if I am. I'm a grown ass man and I can have a drink or two if I want. Now, move out of my way." Rico says slightly pushing her to the side.

"No, I'm not moving until you tell me what the fuck is your problem!"

"My mother died!" Rico blurts out.

"What?" Camela says.

"She...she died. My son's one and only grandmother is dead and gone, aight? Now just...just leave me alone." Rico says trying to push past her.

"Wait a minute Rico...baby just talk to me." Camela says trying to console him, until he pushes her really hard this time and she falls to the floor. She looks up at Rico with confusion and tries to get up.

"Baby...I'm sorry. Here, let me help you." Rico says now feeling bad for putting his hands on her. She gets back up on her feet and slaps him.

"I think...you need some time to yourself Rico." Camela says and heads up the stairs to pack her some clothes. Rico runs after her and when he gets to the bedroom, Camela is packing most or her clothes.

"Ba...baby, what are you doing?"

"I'm leaving Rico! Now move!"

"Leaving? You can't leave me!" Rico says grabbing her arm but she snatches away.

"And why can't I? You come in here drunk, it's in the middle of the night and on top of that you put your hands on me? What is with you niggas?"

"Baby, I'm sorry! Ok?....I'm sorry. I... I just...I just feel so alone since Tony died and...now my momma." Not being able to hold it in anymore, he breaks down and sits on the edge of the bed. "You don't know what it's like losing somebody so close to you." Rico says.

"Rico, I do know what it's like. I lost my best friend in a car accident two years ago, I lost my grandma last year, and I've lost a cousin to cancer only a few months ago. You're not the only one going through this Rico." Camela says.

"I'm sorry. I just... feel so alone."

"...You're not alone Rico. You have me and about to have a precious baby here with you." Camela says sitting next to him.

"You right. It won't happen again."

"Come here." Camela says and leans Rico on her shoulder to console him..

~

After a long night of mourning over the death of his mother, the next day Rico had to suck it up for the moment and head over to the warehouse to help set up.

As he was driving, he couldn't help but notice a black SUV following him since he got off the freeway. He got that same vibe that he had when the guy in the airport was following him around. Rico pushes the gas and speeds up a little more. The SUV does the same and now he knew for sure he was being followed. Rico quickly busted a U-turn and headed the opposite way. The black SUV does the same and now they were in a high-speed chase. Whenever he made a left, they made a left. Whenever he sped up more they did as well.

Rico saw the traffic light was about to turn red, but knew if he stopped they would catch up to him. He sped up a little more while the light was still yellow, but as soon as he drove over the crosswalk the other light had turned green.

Crash! Rico's car is hit by another car and spins out of control. He tries hitting the brakes and crashes into a nearby fire hydrant. When his air bag deploys, it knocks his head back and his vision gets blurry until he eventually passes out.

Beep....beep...beep...

The sound from the heart monitor wakes Rico up as he flutters his eyes open. At first he is just staring at the ceiling until he looks over and sees Camela, Pop, and Chris standing there.

"Where am I?" He groans.

"You're at Grady man. You got in a car accident and hit your head, but the doctor said you're going to be ok." Pop said.

"Yeah, baby are you ok? Your car was completely totaled." Camela says.

"I'm fine. Just a little dazed but I'm good." Rico says.

The three of them sat by Rico's side while nurses came in and out the room. After a while Pop and Chris left, leaving just Camela and Rico.

"I got to hear the baby's heartbeat today. The doctor said in another few weeks we'll know if it's a boy or girl." Camela says.

"That's great baby." Rico says.

"What's wrong babe?"

"Nothing, just wondering where the nurse is with my pain medicine because a nigga starting to get a headache." Rico says and just like clockwork a different nurse walked in with her clipboard.

"Hello, my name is Nurse Cannon and...it looks like you've been cleared to go home Mr....Mitchell?...De'Rico?" When the nurse turned around and showed her face Rico couldn't believe his eyes.

"Leah?"

"Oh my God! How are you?" She asks.

"Well...as you can see." Rico says pointing out him being in the hospital.

"Still a reckless driver I see."

"Naw, just...other people and their reckless driving."

"Oh yeah right."

Rico couldn't believe after all these years he would see Leah again. She slimmed up a little bit but still remained thick in the waist and hips.

"Uh-hmm." Camela says interrupting their reunion.

"Oh uh...Leah this is-"

"His girlfriend and soon to be mother of his child." Camela says snobbery. Leah could feel Camela felt some type of way towards her but kept her composure.

"Really? Well congratulations."

"Thank you." Camela still says with an attitude.

"Well...I don't want to take up too much of you guys' time. I'll have the assistant type up your discharge papers and you can go home."

"Thanks Leah." Rico says side-eyeing Camela for her childish behavior.

Leah walked out, but for some reason, with a heavy heart. She thought after all this time if she ever saw Rico again she wouldn't still have feelings for him. Right now her mind was overflowing with confusion and a little bit of hurt from him moving on. Rico, on the other hand, didn't know what to feel, but he did know he wasn't feeling Camela's attitude.

"What the fuck was that all about?" Rico asks.

"What do you mean?" Camela asks.

"The way you were acting."

"Oh, so I'm supposed to just sit here and let you fawn over some old high school girl friend?"

"It don't matter. That shit was real childish."

"Well, you know what, how about I just leave then?" Camela gets up to leave, until two men in black walk in.

"Who the hell are y'all?" Rico asks.

"Mr. Mitchell, we're with the FBI. After you're released we need you to come with us for questioning."

"Kiss my ass. I ain't going nowhere." Rico says.

"Let me make this clear, if you refuse to come with us, not only will we issue a warrant for your arrest, but hers as well." One of the agents say pointing to Camela.

"What?! Rico, what the-"

"Alright, alright...I'll go." Rico forcibly agrees.

After being discharged, he instructed Camela to go home, while he went with the two agents for questioning. When he got there it was the same old questions over and over again.

"So, you're just a regular business man walking around with $250,000 in his pocket?" The agent asks him.

"Yeah. What's so wrong about that?" Rico says.

"Nothing, but only thing is by you not having no job history and no current employment it makes the Bureau feel kind of... suspicious of your actions."

"Suspicious? You want to know what's suspicious? The fact you motherfuckers keep questioning me and coming after me, when I did nothing wrong. You know I'm starting to think this whole thing is about me being Black."

"What? Get the hell out of here,. We just want to know-"

"Want to know what? Huh? Why is it that a Black man can't have a couple thousand in his bank account, but a scheming ass White man can and don't get chased down by the FBI?"

"Look Mitchell, don't play the race hand with us ok." The agents says.

"It's already dealt. Let me ask you something Agents. Do you know how much those White motherfuckers make working on wall street a day? About close to $900 per day. That's 300,000 per year. Now those same people steal, lie, shit even kill if they too for that money. I don't see none of them getting harassed by you two. So this is what I propose...you can let me go and pretend this never happened or I can call my lawyer and sue for harassment and discrimination. I know for a fact you two love your little bullshit ass positions and wouldn't want to lose your job." Rico said smirking. He knew he hit a nerve when things got quiet and the two agents looked at each other.

"Your free to go now, Mitchell, but just know we will still be keeping an eye on you."

"Happy to know." Rico gets up and leaves out the interrogation room feeling like he had won the fight, but knew he hadn't won the battle yet.

Later, he swings by the warehouse to see how things are going and almost everything was ready for distribution. Seeing his vision come to life had him feeling like Nino from *New Jack City*. He meets with a few new connects to talk about product and finally heads home for the night.

Camela is still mad at him for the way he acted towards Leah. Rico kept telling her it was nothing, but if he had to be honest, Leah was all he kept thinking about ever since seeing her earlier at the hospital. Now that he knew she was back in town and where she worked, he was pretty sure he was going to be a frequent visitor. Feelings he thought had died were re-ignited.

Chapter 16

Present day.....

Rico is still being interrogated by Jamil and Kimberly on his involvement in the drug game. Jamil reaches in his suit jacket pocket and pulls out a photo. He tosses the photo on the table across to Rico.

"So if you claim you and this Jax character was never cool, was never friends, then what are you two doing together in this photo? Y'all look real...cozy to me." Agent Jamil says.

"That picture was just for the moment. We were both at the club that night."

"Yeah but that still doesn't explain how two men who are so-called enemies can be in the same room and not have a full-blown shoot out." Kimberly says.

"It wasn't always that way." Rico sighs. In fact, Rico remembers the very moment him and Jax decided to squash their differences and partner up, but sometimes things have a funny way of working out.

2011...

"Ohh I really like these colors together." Camela says. She and Rico were sitting down with a party planner for their upcoming baby shower. Rico thought it was kind of silly to need a party planner for just a baby shower, but since this was Camela's first she wanted it to be special and extravagant.

"What do you think babe?" she asks Rico but he was too pre-occupied with his phone. Since seeing Leah at the hospital, he just couldn't get her out his mind.

"Huh? Oh yeah, that's nice." Rico says distracted.

"Babe, you not even listening." Camela says feeling embarrassed by his lack of attention.

"I am but...just give me a minute. I need to make a phone call." Rico says getting up and going outside.

"I cannot believe...I apologize." Camela says to the party planner.

"No, no it's fine. Here, let's look at some more samples."

Rico walks outside where he was sure Camela couldn't hear him. He finally got enough courage to call Leah's job to talk to her. He waited until the operator picked up and then asked to be connected to the unit she worked in.

"Hello fifth floor?"

"Yes, is Leah Cannon working today?" Rico says into the phone.

"Uh yes, she is. Can I ask who's calling?"

"Um...tell her an old friend."

"Ok, hold on one minute." The person on the other end put him on hold for what seemed like five minutes.

"Hello?" Rico heard Leah's sweet voice.

"Leah?" Rico says.

"Rico? Rico, what are you doing calling my job?" Leah asks.

"I...it was the only way I knew how to contact you. Leah look, I know the last time we saw each other we ended on bad terms but…I ain't gon lie, ma. I missed you. A lot."

"Rico…that's good to know but…things can't just go back to being the same."

"Why can't they?"

"Well, for one, you're in a relationship and about to be a father." She said reminding Rico of him and Camela being together.

"That can change. I mean, here I thought I would never see you again and…I just feel like God might be giving us a second chance."

"God gave us a second chance? How would you know? I've never even heard you talk about God."

"Doesn't mean I don't believe in him." Rico says.

"Look Rico, I've…missed you, too, but I've moved on with my life…Rico, I'm engaged." Leah saying those words felt piercing to Rico's heart.

"I hear that…but engagement don't mean nothing until y'all walk down the aisle."

"Rico…I gotta go. You have a nice life." Leah says and hangs up. Hearing about Leah getting married to another guy honestly had Rico feeling hurt, but he realistically figured Leah would've probably moved on by now like he did. It wasn't nothing to him but a little competition.

Rico walks back inside to Camela and the planner still going over colors and decorations. He sighed and just couldn't wait until this was all over. Only thing he looked forward to was meeting his son.

"This was our most recent shower that we did last week. The theme was Under the Sea."

"They're all so beautiful. I just don't know which one to pick. Babe, what do you think?" Camela asks Rico but scoffed when she saw he was still texting away on his phone. Pop had sent Rico a text saying to come to the warehouse asap.

"Rico! Like really?" Camela yelled.

"Babe, just pick anything. I don't care which." Rico says and goes back to texting.

"I can't believe you. This is your son, too, and you mean to tell me you're too busy texting to help me pick out a design?"

"Camela don't start." Rico says glaring.

"Wait, wait how about this? You can take this catalog with you and we can schedule for another day?" the planner suggests.

"Thank you. That'll be fine." Camela says.

After leaving the party planner, the ride home was quiet. Rico hurries to try and drop Camela off, so he can go see what was up at the warehouse. From the sounds of it, he can tell it was some bullshit.

"You just have to make things difficult don't you?" Camela finally says.

"Man, what is you talking about?" Rico says.

"I'm talking about you acting like you weren't the least little bit interested in helping plan out our baby shower."

"Um, that's because I wasn't. I told you this whole baby shower thing is for y'all women to be planning out. This ain't really a man thing."

"Oh yeah? But y'all niggas don't be saying that when y'all help make the baby."

"That's different. I don't know why I even have to be there. You know your bougie ass parents don't like me."

"First off, my parents are not bougie and they never said they didn't like you."

"Yeah, well your daddy doesn't like me. And another thing, why we gotta invite your bougie ass cousins?"

"Because I haven't seen most of them in a long time, and it's been a while since anybody in our family has had a baby shower, so this is a really big event. That's why I want everything to be perfect."

"Man whatever." Rico says and continues paying attention to him driving. Ever since getting chased down the last time he made sure to stay alert. It was quiet for a moment, until Camela started to wonder who was holding his attention on the other side of his phone.

"So, who was you on the phone with?" Camela asked.

"...Pop why?" Rico says half telling the truth.

"Hmmm. You sure it wasn't some bitch?" Camela says.

"Aww, come on Camela with that shit man."

"I'm just asking. I mean, you're the one who is sitting up here acting like you didn't get caught cheating on me almost a month ago." Camela brings up.

Trying to find a way to cope with his mother's death, Rico got real fucked up one night when Camela was supposed to be on a business trip. He had two bottles of Cîroc that night and ended up inviting two hoes from the hood over. Little did he know that Camela's plane got canceled and she had to turn back around and come home. When she walked in, she caught Rico getting his dick sucked. After them going back and forth and Rico blaming it on him mourning, Camela decided to still stay and work things out.

"I thought we wasn't going to bring that shit up no more. Why you bringing up old shit?" Rico asks.

"Because Rico. I don't trust you! Shit, how I know you haven't been texting that nurse hoe from the hospital?"

"Come on now, why would I be texting her?" Rico says lying.

"Rico, I seen the way you looked at her. And I remember when we first started fucking around all you talked about was Leah. Leah this and Leah that."

"Listen, I told your ass it was nothing. So just drop the shit ok?" Rico says ending the conversation. Rico did care for Camela off the strength she was carrying their child, but the feelings he had for Leah never left. They was just buried deep down inside.

He drops Camela back off at home and heads to the warehouse. Pop, Chris, and the twins were there; supposed to be setting up shop. Instead they were dealing with some bullshit.

"Alright, what the fuck is going on now?" Rico says walking in. He sees everyone standing in a circle surrounding a person tied to a chair.

"Caught this little spy hiding behind some boxes outback. He not trying to tell us who sent him down here, but I already got an idea who might have." Pop says. The hostage looked to be about in his mid-thirties and was sweating from nervousness.

"Oh really? Well, he might answer to this." Rico pulls out his gun and points it to the hostage's skull.

"Come on man! Don't kill me please!" He cried.

"Who sent you? I'm only going to ask you this once." Rico says.

"Man...Jax. Jax sent me."

"Told you." Pop says.

Bang! Bang!

Rico put two shots in the hostage's head almost splitting open his skull.

"Fuck!" Rico yells. "This nigga Jax just not getting the fucking picture."

"Fuck that. We need to go pay that motherfucker another visit so he can get the fucking picture." Pop suggests.

"Oh, you don't think I am? Chris, you and the twins dispose of the body." Rico orders.

"Man, why I gotta do it? Why can't they just do it?" Chris asks.

"Because you're training them. Now do as I say. We'll be back." Rico and Pop exit the warehouse with a mission in mind. Jax was overstepping his boundaries too much nowadays. It was time Rico showed him he wasn't about the games.

~

"Jax!" Rico says busting through Jax's office door with Pop right behind him.

"How did you get in here? How does he keep getting in here?" Jax asks his henchmen.

"Nigga fuck all that! What's up with you sending a spy our way to spy on us and shit?" Pop asks. Jax start chuckling.

"Ain't a damn thing funny Jax. I thought we agreed your territory is your territory and mines is mine." Rico says.

"Maybe we should uhh...talk in private." Jax says signaling his henchman to leave the room.

"Naw fuck that! I ain't going nowhere!" Pop says cocking his gun.

"Please, this will only take a minute." Jax says slyly. Rico eyeballs Jax for a minute trying to figure out what type of shit he was on. Regardless, he had his pistol loaded and ready to shoot.

"Pop, just wait outside the door." Rico says.

"Rico...you sure?" Pop asks.

"Yeah." Rico continues to glare at Jax while Pop steps out and slams the door.

"Crazy friend you got there." Jax says.

"Yeah, well he ain't the only one. What's up with the bullshit Jax? Huh? What's up with the spy and shit?"

"Rico, my boy...I was just simply curious. A few of my boys heard you getting ready to move some big weight in the city and I just had to see for myself."

"By sending a fucking spy?"

"You know...Rico, I been thinking maybe it's time we stop all this territorial nonsense. I mean ATL is big enough for the two of us. Why not partner up?"

"Come again?" Rico was confused why his arch nemesis would want to all of the sudden partner up.

"Just think about it. Two of the biggest drug lords in ATL come together. People will practically be giving us their money." Jax says. Rico whips out his gun hearing enough of what Jax was saying.

"Yo are you working with the FEDs or something?" Rico asks.

"Whoa, whoa calm down now son-"

"I'm not your fucking son. Now tell me are you working with the FEDs?"

"No, I'm not. I just think by us joining forces and coming together we can make two times the money we're making now." Jax says again. Rico still doesn't believe him and would rather take his chances working without his help.

"I don't need your fucking help Jax. Next time you send a fucking spy or any kind of informant to my place of business it'll be a bullet going in your head." Rico tucks his gun away and leaves. Jax just shakes his head, smiles, and figures Rico will be back sooner than later.

Two weeks later....

The day of the baby shower, everyone is gathering at the Hilton Hotel ballroom. Most of Camela's side of the family shows up first along with some of Rico's friend's and whoever they brought with them.

"Mom! Dad! You made it." Camela excitingly says.

"Of course sweetheart. We wouldn't miss this for the world." Her mom says. Camela's father was still not amused by Camela being pregnant by Rico.

"I'll admit that...reject boyfriend of yours surely outdid himself. How much did he put in? $100?" Camela's father sarcastically says.

"Try $100,000 plus tickets to Disney world in everybody's goodie bag. Yeah, we doing it real Beyonce and Jay-Z in this thing." Rico says interrupting and putting his arm around Camela. Her dad remains silent not knowing what to say.

"Come on Joyce. I think I see some seats over here." He glares at Rico and walks away.

"Ignore him. You two look nice." Camela's mom says and follows after Mr. Cross.

"Ahhh, my nigga! What's up?" Rico says greeting a few homeboys from around the hood and their plus one they brought.

"Y'all go head make ya'self at home. Enjoy the festivities." Rico says giving them all dap as they went to raid the snack table.

"Babe." Rico turns around to Camela flaring her nostrils. He knew she did that when she got irritated.

"What?"

"I thought you said you were only inviting a few friends. Not the whole damn hood." She says crossing her arms.

"Listen fuck all that. If you can invite your bougie ass cousins then I can invite some of my boys from around the way....speaking of which, here come one of your bougie ass, country cousins now." Rico says

"Cousin Camela!" Says a lady dressed in an all-blue suit with a dress hat. She reminded Rico of the actress from Half and Half who played the mom.

"Cousin Sidora! Oh my God! How long has it been?" Camela says.

"Too long darling. Now who is the lucky dad to be? You must show me him." Sidora says.

"He's standing right here." Camela says and Sidora's facial expression changes.

"Ohh...uhh...he's not the one from the family cookout in Blue Ridge is he?"

"No cousin Sidora, that was Cedric. This is Rico."

"How you doing mam?" Rico says reaching out his hand for her to shake but she just looked at him as if he was a homeless person on the street.

"Uhh yes…Hi. Oh, darling let's hope he looks everything like you." Sidora tries to fake whisper but Rico heard every word. "Ahh, there are your parents. Let me go say hi. Nice to meet you Tico." Sidora says rushing off.

"Tico? Bitch-"

"Babe, be nice. Ok? Please?" Camela says stopping him from going off on Sidora.

"Yeah whatever." Rico says and walks off.

The rest of the evening, Rico and Camela entertained their guests but seemed separated the whole night. Rico partied and only socialized with his guests and Camela spent most of the time listening to some of her family talk about people including Rico.

"Ok, it's time to open gifts." The planner said over the loudspeaker. Everyone gathered around the stage where there were two chairs set up for Rico and Camela. They both took their seats ready to open presents from their loved ones.

"Ok, this first one is from mom and dad of the mother to be." Camela unwrapped the big blue box and opened it.

"Awww, a rocking horse! Thanks mom and dad." Camela says to her parents. They both nod their heads.

"Alright, this next one is from…Re…Rein-no?" The planner tried pronouncing the name on the tag.

"Renio! That's my dawg!" Rico says pointing to his homeboy in the back. He digs inside the gift bag and pulls out a big plastic baby bottle filled with toys and other items.

"Good looking." Rico says in approval.

"What you wanna make of it? We can go!" A voice from the back said. Everyone turned their attention to the commotion and saw it was one of Rico's friends getting into it with Camela's cousin Thomas.

"What's up? Say that shit to my face!"

Bang! Slap! Crash!

Suddenly, the two go at it and start to fight. Somehow, their friends or girlfriends got involved and ended up fighting too. They knocked over some tables in the process creating a big mess and drawing the attention of hotel security.

"Break it up! Break it up! Party over! Everyone leave now!" Security shouted.

"I cannot believe this shit!" Camela says storming off stage. Inside, Rico found the whole situation comical but felt bad how things turned out in the end. He believes by tomorrow after a shopping spree, Camela will forget all about tonight.

After loading half the gifts into his car, Rico looks around for Camela so they could leave. He walks back inside, but before he rounds the corner he hears Camela arguing with her parents.

"Dad, could you please not say I told you so?" Camela cried.

"And why shouldn't I? Honestly Camela, how could you let this...low life impregnant you?! I've sent you to the best schools, paid for you to get through business school, bought you your first house and car! You're going to throw that all away for a life of being some baby momma on welfare?!"

"Alright, that's enough! Camela couldn't help what happened." Mrs. Cross says.

"Like hell she couldn't! Camela...I'm just very disappointed in you and that you choose to be with this...hoodlum instead of somebody respectable. That's all I'm saying."

"I'm...I'm sorry dad." Camela says. Rico couldn't believe his ears. Not one time did Camela take up for him against what her father said about him. Here he was trying to make things work out by being with her and she can't even come to his defense.

Rico leaves back out to the car not wanting to hear no more. He gets on the driver's seat waiting for Camela to walk out. When she finally does, he gave her the death look as she got in the passenger's seat.

"You ready?" Rico asks.

"Yeah." Camela sighed. Rico starts up the car and heads home.

The ride home was so silent you could hear the crickets outside. At every stop light Rico kept looking over at Camela just shaking his head.

"What? Why you keep looking at me like that?" Camela finally asks.

"Because I heard what the fuck your father said about me. About me being a hoodlum and all that shit." Rico says angrily.

"You did?" She asks.

"Hell yeah I did. His words didn't hurt me, because I don't give a fuck what nobody says about me, but the most hurtful thing ever was how you stood there and said nothing in my defense."

"Well...some of what he said was right Rico."

"What?!" Rico damn near almost wanted to reach over and choke Camela for saying that. *Count to ten Rico, count to fucking ten.*

"You know what, you real lucky you carrying my seed because if you weren't ya ass would be walking back to the house right now!"

"Well, it was your stupid friends that started the fight and ruined everything!"

"So fucking what! This is about loyalty Camela. How can you say you love me and don't take up for me when niggas down me?!"

"Rico, I'm not used to all of this. This is all new to me. I've never been with a drug dealer before, let alone been pregnant by one."

"Well, either get with the fucking program or get lost."

"What does that supposed to mean?"

"Exactly what it sounds like." Rico says. Camela being lost for words just pouted the rest of the ride. She didn't think what her father said was a big deal, but now she was wishing she would have said something in Rico's defense.

Rico drops Camela and the gifts off at home and rides to meet a guy named Angelo about co-ownership of a night club. With the FEDs always questioning him about how he makes his money, he needed definite proof next time. It was a win-win plan. More money in his pocket and the FEDs would back down. Another part to his plan was to start trying to expand. ATL was beginning to feel too small and he needed something that was out of state and least expecting.

A few days later...

Rico lands at LAX airport. Not only was this a business trip but somewhat of a leisure trip as well. He was in search of new property like a mansion or nice seaside beach house and to see all of what Los Angeles has to offer. He remembers times when him and Tony would talk about going to L.A. together.

"If you had a place to run away to, where would it be?" Rico asked Tony.

"California. Preferably L.A. I heard the sun is always shining out there."

"Not always. It has to be night time at some point."

"I know that stupid, but can you just imagine driving along the coastline, roof down, wind blowing, and right at that very moment you catch the sun going down." Tony said exhaling the smoke from his blunt.

"I hear that. But what about the girls?"

"Of course. I'm going to get me one of those bad Hollywood, Halle Berry type bitches. So that way I can fatten her ass up." They both chuckled.

"So, when we going?" Rico asked.

"Soon....soon." Tony said.

Rico could almost feel himself shed a tear and cleared his eyes as he snaps out his flashback. His rental car, a Mercedes-Benz G-class pulls up and he heads to the hotel to unwind.

The rest of the day Rico meets up with a few different realtors that showed him some houses, but none of them seemed to catch Rico's attention. One realtor, who sold houses to a lot of big-name celebrities like Usher, Kim Kardashian, and Vin Diesel, showed Rico this huge million-dollar mansion in the Hollywood Hills. He liked it but right now decided not to close on it. In all this, Rico was thinking of his kids if they ever needed to get away or hide out somewhere as well. With this lifestyle came a target on your back and he was going to make sure to instill that on his son and other kids to come.

Getting tired Rico heads back to his hotel room. He kind of felt lonely being there, but right now him and Camela were on bad terms. Otherwise, he would have brought her with him.

Bzzzz...bzzz

Rico heard his phone vibrate and saw it was a number he didn't know. Thinking it might be the FEDs trying to get the drop on him he ignored it, but the number called right back. This time he answered.

"Hello?" Rico says.

"Well, I'll be damned...Rico, it's me man." A male voice says.

"Me who?" Rico asks.

"Rodney. Rodney Waters from high school?" Rico quickly thought if he knew anyone named Rodney and suddenly it all came back to him.

"Rapping Rodney?" Rico asks.

Rodney was always trying to rap and bust rhythms in the cafeteria and in class. Some of them were good, while others would have got him swept off of stage at the Apollo.

"Yeah man. It's me! Damn, how can you forget your very first corner boy?" He says. Rico had recruited Rodney when he started selling weed at school.

"Naw, naw I ain't fo'get. How you get my number anyway?" Rico asks.

"Hey, when you big time and you practically run L.A. you can get anybody number."

"Oh, you big time like that huh?"

"You know it. Only now they call me Rodmoney. My rap

career has took off over the past year. I'm talkin' million-dollar contract, big ass house, jewelry, and the whole nine."

"That's good man. I'm happy for you."

"Well hey, what you doing tonight?"

"Nothing much, probably about to turn in for the night."

"What?! Man you should roll with me to this club in Hollywood. The label throwing me an album release party and it's going to be all the way turned up."

"You don't say?" Rico gave it some thought and he knew it was bound to be a gang of women there. He thought about Camela and all, but her loyalty was still in question after what happened at the baby shower. *What was it that Tupac said? To live and die in L.A.*

"Yeah sure. I'll meet you there."

"Aww, hell yeah! I'll shoot you the address."

"Aight." Rico hangs up and immediately starts getting another call. He saw it was Camela and wasn't in the mood for her right now. He ignored her call and started getting dressed for the party.

An hour later, Rico walked into Club *Aces* and looked around to see if he saw Rodney. He had on a fresh Ralph Lauren button down with some Tommy jeans, and a fresh pair of air forces. Women walking by was hypnotized by his appearance. He spotted Rodney over in a VIP section and went over.

"Excuse me, VIP guests only." The security guard says blocking his way in.

"I am VIP." Rico says.

"Oh yeah? You on the list?"

"Man, I don't gotta be on no list. Just go tell Rodney I'm here."

"Yeah right. Nice try. Now be gone." The security guard said shooing him away.

"What? Nigga you better come correct before I-"

"Rico!!! I was beginning to think you wouldn't make it. What seems to be the problem here?" Rodney said walking over with a bottle of Courvoisier in his hand.

"Yeah, this bitch ass toy cop wasn't trying to let me in." Rico says.

"Hugghh, Deion did I not tell you to do your job correctly?"

"I am. You said-"

"Ahhh! Speak only when spoken to. Now Mr. Rico here is a very special guest of mine, ok? Don't make me fire you and you go back to doing security at Wal-Mart. Now go fetch me and my guests another bottle." Rodney orders him. The security guard sheepishly walks over to the bar.

"Daaaaamn!" Rico and Rodney laugh.

"Somebody gotta tell him. Excuse me everybody. I'd like to introduce a very good friend of mine Rico. Rico...everybody!" Rodney introduced him. Everyone in Rodney's posse waved and spoke.

"Look, drink up man. We got open access to the bar courtesy of my record label."

"I see nigga. You over here drinking like a fish."

"Hey, this is how stars live out in L.A." Rodney says. Rico's phone vibrates in his pocket. He now has three missed calls from Camela. He ignores it and turns his phone off. Tonight, he was going to relax and have some fun.

"Hey, this next one goes out to my dawg Rodmoney! Rod-money in the building!" The DJ shouted out. The spotlight shined over in their direction as Rodney waves out to the crowd.

I gets money, all day
Every fuckin day
When it comes to this money
It ain't no fucking game...

The DJ started playing Rodney's song and the whole club began dancing. Rico bobbed his head as he admitted it sounded actually good. He poured him a glass of Jim Bean that was on the table and made a toast to Rodney for his success.

"Hey, you're Rico right?" A thick, mixed girl scoots over next to Rico. She had long, naturally curly hair and smelled like Victoria Secret perfume.

"Yeah." Rico answers.

"Wow, so you and Rodmoney must be really close for him to brush off his security like that."

"Yeah, we go back. What about you pretty. What's your name?" Rico asks.

"Maria and that's my friend Layla over there." She said point-ing to a Latino girl.

"Ohh ok...nice." Rico flirts.

"So uhh...what you getting into later?" She asks. Rico al-ready knew that was code talk for *Can I get some dick?*

"Well uhh...actually me and Rod was thinking of having an after party back at my place."

"Really?" She says twirling her hair with her finger.

"Yeah...hey Rod!" Rico called over to Rodney who was flirting with groupies. When he looked over, Rico motioned his head towards Maria and Rodney started cheesing.

"Yesssir!!!" Rodney yelled out.

"So, what's good? You wanna kick it with us after?"

"Sure, is it ok if Layla comes along?" She asks with seduction in her voice.

"Absolutely." Rico throws back the rest of his drink preparing for a good night.

After the party, Rico, Rodney, Maria, Layla, and two more groupies headed back to Rico's suite. Being drunk and horny, one thing led to another and next thing Rico knew all six of them was having a full-blown orgy. If Rico wasn't trying to keep a low profile, he would've taped the whole thing.

"Man this is the best night of my fucking life!!!" Rodney yelled while anal fucking the groupie he met at the club.

The next morning...

Rico opened his eyes that started to burn from the light of the sun through his window. He realized he was laying on the floor and the room was trashed. The last thing he remembers was Rodney leaving with his two hoes which left Rico to finish fucking the night away with Maria and Layla. When he looked up he saw two pairs of legs that belonged to none other than a pissed off Camela.

"Babe...Camela what are you doing here?" Rico says jumping up.

"No! The question is what are you doing here and why you not answering your phone?! Rico I called you at least twenty times last night!" Camela yelled.

"Wait...how did you get here so fast?"

"I caught the red eye leaving from Atlanta last night. You would've known that if you would've picked up the phone! Rico what the fuck's going on?!"

"Hey, can you guys keep it down? We're trying to sleep." A drunk Maria said standing in the doorway of the bedroom with Layla standing behind her.

"Oh my God!" Camela feeling overwhelmed runs out the suite.

"Baby! Wait a minute! Babe!" Rico tries to grab her arm but she turns to him and smacks him so hard her hand print appeared on his face. Camela walked down the hallway in tears of Rico's infidelity once again. All he could do was stand in the doorway and feel guilty for what he had done.

Later once Rico finally sobers up, he meets with another realtor and he shows him a different mansion in Malibu. Rico decides it wasn't really his style and makes up his mind that maybe L.A. just wasn't the place for him. They wrap up and he books the next flight home.

Hours later...

Upon returning home, he sees a note that Camela left on the kitchen counter. She says that she has gone to stay with her parents for now until they can figure out how to raise their son separately. Rico felt bad for fucking up, but he knew if he just gave Camela some time it would blow over.

Bzzz.

Rico receives a text from Joaquim saying everything was finally set up at the warehouse. It pleases Rico when he comes home to good news instead of some bullshit. He sees another text from Pop saying he's sick and can't go pick up the drop from one of the trap houses. *If you want something done guess you gotta do it yourself.*

On the way to collect the drop himself, Rico tries his luck and calls Camela. Just like he expected it went to voicemail. There was no way Camela thought she was just going to take his son from him over no bullshit like this.

"Get out the car now!" Rico is suddenly snatched out his car at the stop light by two big guys and thrown into the back of a black Suburban. When he sees the person behind all this is Jax, he just sighs.

"You must have a fucking death wish Jax." Rico says brushing his shirt off.

"Well, I had to get your attention somehow. You been ignoring my calls Rico." Jax says.

"I just got back into town. Now what do you want?"

"You know what I'm going to say."

"You right. And the answer is no."

"You know Rico, I understand you got pride and I respect that. But that pride of yours is going to block a lot of your blessings."

"Then so be it, but I'm not going against the grain and become partners with the likes of you."

"Haha, I swear you young niggas just don't know when you got a good opportunity on the table and how to take it."

"Jax, why are you doing this anyway? Why now?"

"Like I said before, we can do more if we work together. Jax Johnson and Rico Jefe. We'll be like the drug dealer version of Shaq and Kobe." Jax says with a sly smile.

"Man whatever. Can I go now?" Rico says unlocking the door.

"Yeah, yeah but you just think about it." Rico opens the door to climb out the car. "Oh Rico, one more thing...I heard about your dad's overdose last week. I'm sorry for your loss." Jax says.

Rico froze after hearing now his father was dead. Even though now he wanted nothing to do with him, a part of Rico never gave up hope that one day Dewayne would come to his senses and make up for everything he did. He now truly felt alone in this world.

Chapter 17

Ball so hard motherfuckers wanna fine me
That shit cray
That shit cray
That shit cray....

Rico is sitting in his VIP section of his new co-owned night club *The Chase.* He sips on his Jack Daniels as he watches his workers discreetly come bringing in duffle bags either filled with money or drugs. Rico has been laundering money through the club for only a few weeks, but so far there has been no word or sign of the FEDs since doing it. Rico looks out on the dance floor watching a few beautiful women that caught his eye. Camela still wasn't talking to him, but he knew she was due any day.

When he saw Jax walking through the door, Rico wasn't surprised. In fact, he had summoned him here so they could really sit down and talk like men. Even though he wanted nothing to do with Jax, his plan to make more money together didn't sound too bad either. It was just going to take time for Rico to build trust with Jax because something about him still rubbed him the wrong way.

"Heard you wanted me here. Nice club." Jax said walking in his section.

"Look, sit down. I don't have all night." Rico says.

"Well, what can I do for you?" Jax asks.

"I want to talk about your plan about merging together.

What's your motive? Why all of a sudden now?" Rico asks.

"Just...a change of heart I guess. When I first heard about you, Rico, I thought to myself...oh, he's just another young, dumb nigga who thinks he's doing something." Jax laughs, but Rico didn't find it funny.

"Tread lightly." Rico says pouring a cup of Patron.

"Right...so once I heard about you getting a warehouse and basically taking over the other side of Atlanta I then said to myself, hmm this youngin might be on to something."

"I am. The best product right now is coming from places like Cuba, Guatemala, and even Jamaica."

"See, and with your different connects plus the territory I have. We can make a killing. We can run this town." Rico inhales on a cigar he had been smoking and ponders on what Jax is saying. Before he could answer, a young-looking guy with a camera walked into the section.

"Hey fellas. I'm Freddy, the new club promoter. Do you mind if I take a picture of you two for our club's website?"

"No get lost." Rico says.

"Hey, come on Rico. Live a little." Jax says. Rico sighs and figured what can one little picture hurt.

"Fine one picture, then beat it." Rico scoots up on the couch he was sitting on to get in closer for the picture.

"Ok and...perfect." *Click!*

Freddy snapped the picture of the two drug lords and walks away to take more of other guests.

"Well uhh...you don't have to make a decision tonight, but you let me know by tomorrow." Jax said looking over across the club. Rico looked in the direction he was looking and saw he was saying what's up to a strange looking group of niggas.

"You know them or something?"

"Yeah, yeah...just from around the way."

"Them niggas on some gay shit. They been mean mugging the shit out of me all night."

"See Rico, you need to relax a little. You're so paranoid. Just chill out, smoke your cigar, and try to come up on some pussy while you here." Jax says.

"Hmmph, that won't be a problem for me." Rico says putting his cigar back in his mouth.

"Hahaha! I see. Well, let me get out of here. I have business to tend to. You think about what we talked about." Jax says and exits the section.

Rico would have to give it a lot of thought and needed more than just twenty-four hours. When he looked back across the room the same group of niggas was still there, but the main one giving Rico cold glares looked like the leader. Rico was strapped as always and ready for whatever.

"Hey there." Rico snapped out his killer thoughts when a beautiful, brown-skinned woman came up to him.

"Well hello there." He said back licking his lips.

"You mind if I sit?" She asks.

"Naw, not at all." Rico scoots over.

"So, what's your name?" Rico asks.

"Brenda."

"Oh ok, Brenda. I'm-"

"I know who you are. The whole city knows who you are."

"You don't say? So, what's a pretty thing like you doing here by yourself?"

"How you know I'm by myself?"

"I seen you when you walked in. If you was here with someone or even meeting someone here you wouldn't be over here talking me. Now would you?"

"No, I guess not." Brenda blushed. Them flirting back and forth is suddenly interrupted by the same guy who was eyeballing Rico.

"Hey nigga, you talking to my girl?" He said aggressively.

"Excuse me, but I am not your girl anymore Jerome."

"Since the fuck when?"

"Since you had bitches calling your phone at three o'clock in the morning."

"I told you that shit was nothing."

"Oh yeah, whatever."

"Yeah well you don't need to be over here talking to him." Jerome says pointing to Rico.

Rico chuckles to himself over the stupidity this nigga was displaying. He slowly stands up and steps closer to Jerome. He lifts the side of his shirt showing a black Beretta gun.

"I don't know if you stupid or just dumb, but here's what's going to happen. Yo ex-bitch is going to leave with me, I'm going to take her home and fuck her brains out, and as far as you... you're either going to leave this section on your own or in a body bag. So, choose wisely." Rico smirked. Jerome stood there for a minute looking like he wanted to jump at Rico so bad, but instead he just walked away still mean mugging.

Rico and Brenda laugh and go back to having conversation. Hours later, after a few more shots, they went from talking to Brenda slow grinding in his lap. Now feeling hornier than a nigga on ecstasy, Rico was ready to take Brenda back to his place and settle down for the night. He was supposed to meet up with Pop and Chris after the club let out, but he decided he would text them in the morning to meet.

"Haha! Oh my gosh, I can hardly stand up!" Brenda said laughing as they both exited the club from the back door.

"I know and I'm loving every bit of it." Rico says drunkenly kissing on her neck.

Pop! Pop! Pop!

Bullets pierce Rico's body from the back. He slumps to the ground starting to bleed.

"Ahhhhhh!" Brenda screamed.

Rico's vision was getting blurry but that didn't stop him from seeing who the gunman was... Jerome. He couldn't hold his eyes open anymore and blacked out.

~

Shit....where the fuck am I? Rico looked all around and saw nothing but white. Last thing he remembered was leaving the club with Brenda and then being shot from behind. Fuck! Am I dead?

"Ohhh my Rico." A familiar voice said.

"Mom?" Rico looked all around but didn't see anyone.

"Rico...what are you doing with your life? I told you to make something of yourself."

"I am mom."

"Not by putting your life in danger...I understand you must live

your lifestyle but there are more important things ahead for you than this."

"Like what?"

"Your son." Rico paused when he heard that.

"Mom I...I have to show my son I'm a man. I can't let him struggle like me and Tony did...and why can't I see you?"

"Rico...it's time to go now. But remember...show your son you are also his father, not just with your money. But with your heart.... I love you."

"Mom?! Wait! Mom?!"

Beeep....beep....beep...

"Mmm....mmm..." Rico opens his eye to a bright light from the hospital room ceiling.

He tries to collect his thoughts and lifts his head to see he was yet again in the hospital, but this time alone. When he looked down, he could see three wound patches stopping the bleeding coming from his abdomen and chest.

"I gotta get the fuck out of here." Rico says trying to climb out of bed, but for some reason couldn't move his legs. He had no feeling in his legs at all and panicked.

"Nurse! Nurrrrse! What the fuck?! Nurse!" Rico cried out.

"Whoa, whoa hey Mr. Mitchell; it's ok." A older gentleman in a white lab coat came in and says.

"What the fuck is going on?! Why can't I feel my legs?!" Rico yells.

"Wait. If you give me a minute I can explain. Now, my name is Dr. Alex and I must tell you that you came in with some serious gunshot wounds."

"Yeah no shit! Now get to the point, Doc."

"Well the bullets we extracted from your body didn't damage any major organs so that's a good thing. However, two of them did cut through some nerves causing damage which would explain the loss of feeling in your legs." The doctor says showing Rico his x-rays.

"So....I'm never going to walk again? Is that what you're telling me? Or worse....you going to cut my legs off?" Rico asks fearing the answer.

"No, no. The loss of feeling is temporary. With the right treatment and therapy, you should be back walking in as little as a few months. You just got to have patience."

Rico throws his head back on his pillow not believing what he was hearing. *No walking for a few months?* Only thing that was on his mind now was revenge.

"Um...I believe you have some friends in the waiting area for you. I'll let them know that you're awake." Dr. Alex says and walks out.

A few minutes later, Pop, Chris, and the twins walk in. He isn't sure how he's going to break the news to them, but he knew he had to.

"Yo dawg...you aight?" Pop asks.

"Yeah...how did y'all find me?" Rico asks.

"When we got to the club one of the bartenders said she seen you leaving out with some chick through the back and your car was still parked outside. When we left through the back to find you...you was laying in a pool of blood. Nigga we thought...you was dead." Chris says.

"I should've been, but you can't kill a real nigga." Rico

chuckled.

"So what's up? When they say you getting out of here?" Pop asks.

"I...I don't know. Actually, the doctor said I can't use my legs until my nerves heal up." There was silence over the devastating news of Rico not being able to walk.

"Hey...man you won't believe who we saw upstairs." Pop says.

"If it ain't the nigga who shot me, I don't care." Rico says.

"Camela had the baby Rico. Little nigga look just like you." Chris says. Rico was stunned at the news of his son's birth. *Maybe that's why my mother was telling me to get my shit together.*

"Camela's upstairs? In this hospital?" Rico asks.

"Yeah. Funny how that worked out huh?" Pop says.

"Well nigga, don't just stand there! Find me a wheelchair so I can go see my son." Rico demands. They start scrambling around the room to find Rico a wheelchair. When they pull one out the bathroom, Pop helps him into it. They let the nurse know where he was going and Pop took him to the maternity ward.

When they get there, they stop and ask the nurse for Camela's room number. Pop rolled Rico to the room and got there to see Camela holding their son in her arms.

"Rico...what happened? I heard about the shooting." Camela says.

"I'm fine. Pop, give us a minute." Pop lets go of his wheelchair and gives them some privacy. Rico rolls over to Camela's bed to get a good look at his son.

"I named him Tony...after your brother. I know how close

you two were." Camela says. A spark of happiness ignited in Rico hearing that his son would carry on Tony's name.

"Thank you Camela." Rico says.

"You're welcome. Now what's this I hear about you being shot? What happened?" Rico tells her about him not being able to walk.

"Wow...I'm so sorry Rico."

"It ain't no big deal. The doctor said I should be back walking in no time. In the meantime, I want you and my son to come back with me.

"Rico....I don't really know about all of that."

"Let me rephrase this....I wasn't asking Camela. If I'm going to be spending a lot of time at home, I want my son to be there. No questions asked." Rico says.

Three days later, Rico is discharged and heads back home. The doctor has set up for a live-in nurse to come by and help him with his legs. When returning home, he never realizes how many steps he has until now. Pop and Chris carried him up the steps. From there, Rico is greeted by the nurse, who he works with to do a light workout. He sent a car to pick up Camela and the baby and was just hoping this would work out. Later that day, Camela is walking through the door with baby Tony in her arms. They converse over dinner, while bonding with their child.

That night, Rico transfers himself to his wheelchair and goes to the bathroom. He tries to remember how the nurse showed him how to transfer from the wheelchair to the toilet. Rico slowly gets up using his arms and accidentally ends up falling.

"Hugh...this is going to take some getting used to." Rico says just laying there.

The next morning while eating breakfast, he hears the doorbell. He sends the nurse to open the door and in walks Jax.

"Well, I see you got people waiting on you hand and foot. How you doing Rico?" Jax says.

"I'm good. This shit just temporary for another few months. I wanted to talk to you about my decision."

"Yes?"

"After much speculation....I've decided partnering up wouldn't be such a bad idea. Especially now that I'm going to be taking some time off."

"Great. I'm glad you've decided wisely. How do your boys feel about it?"

"I haven't told them yet, but I will this afternoon. Jax...I'm telling you now if there's any funny business-"

"You have my word Rico. I will make it my life to make sure everything runs smoothly." For some strange reason, Rico felt like he was starting to trust Jax's word, but he still had some doubts. At the moment, he had no choice or otherwise his empire would flop.

"I'm going to go. Much work that needs to be done. You get some rest now." Jax says and leaves.

Later that day, Chris and Pop come by the house. Rico was dreading telling them about him and Jax, but he lived by a street code to always be brutally honest instead of untrustworthy and secretive.

"Haha, damn nigga. You got your own nurse and shit." Chris joked.

"Haaa, yeah does she change your diaper and feed you too?" They both laughed.

"You want me to shoot you both in the legs so you can find out?" Rico fired back.

"Hey man, chill. We just came over here to see how you was doing." Pop says as they sat on the living room couch.

"Look...what I'm going to say, you both might not like, but I been talking to Jax and as you two know he's been trying to get me to partner up with him."

"Yeah, weird ass nigga." Pop says.

"I...decided it wouldn't be a bad idea. In fact, I've asked him to partially take over while I'm down right now."

"Yo...what?" Pop asks.

"Pop man, listen-"

"Naw, you listen, how the fuck you gon let this bitch ass snake halfway take over without even telling us about it first?" Pop says angrily.

"I'm telling you about it now. At the end of the day, Jax still knows who the boss is and can't make moves without my say so."

"How? How you know he won't go behind your back like he's done so many other motherfuckers?!"

"Rico...Pop's right man. Jax...he's a snake. He's no good."

"I have to do what's best. Not just for me but for all of us. I can't move how I used to because of my legs. So, the best move to make at this moment was to partner up with Jax and make shit work."

"Wait a minute...why not just let me take over until you get back? I been helping you run shit since the beginning."

"Pop, no offense but...it's not that simple."

"But it's simple for you to let Jax in?" Pop says and Rico is silent.

"Ohhh, I see how it is. Cool then, I'm out." Pop says and heads for the door.

"Pop?!" Chris calls out to him.

"It's ok. Let him go. Sooner or later, he'll come around."

"Well...I understand your decision man. We all gotta do what we gotta do."

"You already know, but at the same time, I still don't entirely trust Jax as of yet. So, when you at the trap or the warehouse just keep your eyes open. Anything suspicious and that's the end for that nigga."

"I gotchu Rico."

Chapter 18

Over the next month, Rico has been home healing and watching his son grow. He has now managed to transition from being in a wheelchair to a walker but still had minor trouble keeping his balance.

"Ok, take your time. Don't rush." The nurse said coaching him. Rico was doing his daily therapy session which now consisted of how many steps he could take without the walker.

He held onto the wall as he made his way down the steps. Once he let go he was stunned that he could hold his balance, but after a few more steps he ended up falling.

"Shit!" Rico yelled.

"It's ok, Mr. Mitchell. You can try again?"

"Would you just shut up! Obviously you don't know what you're fucking doing. Otherwise, I wouldn't keep falling!"

"Now hold up, Mr. Mitchell. I been working with you for six weeks now and have had to put up with your nasty attitude along the way. Now if you want my help fine but you will not talk to me that way."

"I don't give a fuck about what you talking about right now. Do your fucking job!" Rico yells.

"That's it. I'm leaving, and also, I quit!" The nurse says walking away and leaving Rico on the floor. She walks to the front door and grabs her purse and coat. As she gets ready to walk out,

Camela and the baby walk in.

"Chile, I don't know how you put up with him. Good luck." The nurse says and storms out.

"Rico?" Camela says and when she finds Rico laying in the middle of the floor she can't help but start laughing.

"Oh, you think this shit is funny?" Rico says.

"Hehahehe." Once Camela starts laughing so does the baby.

"Oh, both of y'all think this is funny?" Rico tried his hardest not to crack a smile but just couldn't help it. All three of them started laughing at Rico looking like a real jack ass.

"Ok, ok, can you help me get up?"

"What's the magic word?" Camela teased.

"If you don't help me get up off this fucking floor!" Rico yelled playfully. Camela put the baby in his playpen and helps Rico off the floor and over to the couch. As soon as he sat down, the doorbell rang.

"I'll get it." Camela says. When she opens the door, it's Chris coming to drop off this week's profits.

"What's up boss?" Chris says walking in the living room.

"Nothing much."

"Here's this week's profits." Chris says giving him a black duffle bag.

"Damn, how much in this motherfucka?"

"I don't know but you would think we robbed another bank with all that money."

"This is from all the traps?"

"Yeah, surprisingly things been going good with Jax being in charge."

"Partially in charge, and I guess you right. Money talks and bullshit walks." Rico says holding up a stack of money and throwing it to Chris.

"What's this?"

"For stepping up and being down to ride. You earned it."

"Damn thanks."

"So...have you heard from Pop recently?"

"Naw. He stopped coming to work the day after you told us about Jax." Chris says. Rico has tried to reach out to Pop and talk things out but hasn't gotten a response. He felt fucked up without hearing from Pop, someone who was supposed to be his right-hand man.

"Aight man. I gotta get out of here." Chris says. They dap each other up and Chris leaves. Rico sat there on the couch deep in thought.

"And Kobe passes to Brown...he shoots it! Another slam dunk!"

Rico inhaled his blunt while watching the game on TV. He was sitting in the dark with light only coming from the screen, trying to gather his thoughts on how he should approach this situation with Pop. A part of him just said fuck it and let Pop be mad, but another part didn't want to just leave Pop out in the cold. In the end, the reason Pop wasn't working was because of Jax and he held more loyalty to Rico.

"Hey babe...what you doing in the dark?"

"Nothing." Rico says dryly.

"Well, I was thinking since the baby is asleep, maybe we can..." Camela scoots next him and kisses his neck, but Rico moves away. "Babe, what's wrong?"

"Nothing, I just…want to watch the game right now." Camela felt stung that Rico was suddenly turning her down. She hops up off the couch and stands in front of the TV.

"What are you doing?"

"Who is she?"

"What?"

"Who is the bitch that got you turning all of this down?"

"Man if you don't get your black ass out the way."

"It's that bitch from the hospital isn't it? The one who was your high school sweetheart."

"Camela, move out the fucking way!"

"Don't think I ain't see those text messages in your phone!"

"What texts?" Rico asks trying to play off what she was saying. A few nights ago, Rico texted Leah out of the blue after getting her number from a connect from the hospital administration. He told her about him getting shot and she asked was he ok. Which gave him hope that she still cared for him.

"Don't play stupid with me, Rico. I know you been texting that bitch!"

"Blood, if you don't get ya ass out the way!" He said throwing a pillow at her.

"Fuck you Rico!" Camela yells.

"Yeah whatever. That's the postpartum talking." He says.
Rico admits he has been distant from Camela since getting shot. He gets up and calls for his driver to take him somewhere so he can get out of the house.

A few hours later, after driving around, Rico asks the driver to take him to Pop's house so they can talk things out. When he pulls up he sees Pop outside shooting dice with a few homies. He notices that Pop is looking more scruffy than usual, but that's only because he hasn't been working. Rico gets out the car and uses his walker to limp over to them.

"Pop...let me holler at you." Rico says. Pop at first hesitates, but secretly wants to hear Rico out.

"What you doing here?"

"Look...I know shit ain't been the same, but you gotta understand I had to what I had to do. And since making my decision things have been better than ever."

"Pshh really? You think so?" Pop says.

"I know so."

"Do you? Or has being cooped up in that house made you blind to a lot of shit?"

"What do you mean?"

"I'll show you." Pop walks over to Rico's car and they both get in.

Pop instructs the driver to drive to a location Rico has never been to before. When they get there, Pop tells the driver to kill the lights.

"What are we doing here?" Rico asks.

"Just wait." Pop says. Five minutes later a black car pulls up way across from where they were sitting at. A guy in a black hoodie walks out the alley. When he pulls his hoodie off his head, Rico is in shock.

"Yo...yo! That's the motherfucker that shot me!" Rico says.

"I figured. I just wanted to be sure." Pop says.

"Who's that he's talking to in the car?"

"I guess we about to find out." Pop says when they see the car open and Jax steps out.

"I knew it. See Rico, Jax set this whole thing up. You getting shot and losing your legs so that way you wouldn't have a choice but to step down." Rico was at a loss for words but wasn't shocked. He knew sooner or later Jax would do something sneaky.

"Some of the boys at some of the traps say they been catching Jax going in the safes and taking money."

"How is that possible? Chris just dropped off ten bands earlier." Rico says taking a rubber band of money out his pocket.

Pop takes the money out Rico's hand and unwraps it. He sprays a fifty-dollar bill with some alcohol spray and lights it. It was just like Pop had suspected. The bills were counterfeit.

"I say we start shooting now while we got them right here." Pop says.

"No...you can handle the guy who shot me, but I'll handle Jax."

"So does that mean I'm back on?" Pop asks.

"Nigga you was never off." Rico says. They both laugh a little and go into planning.

A few days later, Rico tells Jax to meet him at the port because of some new product coming in. Jax gets out the car and is confused to see Rico just standing there with his cane.

"Where's the new product?" Jax asks.

"You know how they say everyone has a motive Jax? Ever since you came to me and asked me to partner up, I been getting red flags. Yet and still I let you in and agreed to your idea."

"Rico…what is this all about?"

"That guy we saw at the club that night…the same one who shot me….how well do you know him?"

"I…I just know him from around the neighborhood."

"Funny you say that…I did a little digging and that nigga isn't even from here. He's actually from Chicago and the night I got shot was his first time even stepping foot in Atlanta." Rico says and could see Jax knew he was caught. "So do you want to come clean or should I do it for you?" Rico says.

"I don't know what you're talking about."

"This whole plan of yours was just another plot to take my empire. You had me set up, you had me shot, and tried to take over…but I just got one question? Why'd you spare me? Why not just kill me?"

"You….really want me to answer that? You weren't even supposed to survive Rico Jefe. There's only room in this town for one true kingpin. Not some youngin with a dream." Jax says. Rico starts to reach for his gun, but feels one being put to the back of his head.

"Hahaha. Nice try, Rico, but did you really think I was going to come all the way down here unprepared." Rico slowly puts his hands up.

"Time to say good-bye Rico. And oh, don't worry. I'll take care of that pretty little girlfriend of yours."

"You know I would say good-bye Jax, but thing is….Rico Jefe never comes unprepared either." Rico points up and it makes Jax look up. Standing up on the crates surrounding them was at least twenty of Rico's gunmen.

"Time to say good-bye…Jax."

Ratattattatatatat!!!!!!!

Gunshots start raining down making Rico duck for cover. Jax is hit fifteen times and so is his gunman. Once Rico gives the signal to stop fire, he walks over to Jax who is lifeless.

"Consider this the end of our deal." Rico says. Pop walks over to them in his SWAT gear and dap Rico up.

"Hey, I handled that guy for you. All taken care of."

"Thanks Pop...for your loyalty."

"Aight, aight don't get all mushy. Come on, let's go." Pop joked as they left Jax to die. With him out the way Rico could flourish and officially take over ATL and the rest of the south if he wanted to.

Chapter 19

Another month later...

Rico is back in full health and finally walking again. He calls a meeting to let everyone know that he was back and ready to take over.

"Yeah motherfucka, I'm back. I'm walking again. Thanks to everyone for the prayers and well wishes, but now it's time to get back to business. Now, with Jax fucking eliminated, this city is our playground. I'm letting you know now, snakes and any fuck shit will not be tolerated. Unless you want to end up like that nigga Jax. Any questions?" Rico asks. The room was silent as no one dared to speak.

"Good. Now we have a new product coming in from one of my Columbian connects. I want it to hit the streets asap. Tomorrow, I'm going to be out of town, but when I get back, I want at least eighty percent of this product on the street. If you have any questions or need anything you can hit up Pop. He'll be in charge while I'm gone." Rico says.

Him and Pop smile at each other after agreeing Rico would never trust nobody but him to have his back.

The next day...

Rico catches a flight to New York and lands at JFK airport. He was still on the hunt for more property. He planned on looking at some penthouses on Park Ave and maybe something in Manhattan.

As he rode through the city, he decided to take a detour and see his old neighborhood where him and Tony first came to. Everything pretty much looked the same except for a few new businesses and renovated apartments. When he gets to his old elementary school, he gets out and looks on at the kids playing during recess. He starts to reminisce about him and his friends playing on these same grounds. When times were simple.

"De'Rico Mitchell?" A soft voice said. When Rico looked, it was a pretty Hispanic looking woman in a pencil skirt and button-down blouse.

"Yeah...do I know you?" Rico asks.

"Haha, come on. I haven't changed that much. You should remember me considering I was only your girlfriend for a day."

"Akeelah?" Rico asks.

"Yeah, it's me."

"Wow look...look at you. You look great." Rico wasn't lying when he said that. Akeelah had definitely grown up and was more beautiful than ever.

"You look great too."

"So what are you still doing here? What? Are you a teacher or something?"

"Actually, I'm the principal." Rico is impressed and finds her even more attractive. If it was one thing about a woman he liked it was being her own boss.

"So what are you doing here after all these years?"

"Just...visiting. Thought I would take a trip down memory lane."

"Oh ok. Well...how about me and you catch up over some lunch some time?"

"Damn, I wish I could, but I'm only in town for the night. I'm heading back to Atlanta tomorrow."

"Oh…well how about you come over tonight. I have a condo near Times Square."

"Ok. Sure. I can do that." Rico would have been a fool if he told Akeelah no. Plus he knew he still owed her an explanation for him disappearing overnight.

"Here. I'll give you my number." Akeelah takes out a pen and writes it on his hand.

"Ok, I'll come over around eight."

"Sounds good." She says looking him over seductively and walking away.

Later that evening, Rico keeps his word and goes over to Akeelah's place and have dinner. They talked about the good times when they were in school together. He learns that she is recently divorced, has no kids but loves to work with them. Afterwards, they end up chilling on her couch with some glasses of wine.

"Haha, I remember you and Ricardo always got in trouble. Most of the time is was because of him though." Akeelah says.

"Yeah, hey whatever happened to him? Is he still around?"

"I don't know. After we graduated and went to middle school we all kind of went our separate ways you know."

"Damn. I sure would like to get in contact with him. I know he's probably wondering why I disappeared the way I did."

"Yeah…he isn't the only one." Akeelah says sipping some more wine.

"Oh damn. Akeelah, I'm sorry. I…listen it was some shit

with my dad going on and he didn't tell me and my brother. One night I go home, everything's all good. And next thing I know he's packing us in a car to go to Atlanta."

"Wow, that's...that's crazy."

"Yeah, well he's dead now."

"I'm so sorry to hear that."

"Don't be. He was never a really good father no way. I would never treat my son how he did me."

"Oh my Gosh, you have a kid?" Akeelah asks excitedly.

"Yeah, just one. Only a few months old."

"I wanted kids but...my ex didn't. He said having kids would make him feel older."

"Well, you never know one day. Some lucky guy will come along and give you kids and anything else you want."

"Yeah...you know there's this little boy I have as a student who reminds me of you."

"Oh really? Is he handsome like me?" Rico asks scooting over closer to Akeelah.

"I don't know Rico. I just know he's charming, charismatic, determined..." she says as Rico leans in closer to her face.

"You know, you always had a way with words." Rico says and leans in to kiss her. They tongue kiss as he takes both of their wine glasses and put them on the table.

Akeelah climbs onto his lap and takes her shirt off. Rico caresses her titties and starts sucking on her neck. He unbuttons her bra and kisses her nipples. Lifting up her skirt and pulling her panties to the side, Rico fingered her pussy feeling how wet she was.

"Mmm Rico." She moaned his name. He was loving the sound of how she said it.

With his other hand, he pulled out his dick and slipped it inside. Feeling how tight she was, he could tell she wasn't sleeping around since her divorce. Shit, her ex was probably hardly hitting it. He moved her up and down his shaft, while her titties bounced in his face. Every time he sucked or kissed on her neck, he felt her walls tighten. The mood was so intense between them.

"Fuck me! Fuck me hard Rico!" Akeelah whined.

You don't have to tell me twice. Rico stood up with Akeelah's legs still wrapped around his waist. He pins her up against a wall and continues to bang out her box. When she started clawing his back, Rico knew she was about to cum again.

"Oh shit! I'm cumming!"

"Cum on this dick then!" Rico says. Akeelah does just that and cums so hard white stuff came out.

When he felt himself starting to cum, he forgot he didn't have no condom on. He quickly walked them back over to the couch, stroked her a few more times, and pulled out.

After catching their breath, they both went upstairs, had another round, took a shower together, and cuddled up in Akeelah's bed.

"Rico?" Akeelah asked half asleep.

"What's up?"

"What does this mean for us? With you living in Atlanta and all." Rico was caught off guard by her question. Even though he still had Camela living with him, their relationship has been rocky the past few months.

"I don't know...we'll figure that out." He says kissing her forehead.

Back in Atlanta...

*Amazing grace
How sweet the sound
That saved a wretch like meeeeee...*

Everyone stood at the gravesite as Jax was lowered into the ground. The main person standing at the forefront was his son Junior. Him and his mother was hurting by the loss of their loved one. Only thing that was on his mind was revenge on who killed his beloved father. Jax taught Junior everything about the game to the point where Junior was going to take over once Jax retired. But now that would happen sooner than later. After the memorial service, Junior stayed behind to privately say his goodbyes.

"Hey man, what's up?" A guy named Shiek said walking up to him.

"I'm good."

"Yeah, sorry about your pops. This is all so fucked up."

"That's exactly why I need you to find the guy who did this to him."

"Hey man, the streets are talking but they ain't talking that much."

"Well, make them talk. I don't care what it takes. I will find out who killed my father....they will pay."

Chapter 20

Returning to Atlanta, Rico meets up with a realtor to close a deal on another night club. In the middle of signing the paperwork, Pop calls him to tell him mayoral candidate Ronald Grier wanted to meet with him. Rico wasn't into politics, so he couldn't imagine what some asshole running for mayor would want with him. He agrees to meet him at his office across town.

"Mr. Rico Jefe. It is truly an honor." Ronald says as Rico walks into his office.

"Look, I don't got all day. What do you want?"

"Well, I figured me and you could…work out a deal."

"Here we go. What the fuck you mean a deal? What kind of deal?"

"Well, as you know I'm running for mayor-"

"Yeah and losing by twenty points to Sharon Carter."

"But see, that's where you come in at. You are the king in these streets I hear. You control what these people do. They listen to you."

"What's your point?"

"My point is, you help me get more votes for my campaign and I help keep the FEDs and police off ya ass."

"And what if I say no?"

"That's your choice. But I'm pretty sure the police would

love an anonymous tip concerning...Jackson Pelt's murder." Ronald says referring to Jax.

"Pshh...are you threatening me?"

"Of course not."

"No, it sounds like you're threatening me. And I don't take too kindly to threats." Rico says showing his gun.

"Whoa, whoa. Ok, hold on. I think we got off to the wrong foot-"

"You're right. We did. But any man willing to blackmail me must be desperate. So, here's my proposition for you. You keep your fucking mouth shut and I don't have to kill you, and I'll give your idea some thought." Rico puts his gun back at his side. He quickly leaves out.

On the way home, Rico is stuck in traffic because of an accident in the middle of the street. He's been trying to call Camela since he landed this morning but got no answer.

"Come on! Get y'all asses out the way!" Rico says honking his horn. Just as he looked to the side, he noticed a familiar face walking down the street. It was Camela walking with some guy. Rico felt a bolt of rage go through him and jumped out the car.

"Camela, what the fuck are you doing?!" Rico says power-walking over to them. Camela said nothing and just stood there like a deer in headlights. "What are you doing?! What the fuck is this?!" Rico quickly pulls out his gun and points it at the guy.

"I suggest you run." Rico says.

"Rico no!" Camela yells.

Bang! Bang!

Rico fires two bullets at the guy, who was running down the street but missed.

"Rico put that fucking gun away!" Camela says.

"Are you crazy? Two of these should be in you! What the fuck were you doing with this nigga?"

"I was just walking down the street and he started talking to me!" Camela says.

"So what! You tell that nigga you got a man."

"Oh, now you're my man? But you get to sleep with other women, go out of town, not answer your phone, and you supposed to be my man?" Rico didn't want to admit that Camela was right, but she was.

"Man whatever. I'll see you back at the house." Rico walks off getting back in his car and drives off. Later on, he meets up with the guys at one of the traps to relax and have a smoke session.

"Damn blood, is you gon pass the blunt?" Pop says.

"Shut yo ass up." Rico says exhaling and passing the blunt to Pop.

"Damn Rico, so you really think she cheating on you huh?" Joaquim asked him.

"Man, fuck that hoe. Only reason I'm with her is cause of my son. If it wasn't for him I would've been kicked that bougie daddy's girl to the curb." Rico says after telling them what happened earlier with Camela.

"Well, the pussy must be good because it's a lot of niggas out here that's not with they baby momma." Pop says.

"Yeah, but it don't make it right. If you with someone you should want to be with them, good or bad." Abel preached.

"Whoa, who got your panties in a fucking twist Abel?" Rico asks.

"Don't mind him. He just mad because another girl broke up with his ass yet again." Joaquim added.

"Damn. That's like the third one this year. You know it is ok to get pussy right?" Rico says.

"Man, fuck you guys." Abel said taking the blunt and inhaling.

"Hey, you know what I was thinking?" Joaquim says.

"Didn't know you thought about much but go head." Pop joked.

"Heeheehee...funny. Anyway, me and Abel was thinking we should come up with like a name for ourselves."

"What?" Rico asked confused.

"I'm saying you got the Bloods, the Crips, but what if we had our own gang name that people will know us by." Joaquim says. The room fell silent until Pop started laughing.

"Maaaan, get out of here with that lame ass idea." Pop says.

"Actually....I think it's a good idea." Rico says.

"Are you fucking serious?" Pop says.

"What's wrong Pop? Mad you didn't come up with the idea?" Joaquim teased.

"Fuck you."

Knock, knock, knock.

Pop hopped straight up and looked through the peephole.

"Man, open the door nigga." A voice said from the other side.

"Niggas been waiting on you all day with ya slow ass." Pop says opening up the door and Shiek stepped in.

"My bad. All of us aren't rolling in a Benz around town." Shiek hands him the black duffle bag with the shipment from the warehouse.

"What's up Rico?" Shiek says. Shiek came to work for Rico a few weeks ago. Rico didn't have no problem, but it was something about him that didn't feel right.

"What's good with ya." Rico says back.

"Hey, you got the streets on lock right now man. Ever since Jax got offed shit been running smooth." Rico says nothing. He made sure no one told any new workers about him executing Jax.

"Crazy how he died though. I heard when they found him that nigga brains was splattered all across the docks. It took them hours to clean it up."

"Hey, listen here. Let me tell you something...Jax was a fucking snake. He got what he deserved."

"What you mean?" Shiek says.

"Exactly what I said. And matter fact, why the fuck are we talking about this nigga anyway?" Rico says.

"My bad man. I just-"

"Drop it!" Rico yells. Shiek stood there not knowing what to say.

"Hey, I think you should go." Pop tells Shiek.

"Yeah...I'mma head out. See y'all later." Sheik gets his bag back from Pop and leaves out the door.

"Damn man. Where you find this nigga at?" Rico says.

"I know, I know man but he mean well. He just a little stupid, that's all." Pop says.

"Stupidity in this game we playing is dangerous. He's your mans so I'm gon lean off of him, but watch him." Rico says.

"Aight." Pop says back.

"The last thing we need is somebody running their mouth about me killing Jax."

Little did Rico know, Shiek was still outside and heard the entire conversation. Once he got the answer he needed he quickly texted Junior.

Chapter 21

Renovations for Rico's new night club was almost done. He decided to name the club after his late mother; *Serafina's*. He knew she and Tony were both smiling down on him proud at all he has achieved. While standing outside admiring the construction he gets yet another phone call from Chris.

"What's up?" He answers.

"Where are you at?! Man, you need to get here now! One of the traps is on fire!"

"What?! I'm on my way!" Rico dashes to his car and hops in. He speeds off doing about eighty down the freeway.

When he reaches one of his main trap houses, he pulls up to it being engulfed in flames. He sees Chris and Pop trying to hold back Joaquim.

"What the fuck happened?!" Rico says running over to them.

"Somebody fucking threw a cocktail bomb through the window! Man Abel is still inside!" Chris says.

"Abel!!!" Joaquim yells. Rico tries to run in and is stopped by the fire Marshall.

"Sir, I need to get in there! My friend is in there!" Rico says.

"We already have somebody in there looking for him, but I can't let you in; it's too dangerous."

"Man, if you don't get the fuck out the way!" Rico yells. In the midst of him trying to run into the burning house, he is relieved to see an unconscious Abel being carried out by one of the firefighters.

"Abel!" Rico and Joaquim run over to him as they lay him on the stretcher.

"Abel! Abel! Abel, come on man!" Rico says tapping his face but he was unresponsive.

"He's still alive but barely has a pulse. We have to get him to the hospital." The EMT says.

"I'm going with. I'm his brother." Joaquim says climbing in the back.

"Joaquim, call when y'all get there and I'll follow up." Rico says. Joaquim nods to him before they ride off in the ambulance.

As much as Rico was worried about his boy being ok, he had to find out what happened to his trap house and most importantly...why.

"So you mean to tell me...all you motherfuckers sitting around...and none of you know what happened?!" Rico yelled at Pop and Chris because they were supposed to be in charge.

"I'm telling you, Rico; it all happened so fast. Only thing we got was an all-black Camaro riding down the street."

"Did you at least get the license plate?" Rico asks.

"....no." Chris says.

"Fuck!" Rico yells. He was so enraged about what happened he didn't even notice the police officer walking up beside him. "Look, come on man. Now is not the time." Rico says.

"This won't take long. Do you own this property right here?" The officer asks.

"Yeah."

"Really? Because when I ran the address on this place it was reported vacant two years ago. So unless you got a permit for.... whatever it is that you guys are doing, I have to take you in for questioning."

"Man whatever. Fuck out my face." Rico says. The officer forcefully grabs Rico and cuffs him. "Come on, come on I was going to get a permit. I just been busy."

"Yeah, tell it to the judge."

At the police station, detectives are asking him all kinds of questions. Rico maintains his silence and says nothing but wanting his lawyer. The police still keeps him locked up. While sitting in his holding cell, he decides to make a decision he didn't want to do, but had no choice if he was going to get out of jail. He requests his phone call.

"Hello?" Ronald Grier answers.

"Ronald...it's me."

"Ahh Rico. Thought I might hear from you. Heard about your property burning down."

"How the fuck...nevermind. Look, I will agree to help you... if you can get me out of here." Rico figured Ronald was his only hope in bailing him out since him and Camela was still beefing and all his money was stashed away at home.

"I'll make some phone calls and see what I can do."

A few hours later, Rico is free to go and Ronald waits for him out front. While driving Rico to his car, they talk about getting Ronald's numbers up. Rico just prayed he wouldn't have to assassinate him like he did Jax for being a rat.

Chapter 22

A week later, Rico hears that Abel is fine and expected to recover from all the smoke inhalation. While he was at home recovering, Rico's grand opening was tonight for his new club. Him and Camela squashed their beef for the time being and are going together.

While getting ready, he gets a call from Chris saying they caught the person who set the fire. To Rico's dismay, it was Shiek. Rico drops what he's doing and heads to the warehouse to meet Pop and Chris.

"So you not going to tell me why you did it? Or better yet who made you do it?" Rico asks. Sheik was tied to a chair, shaking from fear.

"I told you Rico...I...I didn't do it." Shiek says.

"Really? Because everyone else in this room seems to think you did it. There was explosives and flammable products found at your house when they broke in that motherfucker to get you....I'm going to give you one more chance. Who is he?"

"Man I...I can't say." Shiek whines.

"Hmm...ok." Rico nods his head and walks over to his tool box. When he turns around, Rico is holding a chainsaw pulling at the string.

"Aww, come on man!" Shiek cries out.

"One last chance Shiek." Rico says.

"I told you I don't know nothing!"

"Ok." Rico slams the chainsaw into Shiek's leg making blood spurt out everywhere.

"Ahhhhhhh! Ahhhhh!! Aghhhhhhhhhhh!" Shiek screamed out in pain. When Rico was done, half of Shiek leg was hanging off his knee.

"Still not going to talk?"

"Ok! Ok!...his name is...Junior."

"Who the fuck is Junior?"

"He's Jax's son. He wants revenge for you killing his dad. He paid 40k to set the trap on fire and get information."

"Hmmm...makes perfect sense. I didn't even know that old motherfucka had kids. As for you being a rat...well there's only one thing left for you." Rico reves up the chainsaw and swing it at Shiek's neck chopping his head off.

"I want all the information you two can find on this Junior motherfucka. I want to know where he sleeps, who he knows, hell and even how many breaths this nigga takes a day. And don't take all day. You know the grand opening is tonight." He says to Chris and Pop.

"You got it boss." Pop says. Rico wipes the blood off his face and leaves so he can resume getting ready.

Later that evening, Rico's club is packed. Music playing, everyone dancing, and a line was still wrapped around the corner. His friend Rodney even came through with his crew. Rico arrives with Camela on his arm in his brand-new, cream white Bentley. They all go back to Rico's very own VIP room that was made of glass walls so he could still see everything. While partying, Rico looks at all his friends and thinks back to when he had nothing. From having to leave his momma to being basically molested just for food and shelter. Rico would have never thought he would be here on top of the world.

"Aye! Aye! Everybody listen up!" Rico yelled over the music. Everyone stopped dancing and focused on him.

"I just wanted to say...we have had a successful summer. Even with a few cracks in the road, they still couldn't stop us. I don't think nobody can truly say they got it out the mud more than we have. I'm proud of all y'all hard work and look forward to an even more successful winter. I gave a lot of thought to an idea that was put in my ear and in honor of the twins, who couldn't make it tonight, I decided to come up with a name for our clique....a toast to Jefe Gang."

"To Jefe Gang!" Everyone said and sipped their drinks.

"Aight! Let's turn up!" Rico yells and signals the DJ to turn the music up.

Welcome to my hood
Everybody know everybody
And if I got it everybody got it...

The club was super turned up off the DJ Khaled track. Rico and Camela threw back shot after shot, while flirting with each other. He couldn't help but notice how good she was looking in her skin tight leather dress. He takes her hand and leads her to his private office that he had built.

Rico starts kissing on her neck, while unzipping her dress. Camela unbuttons his Versace shirt and caresses his muscled chest. He pulls her panties down and lifts her up putting her legs around his waist. He shoved his dick in her wet, hot pussy making her screech.

"Oh shit! Oh fuck!" Camela screams out.

Rico bounces her up and down making her hair go in all directions. He gripped her ass cheeks and went harder and deeper. The way her shit felt, he didn't want to pull out.

"I love you Rico." She whispers. Not knowing what to say Rico falls silent.

"I know you do." He says and continues stroking her.

The party let out around three in the morning. Rico tells Camela to wait for him in the car, while he goes to question Pop and Chris about what they dug up about Junior

"Soo...what did you find out?" Rico asks.

"Nothing. It's like this nigga's a ghost. Even people on Jax's old territory haven't heard of him." Pop says.

"Nobody just burns down a fucking trap house and goes missing. This nigga obviously trying to send a message and we gon give him a answer."

"Don't worry, Rico; we'll find him. Look, just relax, go home, enjoy your girl, and we'll handle it." Chris says. Rico smirks a little bit.

"This nigga always trying to remain hopeful." Rico jokes.

"I got to. Shit, you never know when it might be your last day on this earth."

"True. Aight, well I'll see you niggas in the morning." Rico says.

Screeeeeech!

They all turn around to some loud tires from a car speeding towards them.

Pop! Pop! Pop! Pop!

Gunshots rang out aiming for Rico, Pop and Chris. They all

duck and hit the ground but that doesn't stop one of them from getting hit.

Chapter 23

Chris!....Chris!....I'm here man! I'm right here!

Chris had gotten shot and was losing a lot of blood. The last thing he remembers was talking to Rico and Pop in the parking lot of Rico's new club, and now he could hardly see and was on a stretcher with an oxygen mask on his face. When he looked up, he saw Rico running beside him and Pop.

"I'm right here man! We right here Chris!" Rico says. They were running down the hallway at Grady Hospital on their way to shock trauma.

"I'm sorry, sir, but you two have to wait outside." A nurse said stopping them at the double doors.

"Man, what you talking about? That's my homie! I gotta stay with him!"

"I'm sorry but it's hospital policy. You have to wait in the waiting room."

"Rico, come on man. He's going to be alright." Pop says trying to calm him down. Rico takes his advice and they both go to the waiting area.

There is mostly everyone who Chris knew including his family and girlfriend Rico is sitting next to Camela trying to remain calm.

"Babe, you're still bleeding." She said pointing to his arm where a bullet hit.

"It's just a flesh wound. I'll be aight." He says.

"Hey." Pop motions for him to come over to him so they can talk in private. "I just talked to his mom and his girl. They're pretty shook up." Pop says.

"As they should be. Somebody gon come shoot up my party? At my club on opening night? That's bullshit."

"And...she's pregnant." Pop says referring to Chris' girlfriend.

"Shit. Man, he gotta pull through this....he gon pull through right?" Rico asks. Before Pop could give him an answer, Rico storms over to the nurse desk.

"Excuse me. Have y'all heard anything about my friend yet?" Rico asks.

"No I have not."

"Well, can you call back there? Walk back there or something?" Rico says getting loud.

"Sir, you need to have a seat and wait."

"Fuck waiting! We been waiting for hours now!"

"Sir, either you go have a seat or I'm going to have to call security." The nurse says.

"Rico, come on, you making a scene." Pop says intervening.

"Naw, fuck that! We been waiting for hours! We deserve to fucking know what's going on!" Rico knocked a vase off the nurse's desk making it break into a million pieces.

"That's it. I'm calling security." The nurse says picking up the phone.

"Rico, come on nigga. This not the way to do things." Pop says.

"Man, fuck that!" Rico pushes Pop off him and tries to open the double doors but can't without the nurse buzzing him in. He starts to kick the door.

"Hey! Hey! Come on, buddy, you're out of here." Two security guards say trying to grab Rico.

"Man, get off of me! Get off of me!" Rico yells acting erratic.

"Hey, I got this." Rico calmed down a little bit when he heard Leah's soft voice. He looked over and saw her hand grab his wrist. It all happened so fast he didn't see Camela's face at the whole thing.

"I got this." Leah tells the security guards. They look at each other and let Rico go.

Leah takes his hand and leads him around the corner. Camela was so stunned but knew that now wasn't the time to be acting out about this. Although she had plans on doing it later.

"Rico, what is going on? What happened?" Leah asks.

"My...my...my mans got shot." Rico cries.

"What?"

"These fools shot at us...and now my homie is laying in there fighting for his life and nobody won't tell us nothing." Rico breaks down. Leah feels sad for her old high school sweetheart and wants to do something to help.

"Meet me by the cafeteria." Leah says. Rico stands up from his slump and immediately hugs Leah.

"Thank you." He says. She contemplates on caressing his back but does it out of sorrow anyway.

After waiting for Leah for what seemed like a long time, he finally seen her walking towards him standing next to the cafeteria.

"Well? How is he? Is he good?" Rico asks.

"I'm...I'm sorry Rico. The doctors did everything they could...he just didn't make it." When Rico heard those words his heart felt like it was breaking.

"They already alerted his family...Rico, I'm so sorry."

Rico begins to slouch to the ground and cry. He couldn't believe his homie Chris was gone. Rico had never truly cried before, but now he didn't care who seen him. This was hurt he would never get over.

A week later....

Everyone is exiting the church after Chris' funeral service. Rico is standing off to the side alone thinking of nothing but revenge. He still hadn't managed to find out any info on Junior and it had him ready to just tear the city apart.

Even though Camela still felt some type of way about him talking to Leah at the hospital, she could see the love of her life was hurting. She walked over to comfort him.

"Rico?...you ok?" She touches his shoulder but he snatches away. "Rico...I been thinking...maybe this is a sign to move out of Atlanta. All this killing and useless violence...look where it's gotten us."

"I'm not fucking leaving. This is my home."

"Rico, people move out of state all the time. Think of me... your son." She touches his shoulder again. This time he takes her hand and lifts it off his shoulder.

"Camela...listen, if you truly, truly want to move and it means that much to you...then do it by yourself."

"Wha...what are you saying?"

"What does it sound like I'm saying? You're a good mom. You can raise little Tony on your own."

"Rico I...I thought you loved me?"

"Key word...you thought. Love will get you killed out here in these streets. So, like I said if you want to go...go." Camela feels heartbroken.

After all she sacrificed to be with Rico, and he still gave her the shit end of the stick. She couldn't believe she was in love with a man who didn't love her back. Camela storms away deciding to catch a Uber home since they drove in Rico's car.

Rico watched as she walked away, but also caught a glimpse of Chris' casket being carried out to the hearse. It was then Rico made a promise to himself to find Junior, avenge Chris's death, and put an end to all this. And he put that on Jefe gang.

To be continued.....

Letter to my readers:

I would like to thank you all for following along and supporting me on this journey. If you are new please stay tuned because this is only the beginning.

Follow my Facebook and Instagram pages:

Facebook: Tink Richardson books

Instagram: author_tinkrich

Made in the USA
Monee, IL
04 February 2021

59086457R00154